Jack Lack is an eleven-year-old autistic boy who struggles to grasp the absurdities of so-called "normal" life, first in his public school classroom for behavior-disordered delinquents, then in his extended family of sinister cousins and eccentric adults. Wherever Jack goes, he is unfairly blamed for every mishap or wrongdoing, and in this comic novel of self-discovery, he sets out to prove his innocence. As he collects clues, a question forms in his mind: Are all these misadventures unrelated events, or is someone:

Out to Get Jack

"I have known James Williams most of his life, and I have seen him transform from a shy, echolalic five-year-old into a thoughtful, articulate teenager. What he has to say about children who struggle with immense disabilities is valuable not only to the families who must struggle alongside them but to the teachers and professionals who endeavor to understand them. Out to Get Jack beautifully demonstrates that we all have a lot to learn, and gifted thinkers such as James can help show us the way."

—Annabel Stehli, Author of *The Sound of a Miracle: A Child's Triumph Over Autism*

Out to Get Jack

by James Williams

*Where do you draw the line between obedience
and standing up for yourself?*

First edition printed in Canada, 2003
Second edition printed in the United States of America, 2011

ISBN-10: 141201249-X
ISBN-13: 978-141201249-2

National Library of Canada Cataloguing in Publication Data

A cataloguing record for this book that includes the U.S. Library of Congress Classification number, the Library of Congress Call number, and the Dewey Decimal cataloguing code is available from the National Library of Canada. The complete cataloguing record can be obtained from the National Library's online database at: www.nlc-bnc.ca/amicus/index-e.html

www.jamesmw.com

For everything there is a season, and a time for every matter under heaven.

ECCLESIASTES 3:1

Chapter 1

It was a typical day for Jack Lack, who had autism and was misunderstood. Although this was not the typical day of many boys in the village of East Germantown, Indiana, it was for him. It had actually been like this for the eleven years that he'd been alive.

First, he woke up and was forced to eat food he hated for breakfast. It was supposed to cure him, but instead made him sick. Then he took the medicine that would stop him from acting rebellious, though it had no effect, since Jack already spent most of his life trying to be obedient but didn't know how. After that, he reluctantly walked to the Cooper School at the corner of Paine Drive and Sufferin Street, only to be tardy because he got into a fight with the school bully, Mark McMann, on the playground.

The bully could not accept the fact that Jack's first and last name rhymed, and felt that teasing him could somehow change this. But Jack wasn't the only one who was teased by Mark. Indeed, he was so mean that *everyone* shuddered when you said *his* name.

McMann also looked like a bully with his bulging muscles and angry-looking face, unlike Jack, who had arms as thin and mousy as his stringy brown hair.

When he finally got into the school building, Jack was ten more minutes late to his class because of his shoelaces. It was a school rule that everyone had to change from outdoor shoes to gym shoes at the start of each day, and it was his therapist's rule that he *had* to have lace-up shoes, even though he couldn't tie them. When everyone else was safely at their desks or standing saying the Pledge, Jack was still in the hall, tears staining the dirty, knotted shoestrings. Sometimes the hall monitor would find him sniffling, and give him a tardy slip.

But even when Jack got into class, he usually missed what his teacher taught him, because she talked too fast and always too loud.

On the other hand, Jack was put in a class of rebellious boys, so it didn't matter that he didn't understand anything. The entire class was considered hopeless. Jack didn't fit in that class because he was short and slight, while all the rebels were strong and hardy because of the exercise they got by running around the classroom during frequent revolts. Such revolts were usually started by Larry, Moe, Curly, John, Paul, George, or Pete, but Jack was generally blamed for them because he lacked the verbal skills to talk his way out of things.

This was a group of kids who wouldn't do anything you wanted them to do. But there was something different about Jack. The other kids misbehaved on purpose, but he did so because of his autism.

Fortunately, Mrs. Walter, the teacher, seemed very patient, although in truth, the school's dark secret was that she was paid a lot more than the other teachers. That was the reason she never quit.

The class riots were always destructive, like the time one of the students took a knife and stabbed the class clock, or the time that the walls of the classroom were defaced with something so obscene, I could never tell you without having to be censored. In fact, every time there was a riot, some new security procedure was implemented to prevent that type in the future. But the students always found something new, and worse, to do.

The classroom was called "THE BD AND JD CLASS-ROOM" because Behavior-Disordered individuals and Juvenile Delinquents usually got along well together—even though the BDs had chemical imbalances whereas the JDs were just plain evil. Jack was the first person to be there because of autism. He didn't qualify for the kinder, gentler autistic classroom down the hall because he could talk and did well on spelling tests.

All the things the teacher needed were locked up in closets, because if these kids had access to them, they would use them as weapons. Although every room had a button to call the school office via the P.A. system, this room had five call buttons. Instead of having only one PUSH TO CALL button, the buttons said:

PUSH TO CALL OFFICE
PUSH TO CALL in a COMPLAINT
PUSH TO CALL for HELP
PUSH TO CALL in case of FREE THINKING
PUSH TO CALL for RESPITE

On this day, Friday, October 5th, there had been no riots yet. Not even a food fight at lunch. The class was doing Social Studies, and Mrs. Walter was teaching kids about the Revolutionary War, a thing that she had been trying to teach them for four weeks, but because of the weekly revolts, she had always been interrupted.

"And so, in the Battle of Yorktown, we beat the British because they did something very stupid. General Cornwallis hid out in Yorktown, a city near a river. Because of the river, there would be only three ways for him to escape in the event of an attack. What I mean is, American troops were—"

"Will you please state the date and year?" Moe demanded suddenly, and Jack got scared. This meant that a riot was starting or could start. Jack did not know why he knew; he just did. He also knew that because he never participated in these fights, he was called "the retard" by Moe and everyone else.

"What did you say?" asked Mrs. Walter.

"The boy asked you to please state the day and year!" Larry shouted, sounding angry. "So answer the question!"

"Moe and Larry, why did you call out again? You should have raised your hand, as it says in your behavior goals. You are to raise your hand successfully eighty percent of the time, or during four out of five attempts to gain attention, with eighty percent accuracy, and a ninety-five percent confidence interval. This is stated in your Individualized Education Plans."

"Answer the question," growled Larry.

Mrs. Walter went on, "Because of that, *I* won't make my career goals this week, and *you* just lost your teasing-tolerance privileges. I will not protect you from any bullying for one whole week. And I won't tell you the date and year, Moe, because you already know," said Mrs. Walter.

Curly cut in. "We want to make sure that what you are teaching us will help us in the future. We don't think so, as we are learning about what happened in the late 1770s. It has already happened. We should move on. We want to learn about the present. After all, we *are* in the twenty-first century, and the third millennium, and twenty years later, when we are all grown up, we will need to worry about over-dependence on computers, ozone depletion, and global warming."

"We will never need to worry about the military mistakes made two hundred years ago," added Moe.

"So what do you think I should teach you?" asked Mrs. Walter, pretending to agree.

"If we are coming here to become working people of society, you have to teach us the right stuff, not a bunch of crap that we'll never use. Now, answer my question!" said Moe as if he had won an undeclared battle.

"YEAH!" shouted every other student except Jack.

"I do not need to answer that question. You are already getting yourself into big trouble."

"The kid asked a question, so answer it!" shouted John, the student who always stuck up for Moe.

"YEAH!" shouted every student except Jack.

"No, I won't. You're just children. I am an adult, and besides, I am the teacher. You must obey me, but *I* don't have to obey *you*," said Mrs. Walter sharply. "And because you also called out, John, you're going to lose ten points. No big surprise for you this afternoon."

"Oh, no!" cried John mockingly. Then he got up and threw a pencil toward the one small, barred window, where it bounced off the glass.

"Can you p-p-please stop it?" Jack whispered. "I-I-"

"Traitor!" said Moe. "Remember, retard, unless you shut up, we're gonna beat you up on the playground."

"That's one, Moe," warned Mrs. Walter.

"I don't care about your 'one-two-three' method."

"Why are you blaming us?" asked Moe. "You teachers tell us to answer the questions that *you* ask. So we only ask for you to practice what you preach. Remember the golden rule."

"Yes, I do. But that is totally irrelevant to what is going on here. As it is only my job to educate you, I do not have to answer questions that are not important for your education. That's *two*," said Mrs. Walter.

"You did not answer our question when we asked nicely. So learn the *hard* way," said John.

"Everyone, chant with me," said Paul.

And everyone except Jack started chanting: "ALL WE ARE SAY-ING . . . IS ANSWER THE—"

"That's *three*, class!" screamed Mrs. Walter. "Everyone, go to the principal's office now!"

"We won't," said Paul. "We hate school, and we're sick of your martial laws. Everyone, get up and chant."

Then every student (except Jack) got up and marched around the classroom chanting.

"Rules are for your own good. Look at you now! You'll never be functional members of society," said Mrs. Walter, even though she knew she couldn't be heard over the chanting of the boys.

Suddenly the chanting stopped.

"And that's because of school," George replied, "which teaches us to repress our anger and will doom us all to dying of cancer and heart attacks in our fifties. Do you think we remember *anything* we're taught? Well, we don't, so there's no reason why you should teach it."

Mrs. Walter rushed to her desk and pushed a button labeled: PUSH TO CALL in case of FREE THINKING.

Then everyone except Jack marched toward the door and left the classroom. He dropped to his knees and hid under his desk.

"Come back this instant!" Mrs. Walter screamed, forgetting that she had just ordered her students to go to the principal's office.

The P.A. system came to life.

"Yes?" asked Mrs. Bolony, the school secretary. "Is there another riot?"

"Yes, and they're on their way to your office. Think of something good to punish them with."

"Hmm, let me go ask the principal. I'll be right back."

In a few minutes, all the rioting kids had returned with the janitor's spray painter.

Then suddenly, Moe commanded: "STOP!"

Everyone stopped.

"Where's Jack? He didn't listen to his teacher and leave the room. He's the one who should be punished."

"There he is," said Paul. "Let's beat him up." He didn't really mean it, since in his heart he was not a violent person, only angry.

In a show of defiance, though, he hauled Jack out from under his desk and punched him lightly—for show—in the stomach, Jack's most sensitive area due to his autism.

Jack shrieked.

Moe taunted, "You're a traitor! And besides, your shirt's on backwards! *You'll* never be a productive member of society!"

It was true about the shirt, by the way. Jack *had* put it on backwards.

"Yeah, why can't you be like us? Maybe your cerebellum's on backwards," said Pete.

Everyone except Jack laughed.

"QUIET!!!" screamed Mrs. Walter, who was done talking to Mrs. Bolony.

No one listened. John moved toward Jack with an outstretched fist. Jack shrieked again.

Then suddenly, there were three loud thumps, as sharp as gunshots. Jack slumped into the fetal position under his desk again. His heart was pounding so hard, he thought he would drop dead. He wondered who'd been shot. But actually, to tell the truth, the principal had arrived and had knocked on the classroom door.

Because of Jack's sensitive ears, the knocks had sounded like gunshots.

"What has been going on here?" the principal demanded.

"There has been another riot," said Mrs. Walter. "The students have rebelled…again…and it was impossible to teach them about the Revolutionary War."

The principal entered the classroom, sat down in the nearest chair, and rubbed his eyes.

"Why are you all like this?" he asked wearily of no one in particular.

No one in particular heard him.

Then Dr. Drake noticed Jack underneath his desk in the fetal position.

"Which student is this?" asked Dr. Drake.

"Oh, that's Jack, who's probably the most rebellious. He's the one who always has those episodes during fire drills. He complains that he has sensitive ears although no other student complains during a fire drill. He also complains of bullies when we all know it's his own fault he's being bullied. If only he could learn to get along with his peers. It's in his IEP goals, but—"

"Isn't he the boy with autism?"

Mrs. Walters harrumphed. "That's what they say about everybody who's weird these days. Just look at him. It's obvious he's just a fighter."

Dr. Drake looked again at the trembling form hiding under the desk.

"But what can we do?" he said. "The kids in your class are naturally bad."

Then suddenly there was a loud

RRRRRRIIIIIIIIIIIINNNNNNGGGG

and all the kids ran out of the classroom. Jack was now in total shock, so he kept hiding even though he knew he would be bullied big time for not doing what his classmates were doing.

"Wait a minute! That's not the school bell! That's an alarm!"

"Somebody must have set the noisy clock-radio again!" Mrs. Walter said.

Now to most people, it was just an annoying buzz, but to Jack, it was like the explosion of the bomb over Hiroshima—

right next to his ear.

"After them!" Dr. Drake cried.

"I'll get them!" said Mrs. Walter. She ran out to the hall and screamed, "STOP!!!!!!!!!!!!!!!!!!!!!!!!!!!!!!!!"

Then suddenly, all the teachers in the neighboring classrooms in that hallway rushed to their doors and shouted back, "BE QUI-I-I-I-E-T-T!!!!!!!!!!!!!!!!!!"

"What has happened here?" said Mrs. Hevin. "Our class is taking the Houston Aptitude Test for Education, and no one can listen because of the racket!"

"Our class is also taking that test!" said Mrs. Helton.

"Well, somebody better help me catch those kids!" cried Mrs. Walter.

But it was too late. The kids had left the school, to everyone's secret relief.

"Well, I guess all I can do now is get back to the classroom and get ready for another day on Monday," said Mrs. Walter with a sigh.

"Even though normally I'd send out the truant officer," said Dr. Drake, who had followed her into the hall, "it's already two o'clock. There's no use getting them back now."

So Mrs. Walker shuffled back down the hall, only to discover there was one student still in her classroom.

Chapter 2

"Jack! What are you doing in here!" said Mrs. Walter.

"I—I did not leave," whispered Jack from under his desk.

"I can see that," she said, and rolled her eyes. "For your part in the riot, I am going to give you a detention. You must stay after school until five o'clock tonight."

"But I didn't do it! It was—" said Jack.

"I refuse to accept your pleading of innocence! Why do you always try to pin your crimes on other people! You are not going to get through life doing that!" screamed Mrs. Walter.

"But the—"

"Stop making excuses, Jack! You're too old for that! Besides, look at the condition of your ripped clothes! You must have beaten yourself up to hide the fact that *you* led the rebellion! You just wanted to get others in trouble and now you're lying low. Admit that you did that!"

Although Jack was scared about getting in trouble, he thought this was funny. It didn't make any sense.

"I a—am innocent!" said Jack.

"Stop lying to me! I have all the evidence! You did not leave the school with the others, hoping to set them up, and you beat yourself up to try to get them in trouble. When a person tries to get others in trouble, HE will get in trouble. Now I will not take any more of your complaints! You are getting two hours of detention! I am taking you to the principal's office and you will not leave tonight until five o'clock!"

"But my mother yells at me when I'm late!" said Jack, coming out from under his desk and shaking all over. In the past, he would have played frozen, shut down his nervous system to cope with the stress, like those lucky autistic kids down the hall. But Jack's mother had taken him to therapists who used punishments and cattle prods to train his nervous system NOT to shut down in the face of unbearable terror. Now he couldn't play frozen even though he wanted to.

"Well, that's your problem, Mister. Maybe you should have THOUGHT of that before you led the rebellion," said Mrs. Walter.

Then they went to the principal's office, where Dr. Drake was filling out an immense stack of forms.

"Mrs. Walter? What are you doing here?" asked Dr. Drake.

"We have found the person responsible for the rebellion," said Mrs. Walter. "It is Jack Lack."

"Are you sure? As far as I know, bullies never reveal themselves to adults. Remember the sexual assault last year? It took us two months to find out what really happened," said Dr. Drake.

"I'm sure. After all, he did not leave the building when everyone else did, and he beat himself up to make it look like the others did it to him. That means he is a coward, as cowards hurt themselves to make others look guilty," said Mrs. Walter.

"I see," the principal said. "Well, that's quite a bit of evidence against him."

Jack decided to keep a straight face and to hide any laughter as they continued to talk nonsense.

"It's sad. A boy like you trying to make trouble," Dr. Drake continued. "But people who try to make trouble will always get punished. So remember that, Jack. Crime does not pay."

"So I think we should make him sit here for two hours. Is that a good punishment for a riot?" Mrs. Walter said.

"Yes, I believe so. And we will not excuse him from his homework. I believe he has a lot?" asked Dr. Drake.

"Oh, yes. A lot," said Mrs. Walter.

Jack's heart sank. Two hours! His mother yelled at him when he was a minute late! And he was innocent! It was Moe's fault! He started the riot!

Jack sat down in the detention chair, and his thoughts raced around in circles, as always. Images appeared like pop-up ads on the computer screen in his head. Whenever he couldn't pay attention to the outside world, he'd try to explain about the pop-up images—try to tell people to think about how annoying they were on *their* computer—but of course, they never understood.

Why wasn't Moe getting in trouble? In Jack's mind, he saw a pop-up website of menacing fists. Because the universal unwritten code of school states that the truly guilty always get away with their crimes. Therefore, school follows the edicts of the 1500s—guilty until proven innocent, meaning that a person could be charged with a fake crime, but because it was fake, there would be no evidence proving him innocent, and therefore he was guilty. Fortunately, in school, you weren't guillotined or subjected to a swift, cruel death for doing something bad, like the millions who died that way in the 1500s and during the French Revolution. In school, you died slowly, day after day.

Even though it is never acknowledged, in school, the one who is innocent gets blamed. The innocent and the helpless are the ones who suffer. *A school, then, is actually a microscopic version of a feudal society,* Jack thought, with the principal as a king, the students as peasants, and autistic students as slaves. No one is able to do anything without the consent of the party above him. Also, students made up the most population in a school (like the peasants). A pyramid appeared in his mind.

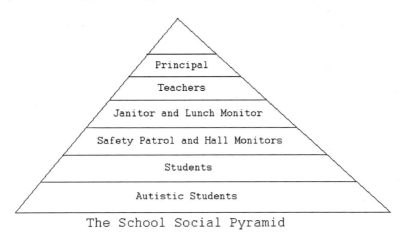

The School Social Pyramid

And each party was in control of the party below it, though no one had control over the party above it.

And to think he lived in America, which was supposed to be a democracy. School is a pre-Revolutionary place, Jack decided.

Like the Catholic Church, which had just decided they were wrong about Galileo four hundred years after he died.

"But aren't you going to tell my mother about this?" asked Jack as soon as he could clear his mind.

"We'll call her and notify her you aren't coming home until five o'clock tonight," said Mrs. Walter.

Then Mrs. Walter left.

"I hope you understand what you have done and the consequences of it, Jack," said Dr. Drake. "And I hope you will never do it again."

Jack understood nothing. Except the stupidity of the adults around him.

* * * *

It was finally 5:00 p.m.

"Okay, Jack, you may go," said Dr. Drake. "I'll see you in one month."

"One month?" asked Jack. "Today is Friday, October fifth. Shouldn't I be seeing you again in three days?"

"I just had a talk with your mother. You'll find out when you get home."

So Jack walked home slowly, knowing he was safe only until he stepped into his house. As he got closer, he took smaller and smaller steps. When he finally entered, he found both his mother and father at the house, which was strange because his father usually got home from work one hour later. His job had long hours.

"We just heard on the news a group of kids ran out of your school today. I'm so happy you aren't one of them, and you are still willing to obey your teacher," said Jack's mother, Susan. "I'm proud of you."

This confused Jack, since he had assumed she would scream and yell at him. But then he could never predict what other people did, since usually their behavior made no sense.

"We've been waiting for you. Something has happened in the family," said Jack's father, Marvin.

Chapter 3

"Your Aunt Eva is going to be remarried," said Jack's mother happily. "We have been invited to stay at Uncle Hayes and Aunt Mary's house in Russiaville for a month to plan the wedding. We are also going to say good-bye to old Aunt Edna, who's dying of mysterious causes. We'll be leaving tomorrow. And your school said it was okay if you left—you know they're always happy when you're gone."

"Didn't you know we were going before this moment?"

"Oh yes, we did," said Jack's mother. "But since you hate changes, we didn't want you to worry. We decided to spring it on you at the last minute."

"But that's twice as bad! I hate changes that are, as that famous autistic savant says, shoved in my face!" said Jack.

Terror struck Jack's heart. Not only did he hate change, he also hated family gatherings, especially ones with his mother's family because they all believed in the assimilation method, meaning that everyone must assimilate into the majority and not get their needs met in order to please the majority. And Aunt Eva and Uncle Hayes were two of his mother's siblings. What was weird was that Uncle Hayes and Aunt Eva both *looked* like loving people. Uncle Hayes had warm brown hair and a smile on his face, and Aunt Eva smiled a lot, too. They looked like they'd never hurt anyone, but inside they were mean. The reason why they were so mean was because Grandpa Charles Thatcher and Grandma Martha Thatcher (originally Milne) were mean parents. Their children became mean parents, which then made each coming generation mean.

They believed that children had no rights. The only nice relative from his mother's side was her weird brother Frank. When he was eighteen, he changed his last name to Thoms, after his beloved Sunday school teacher. He wanted to think for himself. He also did it to give himself a better name for his books, as he was a successful author. Jack had a strong rapport with Frank, since his uncle was the weirdo of his generation.

So, here was his mother's family tree:

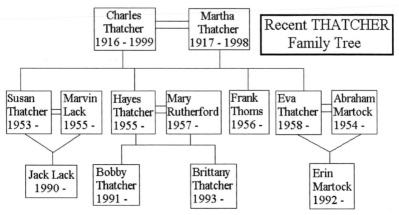

NOTE: Frank Thatcher changed his name to Frank Thoms in 1985.

Charles and Martha were older than usual when they had children, because at first, they didn't want them. Finally, they decided that either they would have them before they were ready, or die childless. And the reason why Frank Thoms and Hayes Thatcher were born a year apart was that Frank was an accident, something his parents never let him forget. Whenever Martha introduced her youngest son, she'd say, sighing: "I don't know where we failed with Frankie, but we did." That scared away all the girlfriends he ever brought home, so he never married.

Jack was studying the family tree he saw in his head (the same chart you just saw above), when his father began to start to talk in an angry way. "And Jack," he said. "I want you to be on your BEST behavior. No talking at all unless it is an emergency. You are not the center of attention and your needs don't count because children are of lesser importance than parents, especially in Uncle Hayes's house," said Jack's father.

"Unlike our house, where everything revolves around you," added Jack's mother. Then, with a sigh: "I don't know where we failed with Jack, but we did."

Your needs don't count because you're a child. That was the theme of the house they were going to. Jack had a lot of memories of that statement, which was told during every gathering. In fact, Jack remembered every time he had been thwarted there. As he got older, he could detect a presence of evil and rejection in that house, saying to him, "You are not welcome in this domain."

He felt sorry for his cousins, who were treated like second-class citizens 24/7. His cousins were also outcasts because of the policy of putting their friends to work once they entered the house. Other kids refused to play with them, because "play" meant things like hauling wood for Uncle Hayes and beating rugs for Aunt Mary. Because of these events, his cousins were horrible brats. Cousin Bobby was the only cousin who wanted to play with Jack, but that friendship was banned by Uncle Hayes two years ago when Jack started teaching Bobby the state capitals, something only "autistic" boys were interested in.

At least once a year, everyone came together and all the children were treated like slaves. The cousins went to a year-round school that started in August each year, with three separate months off during the year: October, March, and July, which compensated for no summer vacation. Sometimes, therefore, the family gatherings lasted an entire month, usually in July, but now, it seemed, the month of October would be the unlucky one. These month-long family visits were supposed to teach Jack social skills and appropriate family interaction. Unfortunately, he usually left more autistic and shut-off than when he arrived.

For example, three years ago, on July 23rd, 1998, Cousin Erin (Aunt Eva's daughter) wanted to go to the zoo. Aunt Eva promised that she would take Erin to the zoo with Cousin Brittany, Bobby's sister. Meanwhile, Aunt Eva's then husband Abraham was to take Jack and his nephew Bobby on a boat tour along the nearby river. (This was one year before Bobby and Jack were banned from interaction.) Jack said to his Uncle Abraham, "I don't want to go."

Eva offered to take Jack to the zoo, but he repeated, "I don't want to go."

Uncle Abraham said, "Well, we can't leave you here. Besides, I am an adult and therefore have total authority over your life like the other adults present. I will force you to go on the boat tour.

Remember," and then everyone else there said it along with him, "CHILDREN COME LAST." This was the motto of the household and was even posted as you entered the house. "And since you are under eighteen, you are a child. You have no say and therefore must do what everyone else does," declared Uncle Abraham.

"But I still don't want to go," said Jack.

"You HAVE to go. You have no say in my house," said Uncle Abraham.

So he was forced to go. When he got into the car, he immediately played frozen, hoping to hurt everyone. But they were only too happy to see him not complain.

At the last minute, though, Cousin Brittany decided that she did not want to go to the zoo—she wanted to go on the boat tour. The adults said, okay, everyone would go on the boat tour.

Hearing this, Cousin Erin said she still wanted to go to the zoo.

"No, you can't," her mother said. "It's no longer an option."

"Why not?" asked Erin.

"Because Brittany is not going and therefore a trip to the zoo is no longer special. Since today is a special day, we can only do special things. A trip to the zoo by yourself is ordinary, since I take you all the time."

"But you promised!" said Erin.

"I *PROMISED* YOU AS LONG AS BRITTANY CAME, AND SHE ISN'T COMING!" roared Aunt Eva. "AND BESIDES, YOU'RE NOT GOING BECAUSE I SAID SO! When I was a child, I learned that children do not question!"

"In my school, I learned that people should always keep their promises," said Erin.

"That's one, Erin," her mother warned. Then Eva turned to her brother Hayes and said, "I just got her re-diagnosed. She doesn't have ADD, as we thought, but ODD: oppositional-defiance-disorder. We're in the process of changing her meds."

Uncle Hayes nodded sympathetically. "Changing meds is always a challenge. When we changed Brittany from Tenex to Depakote—"

"You're a hypocrite!" screamed Erin. "You've taught me to keep my promises! Shouldn't you practice what you preach!"

"That's two, Erin," her mother said.

"But you're not listening to me! That's not fair!" Erin persisted.

"THAT'S THREE!!" roared Aunt Eva. "DO YOU SEE THAT MAPLE TREE OVER THERE? THAT IS THE "ISOLATION TREE." NOW GO THERE AND DO NOT COME BACK FOR TEN MINUTES!"

"But Mom—"

"Twenty minutes, Erin," said Eva, calming down a bit since she was once more in charge of herself.

Jack felt sad for Erin, even though she was very mean to him in return for the rest of the month.

She was still mean to Jack a year later, on July 5th, 1999, when everyone decided to go shopping together. They went to the nearest market, called *Fresh Foods*. To teach their children the value of owning things, Hayes and Mary allowed them to go and find one thing that they would like to get from the store. Since Jack was present, they let him get something, too. According to them, he was old enough now to get things on his own, and besides, it would be good experience for him to have a little independence, despite the fact that Jack was under a cloud of complete terror every time he was supposed to act independent.

"Now remember," said Jack's mother. "You can only get one thing at the store, so make sure it's the thing you want. And then come right back. If you get lost, you should go to the clerk at the Customer Service Desk."

Because he was autistic, he had trouble understanding people. He was wondering why they would tell him to get lost when they really wanted him to get something and return with it. *Why would they give me two contradicting orders at once?* Jack thought. He didn't always understand little words like "if," which didn't represent an object or something he could see. But always desperate to follow orders, he decided that he was supposed to go get lost and go to a clerk, since three years ago, they had given him the order, *"If it is cold outside, go put on a coat."* On that day, it was cold outside, so he put on a coat and his mother praised him. Jack assumed that "if" was just another way of saying "do it." And to him, this was the exact same situation.

So he planned to follow both orders in this way—first to get the thing that he wanted, and then on his way back, to get lost and go to the clerk.

To make everything seem authentic, he got the thing he wanted, then wandered around the store for a while before going to the clerk.

"My name is Jack Lack, and I'm lost," said Jack.

"Do you know the name of your mother and father?" asked the clerk.

"Yes. Their names are Marvin Lack and Susan Lack," said Jack, who was now realizing that he was talking to someone he didn't know and therefore he was disobeying his parents' other rule: *Never talk to strangers.* Now he had three rules to juggle, and he was getting confused.

"Will—will you hurt me if you know my name?" Jack said.

"No, I won't. If I did, I would go to jail," said the clerk.

Then the clerk, doing his job, turned on the P.A. and announced: *"Will Marvin and Susan Lack come to the service desk? Their son Jack is waiting for them."*

Back at the entrance of the store, terror struck into the hearts of the adults.

"Stay here, Marvin. Let me and Mary go find Jack," said Uncle Hayes.

"What has my son done now? I thought autistic kids were *good* with directions!" wailed Jack's mother.

"Well, let's let your brother find out what happened so we can punish him!" said Jack's father.

So Hayes and Mary ran to the desk and found Jack, who had a big smile on his face. He had followed two directions successfully and was waiting to be praised.

"JACK!" screamed Aunt Mary. "WHY DID YOU GET LOST? I THOUGHT AUTISTIC KIDS WERE SUPPOSED TO BE GOOD WITH DIRECTIONS!"

"My mom told me to go to the clerk!" said Jack.

"WE DIDN' T TELL YOU TO GO TO THE CLERK! WE TOLD YOU TO GO TO THE CLERK ONLY IF YOU GOT LOST!" roared Uncle Hayes.

"Excuse me, but your son was very polite about this," said the clerk. "You shouldn't let him wander around. You should be proud that he decided to go to the clerk."

"He's my nephew," said Uncle Hayes, as if correcting this detail was the most important part of the conversation.

"Still, please don't yell at him. You should reward him for coming to me," said the clerk.

"HOW DARE YOU CRITICIZE THE WAY I DISCIPLINE MY NEPHEW? I AM LEGALLY HIS UNCLE AND YOU'RE NOT!" screamed Uncle Hayes.

The clerk, realizing this guy was a lunatic, decided to keep his mouth shut.

"I JUST CAN'T UNDERSTAND WHY YOU HAVE TO ALWAYS DISOBEY YOUR PARENTS! WE ONLY ASKED YOU TO COME HERE IN CASE YOU GOT LOST! WE DIDN'T ASK YOU JUST TO COME HERE! WHY CAN'T YOU UNDERSTAND ORDERS THE WAY EVERY OTHER CHILD DOES IN THIS COUNTRY?" bellowed Aunt Mary.

"But three years ago…"

"NOTHING IS GOING TO EXCUSE YOU, JACK! NEVER GO TO A CLERK UNLESS YOU HAVE TO! WHY CAN'T YOU UNDERSTAND THAT? DO I HAVE TO SCREAM AND YELL AT YOU UNTIL YOU GO DEAF? WHY DO YOU HAVE TO BE SO STUPID AT TIMES?" barked Uncle Hayes.

"You told me to get lost and go to a clerk!" said Jack. "I *was* following your orders!"

"NO, YOU WEREN'T!" shouted Aunt Mary. "I JUST CAN'T UNDERSTAND WHY YOU'RE ALWAYS FIGHTING US WHENEVER WE WANT TO TEACH YOU SOMETHING! YOU WON'T BE ABLE TO LIVE YOUR LIFE TALKING BACK TO EVERYONE WHO TALKS TO YOU! SOMEDAY YOU'LL HAVE TO ADMIT YOU'RE WRONG!"

"Three years ago my mom said to put on a jacket if it was cold. And I did, and she...she..." Jack stopped. He realized it was hopeless trying to reason with these people.

"THAT'S BECAUSE IT WAS TEN BELOW ZERO DEGREES OUT!" screamed Uncle Hayes. "AND BESIDES, THAT WAS DIFFERENT!"

"How?" asked Jack. "I thought rules didn't change."

Suddenly, Jack's mother came and said, "Everyone is waiting for Jack."

"All right then," said Uncle Hayes. "But I'm warning you. If you do this again, you'll be forced to wash the dishes for the next two weeks."

Then Jack went back to his cousins and his father, who were still at the entrance of the store. All the way home in the car, everyone complained about how Jack had wrecked their trip, talking as if he weren't there.

One year ago, in July 2000, when the whole family got together, everyone except Jack decided to go to the local park. This park was famous for "PARKER'S BUSH," the town's tallest shrub named for Dr. Steven Parker. When they got there, Jack went to the swing just to be by himself, only to be caught by Uncle Hayes.

"Why are you here alone? You're supposed to play with your cousins," said Uncle Hayes in his deep voice.

"No one will play with me and I don't want to play with them!" said Jack.

"That's wrong. You should play with your cousins," said Uncle Hayes.

"They hate me," Jack countered.

This was two-thirds true. His female cousins (Erin and Brittany) hated him, and he hated them back. Their hatred was in total agreement. So why should Uncle Hayes cause trouble and intervene if the cousins were in total agreement?

"I'll play with Bobby," Jack offered.

"No. Bobby is not an option. He's been banned from you until my death," said Uncle Hayes.

Jack refused to play with the girls. So Uncle Hayes punished him. First he called out, "ALL CHILDREN EXCEPT BOBBY REPORT TO PARKER'S BUSH!"

Then every cousin reported to the tree except Bobby.

"Now, Jack," said Uncle Hayes. "Do you see that bush? That is now designated the interaction bush. You must go there and stay there until we leave."

"No," said Jack.

"What did you say?" said Uncle Hayes.

"I said, no," said Jack.

"Well, no is *not an option*. You MUST go to the bush and you MUST play with your cousins!" shouted Uncle Hayes.

"No," said Jack.

"Jack, that's one."

"No," said Jack.

"Jack, *that's two!*"

"NO!" shouted Jack.

"Jack, that's three!"

"NO!!!!" screamed Jack.

"NO IS NOT AN OPTION!" shouted Uncle Hayes.

I have to obey this madman, thought Jack. *If all he's going to do is continue the feud between me and my cousins, let him be. Yet he wonders why we fight.*

So Jack played with his girl cousins, and they all were furious together. Then they realized that Hayes was talking and talking with the other grown-ups, since he was an incessant talker and totally wrapped up in his own problems. So when he was talking, the kids would stop playing. Whenever he looked their way, they pretended to be telling stories. It was the first time Jack had ever cooperated with other children in his life. He was actually starting to like his girl cousins—fellow sufferers, and all that—then it was time to go home, and the girls could openly hate him again.

On the way home, Jack wondered why everyone hated him so much. If God made *everyone* in His own image, why were people so mean to autistic children? Weren't autistic kids also made by God? Maybe God wasn't as nice as people thought He was.

Chapter 4

Night came, and Jack's parents forced him to go to sleep. Bedtime actually came earlier than usual, since his parents wanted him to get to sleep at 8:00 p.m. instead of 9:00 p.m. so they could leave early to get to Uncle Hayes and Aunt Mary's house. They warned him that he had better be ready to leave by 9 a.m., or else. As Jack tossed and turned sleeplessly, he wondered what the "or else" would consist of.

The only happiness he had that night was that he had familiarized himself with the route to their house. Road directions were a sedative to his nerves, the predictable lefts and rights forming calm, organized patterns in his mind. One of the supreme joys of his life was actually traveling on a road that he had previously only seen on a map. It made him feel that life in some manner made sense and the future, in one regard, could be trusted.

Jack lived on King Street, so they would take King Street to Walnut Street and turn right. They would go north on Walnut Street to U.S. Highway 40, and they would turn left. Then they would take U.S. Highway 40 to State Road 1, where they would turn right. They stayed on State Road 1 until they reached I-70. They went west on I-70 for about 47 miles until they reached I-465, which they took north and east 11 miles to State Road 431. From I-465, they went north on State Road 431 to U.S. Highway 31, which they took about two dozen miles north to State Road 26. From U.S. Highway 31, they would turn left on State Road 26, and would head west to Uncle Hayes and Aunt Mary's house, on State Road 26 in the town of Russiaville. In total, the trip took about two hours and was 106 miles long.

Jack got up at 7:00 a.m., got dressed, then he went to the kitchen to eat breakfast. On the table, he saw the usual gluten-free flaxseed cereal he couldn't stand, but noticed there was no juice for him to drink. In their own chairs, his parents were sitting, their orange juice glasses raised up, drinking away.

"How come I'm not getting anything to drink?" Jack asked.

His mother laughed. "That's because we don't want you having to go to the bathroom during the trip. We don't want to stop for you, because we want to get there as fast as possible. If you don't drink anything, you won't have to stop and hold us up." She took a long drink from her glass.

"But I'm thirsty! And my medicine is to stop me from being a brat! How will I take it without juice?" said Jack.

"We can deal with that," said Jack's father.

"*Of course you can deal with it.* You're not the one who's going to suffer from thirst!"

"This is a special occasion, so you must change your expectations. You may drink juice every morning on normal days only. On special days you must sacrifice your comfort for others. So we're not giving you apple juice," said Jack's mother. She took another long, slurpy drink.

Because Jack refused to drink water, he normally drank apple juice in the morning to get some fluids in his body. It was a routine for him. It was also routine for him to take the medicine, which required a large amount of fluids to get the pill to go down.

"Three words: *deal with it,*" said Jack's father. "Now eat, or else you're not eating until dinner tonight."

"But people need fluids in order to survive. I learned that in school," said Jack.

"People don't die after a day without apple juice. They die after a week without it," said Jack's mother. "So eat up, Jack, because the food you see here is all you are going to get. And we can deal with another brat. Where we're going, the house is full of them. Now shut up and eat so we won't be late."

And he did, wondering what they were going to be late *for*, since the wedding was weeks away.

After he ate his breakfast, he realized that if he was forced to go, he wanted to get it over as quickly as possible. Suddenly his mind wanted to go immediately. It became an uncontrollable thought, churning and chanting endlessly. So he asked his parents, "Are we going now?"

"Can't you wait?" cried Jack's mother. "It takes a lot of hard work to plan these trips. You don't see that work. You see a trip handed to you and, therefore, you just enjoy yourself. But you don't see all the sacrifices your father and I make to have a trip like this so that we can give you a good time. All we ask is that you wait patiently while we do all the work to prepare."

Jack stood silent, trying to understand this. If his mother and father *truly* hated planning the trip, then why do it? Jack certainly didn't like the trips that they made. So if they also hated them, why did they all have to go?

After one hour of waiting, it was 8:30 a.m. They had only a half-hour to get out the door at 9:00 a.m., the time that Jack's parents promised they would leave.

Well, then it was 8:45 a.m., and Jack's mind was chanting "Time to go, Time to go" uncontrollably. No one cared that Jack was trying to keep to the schedule his parents had set. It was bad enough that he had to go there, that they had threatened him with an "or else" that had kept him awake in terror. Now they were delaying him from going to the place he was forced to go. It may seem weird to you that he'd be going crazy to go to somewhere he hated, but Jack believed that if a person was going to force you to do something, they should force you right away and not wait around to force you.

At 9:00 a.m., Jack realized that nothing would happen unless he reminded his parents of their schedule. So Jack said, "Mom, it's nine a.m. Aren't we going to go?"

Jack's mother exploded. "Stop complaining, Jack! We are working as fast as we can!"

Jack stood still again, trying to understand. But it was hopeless. His parents would continue to be inconsistent. Finally, it was 10:00 a.m. and he had waited for an additional hour. His parents came into the living room and then said to Jack, "It's time to go, Jack! Stop dawdling!"

His mother pointed at the black-and-white clock in the living room.

"Jack, it's ten o'clock! We were supposed to leave an hour ago!"

"If you hadn't fought us at breakfast, we would have been on the road by now! Why do you always make trouble?" said Jack's father.

"I told you when it was nine," said Jack.

"But we weren't done. Why do you always have to disrupt EVERYTHING that we want to do? Can't you think of others for a change?" said Jack's mother.

"If we keep fighting, we're not going to get out the door," Jack reminded them, pleased at his contribution.

"That's different, Jack. Discipline comes over schedules. *Now get ready.* You should have gotten ready while you were waiting. Why didn't you put your socks and shoes on?"

"You didn't tell me to."

"Can't you use your head? You have a large one, so of course you can think!" said Jack's mother.

"No one told me to put my socks and shoes on," Jack persisted.

"Can't you reason it out? We're already one hour late. Why do you have to make us even more late?" said Jack's father.

"Every time I make my own decision, you yell at me," said Jack.

His mother shook her head, then pointed to the shoes.

Jack put on his socks and shoes and started to go to the car.

"STOP!" screamed Jack's mother.

"What?" said Jack, stopping dead, his nerves paralyzed from the noise.

"What do you think you are doing?" said Jack's mother.

"What?" said Jack.

"We don't want you to go in the car yet. We just told you to get ready," said Jack's father.

"But I HAVE to get into the car in order to get to Uncle Hayes and Aunt Mary's house," said Jack.

"We didn't tell you to go into the car. We only told you to put your shoes on and continue waiting again," said Jack's mother.

"But you didn't..." Jack began, wishing to point out that she had NOT told him to wait, only to—but what good would it do to tell her?

"It's so easy to understand," his mother continued. "Why do you have so much trouble obeying us? We're your parents, and God put you on this planet to obey us until 2008, when you will turn eighteen."

"Okay, enough arguing. *Now* we want you to go into the car," said Jack's father.

So Jack went into the car and waited while his parents took their three suitcases into the trunk of the car (one for each person), and then they set off for Uncle Hayes and Aunt Mary's house.

Jack was silent for most of the trip, even though he was carsick from sitting in the back seat. He imagined rows and rows of train departure times in his mind, to pass the time. This worked for the first hour of the two hours that it took to get to Uncle Hayes and Aunt Mary's house. But then, after one hour, he had to go to the bathroom. He tried to hold it in. This worked for five more minutes, and then he couldn't hold it anymore. So he said to his parents, "Mom! Dad! I have to go to the bathroom!"

"Can't you wait? When I was little, my mother made me hold it in for hours during a car trip, and I didn't complain!" said Jack's father. "She told me it was healthy."

"And you may just be imagining it," added Jack's mother. "You know how you are with water. You say you have to when you don't."

Then suddenly, the car made a strange sound. "What's going on now?" said Jack's father, who was driving the car.

"The car is stalling. It may be out of gas," said Jack's mother. "There's a gas station over there. We can get gas and then Jack can finally go to the bathroom."

So they did. Jack finally got to go to the bathroom, and he was so happy that the car had personal needs that he thanked God for it.

Back on U.S. Highway 31, Jack continued to be silent until finally they got to Uncle Hayes and Aunt Mary's house. Jack now remembered where he was—a place where everybody treated him as a third-class citizen, behind the other kids, who were second-class and therefore a step above him.

Jack got out of the car and rang the doorbell. Uncle Hayes answered it. He was dressed in a suit and tie and wore a mustache, unlike last year when he had shaved it off.

"Come in," said Uncle Hayes.

Jack walked in. The clock nearby read 12:05 p.m.

"Hello, Aunt Mary," he called to his aunt, who was standing on the other side of the room dusting a table. He walked toward her.

"JACK, CLOSE THE DOOR!" she screamed. "A DRAFT IS COMING INTO THE HOUSE AND WE'LL HAVE TO PAY MORE MONEY HEATING IT! AND WHY DIDN'T YOU TAKE OFF YOUR SHOES BEFORE COMING INTO THE HOUSE? CAN'T YOU READ THE SIGN ON THE FRONT DOOR!"

Chapter 5

Jack stood still, confused.

Throughout his life, his mother had preached that when you greeted a person, you had to say a greeting word such as "Hello" or "Hi" before you talked about anything else. It was impolite to launch into the subject you wanted to talk about before saying one of those words. Only autistic people did stuff like that. Aunt Mary was an adult and not autistic. Shouldn't she know about proper social skills?

"JACK, STOP STANDING THERE AND CLOSE THE DOOR!" screamed Aunt Mary. "IT'S GETTING COLD IN HERE! DON'T YOU KNOW THAT HEATING A HOUSE COSTS—"

Jack turned quickly to close the door; then it opened wider.

"What is going on here? Why is the door open?" asked Jack's mother, who came into the house with Jack's suitcase. "Why are you yelling at Jack? I can't believe it, Jack—we're here for less than a minute and you've already done something wrong."

"I'll tell you what happened, Susan," said Uncle Hayes. "Jack came in and forgot to close the door. When Mary asked him to close it, he refused."

"I was about to close it when Mom came in!" wailed Jack.

"You're just making an excuse now. Jack, why didn't you close the door when you came in?" said Aunt Mary.

"I thought it closed by itself. It does in *our* house," said Jack, who turned to try once more to close the door.

"A *likely* story. Well, you'll soon realize that kids know their place in this house. Not like in—"

"Why is it so cold in here?" asked another voice coming into the room. Jack jumped back so the door wouldn't hit him.

It was Jack's father. He had walked in and noticed that Jack had done something wrong. "Jack, did you forget to close the door again?" he said.

"No. I was going to when Mom…and then you…"

"WHY CAN'T YOU EVER LEARN TO CLOSE THE DOOR WHEN YOU ENTER A PERSON'S HOUSE?" screamed Jack's father.

"Marvin, we've already tried yelling at him. It doesn't work. I don't know how you failed with Jack, but you sure did. In our household, he would have been whipped dozens of times by now," said Aunt Mary.

"I DON'T CARE! MY SON HAS GOT TO LEARN!" said Jack's father.

"But I'm innocent!" said Jack.

"YOU HAD NO INTENTION OF CLOSING THAT DOOR, JACK. ADMIT IT!" screamed Aunt Mary.

"Mom, I'm ready to go swimming now!" said a voice from somewhere else in the house. Cousin Brittany came running down the hallway wearing a red bathing suit. "Mom, can we go? You said we could go when family came over. And they're here."

"I'm ready, too, Mom," said another voice. It was Cousin Bobby coming out of the hallway dressed in black trunks.

"Quiet, everyone," said Aunt Mary. "Brittany, stay there. Bobby, you are going to have to leave this room."

"Why?" said Cousin Bobby.

"Just do it. Why do you always have to ask why when you're given an order? You'll never survive the army, Bobby. In the army you are punished for asking *why* you must follow an order. I enlisted for four years, so I know," said Uncle Hayes.

"You know the rule," his mother, Mary, said. "Jack is in the room."

"No. I will not leave this room," said Bobby. "It's a stupid rule and there's no true purpose for it. What's so wrong with Cousin Jack?"

"I told you. He'd make a bad soldier," said Uncle Hayes.

No, you didn't, thought Jack. *You said Bobby would make a bad soldier.*

"He is a bad influence on you. Remember two years ago when you began to act like him?" asked Aunt Mary.

"But I like state capitals! Can't you reconsider?" said Bobby.

"I have said enough," said Aunt Mary. "YOU ARE GOING

TO LEAVE THIS ROOM OR ELSE YOU'RE NOT GOING SWIMMING!"

"Fine. No swimming," said Bobby.

"No is not an option," warned Uncle Hayes.

"Bobby, *that's one,*" said Aunt Mary.

Jack couldn't believe it. She was doing the count-down already.

"I will not leave this room."

"Bobby, *that's two.*"

"I'm sorry. I won't go."

"It's my fault," said Jack.

"It's not your fault," said Bobby.

"That's three!" screamed Aunt Mary. "It's not up to you to decide whose fault it is! NOW LEAVE THIS ROOM!"

Bobby gave a last, longing look at his only male cousin, and left the room.

"YOU MAY ONLY COME BACK INTO THE LIVING ROOM WHEN WE ARE READY TO LEAVE!" she roared.

"In order for us to go swimming, we are going to have to take two cars," said Uncle Hayes, all business again.

"Two! Your van has enough to hold us all," said Jack's father.

"Marvin, remember that Jack cannot be in the same place with Bobby."

"If your son can't be with my son, then what happens when we get to the pool?" said Jack's father.

"The place we are going to is a big complex with four pools. It's in Kokomo. Your son can be in a different pool than my son. If Brittany is in the same pool with your son Jack, they'll be forced to play with each other. That will teach Jack some social skills," said Uncle Hayes.

"That's great. We'll all have a wonderful time."

Then they laughed.

Aunt Mary said, "Well, I'll drive Brittany, Bobby, Susan, and Hayes in the van, and you can take Jack in your car."

Jack decided not to mention that he didn't want to go.

Jack and his father got back into the car, and off they went.

Along the way, Jack fixated on road signs, to take his mind

off the awful carsickness. They took State Road 26 east to U.S. Highway 31, turned left, and took U.S. Highway 31 north to Washington St, which they went northwest on to the driveway of the Duncan Pool Complex on Washington St. and Hoffer Street.

* * * *

The Duncan Pool Complex was in a three-story building. The first floor had the pools, the second floor had a gym, the third floor had a lounge and classrooms, and the basement had the locker rooms. The pools took up the entire first floor, so the locker rooms were down in the basement and there were stairs leading up to the pool from the locker room.

Jack's father came out of the car wearing his backpack, which had their swimsuits and towels.

"We need to go to the front desk and sign in," said Uncle Hayes.

At the front desk, they were met by a dark-haired woman.

"You have guest passes, I presume?" she asked.

"Yes, I do. Here they are," said Uncle Hayes.

"Okay," she said, grabbing and examining them as if to determine whether they were counterfeit. "Now remember, Mr. Thatcher, if your guests do any damage or break any rules during their stay here, *you* are responsible. Do you understand?" said the woman.

"Yes," said Uncle Hayes.

"Thank you. Welcome to the Duncan Pools Complex and have a nice day," said the woman.

Then they rode the elevator down to the basement.

In the elevator, Uncle Hayes said to everyone, "I forgot to tell you. We expect to meet Aunt Eva when we get to the basement."

"AUNT EVA!" cried everyone in delight.

Well, everyone except Jack. Jack knew that Aunt Eva, who was remarrying, was going to be mean to him like everyone else.

Aunt Eva was in the basement, waiting for them. Jack's heart instantly started pounding in horror, as he realized he would have to socialize once more with someone whom he hated. What was worse was that it was sprung on him, or "shoved in his face."

Chapter 6

"Hi there, everyone," said Aunt Eva, who was wearing a black dress. "Cousin Erin couldn't come. She had soccer practice. I came to talk about plans for my marriage. Can you believe it? Soon you're going to have another uncle! His name is Peter Norman, and he is very nice."

"Are you going to join us for swimming?" asked Aunt Mary.

"No, not really. I didn't bring a black bathing suit. I actually came to talk to you and Hayes," said Aunt Eva.

Jack was happy that Aunt Eva was ignoring him. Normally, she would have criticized him for talking too much, or for not saying anything, or for not saying hello, or for only saying hello, or for not saying hello before launching into his favorite subject, or for only saying hello then nothing else. It didn't matter what he said or didn't say—in the past, it was always wrong.

When everyone except Eva had changed into their suits, they went up to the pools. There were four pools in the four quadrants of the room: northwest, northeast, southwest, and southeast. The pools were named Kennedy, Johnson, Nixon, and Ford, with Kennedy and Johnson to the left, and Nixon and Ford to the right.

"Bobby and Brittany, please sit down until we're ready to supervise you in the pool," said Jack's mother. "Jack, come with me."

Jack was happy, because at least he had some time by himself. He knew it wouldn't last long.

"What pool are you going to take Bobby to?" said Jack's mother.

"I don't know," said Uncle Hayes.

"The four pools are named after presidents, so I'm going to give a quiz on presidents, and the pool we go into is the first one someone answers correctly," said Jack's father.

Uncle Hayes glared at him for a moment. Quizzes on presidents reminded him of the quizzes on state capitals that Jack had given Bobby, and which had gotten Jack branded hopelessly autistic and banished from his son. Maybe the whole Lack family had a touch of craziness.

Jack's mother went to Brittany and said, "Brittany, come with me." Then she went to Jack and said, "Jack, come with me."

Then she said to Brittany and Jack, "To choose which pool we are going to swim in first, I am going to give you a quiz."

Uncle Hayes glared at her, too, but said nothing.

"Here's your first question," Jack's mother said. "Who resigned because of the Watergate scandal?"

"Gerald Ford, thirty years ago," said Brittany smugly.

"You were right about it being thirty years ago, Brittany, but it was not Gerald Ford. It was Richard Nixon," said Jack's mother. "Here's the next question: Which president was assassinated in the early sixties?"

"Gerald Ford," said Brittany just as smugly.

"You're wrong again. Next question: Who pardoned Nixon for his illegal actions during the Watergate scandal?" said Jack's mother.

"Gerald Ford," said Jack.

"Hey, that's not fair!" Brittany protested. "He stole my answer!"

"You are right, Jack. We will swim in the Ford Pool," said Jack's mother while Brittany glared at Jack.

The Ford Pool was where Uncle Hayes and Aunt Mary were talking to Aunt Eva. Jack was happy because now he could listen to their conversation. Marvin had taken Bobby to the Kennedy Pool, to be as far away as possible.

They jumped into the Ford Pool and Jack instantly began listening to Uncle Hayes and Aunt Mary's conversation with Aunt Eva at the side of the pool.

"The wedding is to take place on Saturday, one week from today. In the meantime, I would like to stay at your house until Peter and I close on our new house. I left my old house this morning."

"Of course you can stay with us. Susan, Marvin, and their son Jack are also staying," said Uncle Hayes.

"I knew all along that I would need everyone to come up early so that they can help me with the final preparations. Tomorrow we are going to make the final arrangements at our chosen site—the Jones Mark Hotel near the airport. I've hired a catering service for our reception. I couldn't have it at my Catholic church because my last husband divorced me."

Aunt Eva had been married once before.

"Jack! Come here! We're going to decide what game to play first!" said Jack's mother, who was with Brittany in the pool.

Jack swam away, but he could still hear the conversation, as his mother was not far into the pool.

"We're going to play Jump Race," said Jack's mother. "In this game, you jump around the pool until you get to right here in the shortest possible way."

Then she pointed a place inside the pool where they were to stop.

"Okay, ready, set, GO!"

Jack and Brittany began to race, but Jack jumped slowly so that he could catch snippets of the conversation. He couldn't care less about winning.

"On Tuesday we take our stuff into our new home, but we won't stay there for the night until Saturday, our wedding night. So we need a place to stay until then. On Friday we have the wedding rehearsal and dinner. If everything works out right, we'll have a good start to our marriage," said Aunt Eva.

"I must also tell you that tonight, someone is coming to dinner along with all of us; my brother Frank," Uncle Hayes announced to Aunt Eva. "He is a very weird guy, because he believes in everything that we don't believe in and often fights with us, but he is still my brother and therefore is welcome."

"He's my brother too," Aunt Eva reminded him.

Uncle Hayes stopped speaking then, because he had forgotten.

"He'll be delighted to see Jack. They have a strong rapport with each other," said Aunt Mary.

This was true. Out of the entire family, only Uncle Frank could really understand Jack.

"After the marriage, we may also have to attend a funeral in Cyclone," said Aunt Eva sadly. "Aunt Edna is dying at the age of eighty-five. She has liver cancer, and the doctor says she has only a month to live."

Meanwhile, Jack had been so tuned into the conversation that he had forgotten all about the jump race.

Jack swam quickly to his mother. Luckily, the race was still going and his mother hadn't noticed his absence. This was the first time he had gotten away with breaking the rules during a family gathering in a long time, since his parents were harder on him during these events.

So Jack, Cousin Brittany, and his mother continued playing at the Ford Pool, and Jack's father went back to the Kennedy Pool with Cousin Bobby. They switched pools in one hour, and then stayed until the pools closed.

It was time to go home. Everyone left the pool and changed into their regular clothes. Then they walked into the hallway to get to the entrance.

"I guess it's time to say good-bye," said Aunt Eva. "But I'll see you tomorrow."

Then she left.

Jack, along with everyone else, walked to the elevator. In the elevator were four buttons, one for each floor, with the words *PLEASE PRESS* above them. Jack pressed all four buttons.

"JACK!" his mother screamed.

"What?" asked Jack, who realized he was in trouble.

"LOOK AT WHAT YOU'VE DONE!"

"What?" asked Jack.

"I CAN'T BELIEVE YOU! YOU PRESSED ALL THE BUTTONS ON THE ELEVATOR! NOW IT IS GOING TO HAVE TO STOP AT ALL OF THE FLOORS IN THIS BUILDING!" bellowed Jack's father.

"But we're getting off after one flight. It won't affect us," said Jack.

"BUT WHY DID YOU HAVE TO PRESS THE NUMBERS? NOW SOMEONE ELSE WILL BE INCONVENIENCED BECAUSE OF YOU! THEY WILL

HAVE TO WAIT LONGER! WHY DID YOU DO IT?" screamed Jack's mother.

"I did it because it said *PLEASE PRESS* right above the buttons! If it said that, then the person who made the elevator wanted me to press them!" said Jack.

"HE WANTED YOU TO PRESS THE BUTTON OF YOUR FLOOR! I CAN'T TAKE THIS ANYMORE, JACK! YOU ARE ELEVEN YEARS OLD! ELEVEN-YEAR-OLDS SHOULD ALREADY KNOW THIS BY NOW! HOW COULD YOU BE SO STUPID?" yelled Jack's father.

"Why do you have to assume knowledge and expectation on the basis of age?" asked Jack. "That seems even more stupid than what I did."

"THAT'S BECAUSE EVERY OTHER ELEVEN-YEAR-OLD IN THE WORLD KNOWS THOSE THINGS!" yelled Jack's mother.

"I was trying to obey the sign!" said Jack.

"THE SIGN SAID TO 'PLEASE PRESS'! THAT ONLY MEANS IF YOU HAVE TO, NOT IF YOU DON'T WANT TO! JACK, I CAN'T TAKE THIS ANYMORE! WHY ARE YOU MAKING SO MANY EXCUSES WHEN YOU'VE BEEN CAUGHT DOING SOMETHING RED-HANDED!" roared Jack's mother.

Ding!

The doors flew open. They were at the first floor.

"I can't yell at you in public anymore, but remember, if you do anything more, you will be punished," said Jack's father.

So they all walked out of the elevator.

* * * *

At home, Jack was on the computer in the office looking for something on the Internet while Aunt Mary was talking to his mother. Outside it had begun to rain.

Before we continue the story, though, I would like to talk to you about the house that Uncle Hayes and Aunt Mary lived in where Jack was going to stay for a month. It was a ranch house with two floors: a basement and a first floor.

The house had three bedrooms unless you counted the two guest rooms that were in the basement as bedrooms. It was built in 1947. The people who built the house also lived in it. They were a married couple: Agnes and Angus Fredrickson. The house originally resembled a square, but the Fredricksons, ten years after having built the house, decided to make the first floor bigger (which was why the basement was smaller than the first floor).

The Fredricksons lived in the house for twenty-five years until they retired in 1972 and moved into a retirement home. The house was sold to a widow named Mary Chesterson and she lived there until her death in 1985. Mary willed the house to her son, Lloyd Chesterson, and he sold the house to Aunt Mary and Uncle Hayes, who have lived there for about fifteen years.

Hayes and Mary occupied the master bedroom on the first-floor, and Bobby and Brittany had the other first-floor bedrooms. Jack was sleeping in Brittany's bedroom, and Erin was to sleep in Bobby's bedroom. The first floor also contained a living room, where the front door led, a family room, a dining room, a kitchen, where the side door led, and there was a hallway that formed a perfect circle going from the living room, around the bedrooms, and to the family room. The family room, however, wasn't always a family room—before the addition was made on the first floor, it was used as a bedroom. The hall provided access to two bedrooms (each with a closet), a bathroom, a hall closet, the two-car garage, the master bedroom with an additional bathroom and a closet, the office, the laundry room, and the back door. In the living room was the stairway to the basement. The stairway led into the game room, two guest rooms, the laundry room, and the utility room where the water heater, furnace, and electrical breakers were. Jack's parents were sleeping in one guest room, and Aunt Eva was sleeping in the other guest room.

To help you visualize what I have told you, here is a detailed floor plan of the house:

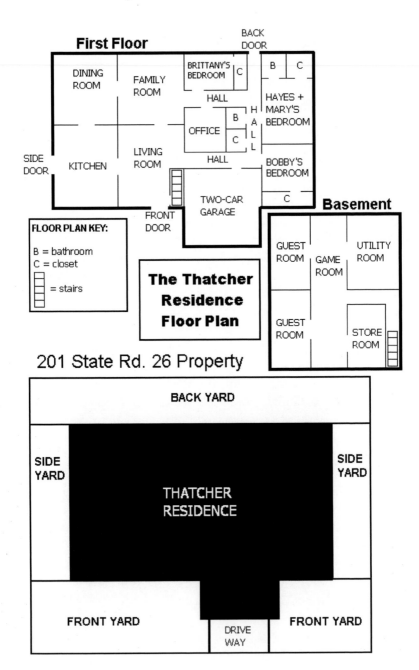

You may return to this map to visualize the house in a later scene. Now that I am done talking about it, the story shall continue:

"Frank is coming tonight at six p.m., in one hour," said Aunt Mary. "We will be going out to eat with him at The Market Grill."

"I just hope he doesn't argue with us and yell this time like he's done before," said Jack's mother. "It set a bad example for the kids. We never yell."

"I'm sure he will. But you have to remember—he hasn't gotten married and his personality has caused him to fail in life. He may be a good writer, but that doesn't mean he's a good person," said Aunt Mary.

"Well, I think we should tell everyone," said Jack's mother.

"Then she screamed to everyone in the living room, "I HAVE AN ANNOUNCEMENT TO MAKE! FRANK IS COMING TONIGHT IN ONE HOUR! WE WILL BE GOING OUT TO THE MARKET GRILL WITH HIM!"

Jack was happy, even though his mother's outburst hurt his ears. Frank was a nice person, and he often argued with his family about how wrong they were to do what they did. Frank was often right, although no one in Jack's family realized that.

Jack wondered how long it would take until the first fight broke out.

Chapter 7

Jack couldn't wait to see his Uncle Frank.

And the good news was, he only had to wait one hour.

"Ding dong!" rang the doorbell at 6:00 p.m.

Cousin Brittany ran to get it.

"Hi, Uncle Frank!" she said.

"Hi, Brittany. I'd like to…"

Aunt Mary entered the room.

"BRITTANY!" she screamed. "WHY DID YOU OPEN THE DOOR?"

"Mary, what is going on here?" said Uncle Frank. "Why are you yelling at Brittany?"

"Because she answered the door. My daughter is not allowed to answer the door when a person comes, because she is a child and it is an adult's job," Aunt Mary lectured him.

"All she wanted to do was let me in from the pouring rain outside, didn't you, Brittany?" said Uncle Frank gently.

"Yes, Uncle Frank," said Brittany.

"You weren't expected until six! I can't believe it!" said Aunt Mary. "A rule has been broken here! I want to see some remorse."

"Remorse? All she did was open a door!"

"She may just have opened a door, Frank, but in our household, only adults open—"

"I'm sure she opened it because she knew it was me!" said Uncle Frank.

Then Frank took off his coat and put it on the coat rack in the house.

Jack looked away from everyone. The angry words were all his overloaded mind could process. He couldn't bear to process visual images of anger at the same time. Gee, Frank hadn't even finished saying hello before the first fight had begun. And now Jack was convinced that Aunt Mary didn't know appropriate social skills. It was the second time she had launched into her subject matter before saying "hello."

"She should be punished," Aunt Mary was saying. "A rule is a rule."

"She didn't intend to do anything wrong!" Frank continued. "It's not like she killed anybody! Other than murder, a person should only get punished if they do something bad on purpose!"

"I make the rules and regulations in this house, and I do not tolerate insubordination!"

"Look at you! You're seething with anger over nothing!"

This is why I like you, Uncle Frank, Jack thought.

"THIS IS WHY I HATE YOU!" Aunt Mary screamed. "THIS IS WHY I'VE HATED YOU FOR TWENTY YEARS! YOU DISAGREE WITH EVERYTHING OTHER PEOPLE SAY!"

"I do not. But I do acknowledge that children have needs. That's why I write books for them."

"I hate your books!" Aunt Mary sneered.

"Well, I'm hungry," said Uncle Hayes, coming in from the other room. "Let's get ready to go to dinner."

Now Jack was really confused. This was the second time an adult had entered the room without saying hello.

* * * *

"So this is The Market Grill."

It was 6:30 p.m., and the kids were starving. Jack hadn't had anything since his dry gluten-free cereal that morning.

"I see, Mary," said Uncle Frank. "We don't have these kinds of restaurants where I live."

"Where do you live now?" asked Cousin Bobby.

"I live in Flora, Indiana, on Elm Street."

"That's off State Road 75," Jack said timidly.

"Why, that's right!" Uncle Frank beamed. "Jack, how did you—"

"Jack," his mother warned. "Remember that no one wants to hear about highways and street directions."

A waiter came to the table. "Hi, my name is Wayne, and I'll be your server tonight. What can I get for you?"

"I'll have the Chicken Vesuvio with red mashed potatoes and some lemonade," said Uncle Hayes.

"I'll have the London Broil with fried mushrooms and some Sprite," said Aunt Mary.

"I'll have the Turkey Barbecue Sandwich with some Pepsi," said Uncle Frank.

"I'll have the Chicken Caesar Salad with water," said Jack's mother.

"I'll have the Garden Salad with water," said Jack's father.

"I'll have the Fried Potato Skins with a Coca-Cola," said Uncle Hayes.

"I'll have the Hot Dog Supreme from the kid's menu with Dr. Pepper," said Cousin Brittany.

"I'll have the Hamburger Supreme from the kid's menu with some Coca-Cola," said Cousin Bobby.

"I'll have the Greek Salad and some apple juice," said Jack.

"Greek salad?" Brittany laughed. "What kind of a retarded food is that?"

"I'm allergic to gluten," Jack said.

Aunt Mary reached into her purse and pulled out a pill bottle. She wrenched off the childproof cap and handed two pills to Brittany, who made a face but put them in her mouth and swallowed them with a sip of water.

"As I was saying," Frank said, "my new story was published three weeks ago. It's called *Children of Ghosts*. It's about these three children whose parents go on a vacation to Detroit, Michigan. The mother asks her twin brothers to take care of the children. They take a taxi to the local train station to board their train to Detroit, Michigan. When they try to buy their tickets, the train is already full, so they decide to go to San Francisco, California, instead. In San Francisco, they hear on the news that the train that they had planned to ride on to Detroit derailed in Lansing.

"Because the parents planned to visit their cousin Lars in Detroit, when he sees the news that the train derailed due to a mechanical malfunction and the people in the front car died, he assumes his cousins are dead because they were in the front car. He calls the twin brothers and informs them that the parents have died. The twin brothers, who believe in ghosts, start to teach the children about their beliefs and take them to the local séance, and they begin to perform daily ceremonies that involve contacting their parents' spirits.

"The children, however, don't believe anything the uncles say, as their parents had told them numerous times there were no ghosts. So it's up to them to find out whether their parents really died.

"Meanwhile, the two parents are having a wonderful time in San Francisco and are unaware of what's going on."

"That's a very interesting story," said Jack's mother.

"By the way, Aunt Eva and her fiancé are coming to our house tomorrow, and they're staying over until the wedding takes place," said Uncle Hayes.

"What's a *fiancé?*" asked Cousin Brittany.

"It's what you call the person you're going to get married to before you get married. For example, after your mother agreed to marry me but before the wedding, she was my fiancée. Another way of saying it is a "husband-to-be" or "wife-to-be," said Uncle Hayes.

"So then, Peter is Aunt Eva's husband-to-be," said Cousin Brittany.

"That's right," said Uncle Hayes.

"Who is Peter?" asked Uncle Frank.

"Peter is Eva's fiancé. They're getting married in about one week," said Aunt Mary.

"No. I meant, *who* is Peter?" said Uncle Frank.

"Peter is the son of a rich lawyer," Aunt Mary sneered. "Does that satisfy you?"

"Well, not really."

"Mom," said Brittany. "Can I have some more water? The pills got stuck."

"Can Uncle Frank come to the wedding?" Jack asked.

Aunt Mary glared at him.

"Why, I'd love to," said Uncle Frank, ignoring his sister-in-law. "Where is it?"

"Jack..." his mother warned, but Jack couldn't stop his

mouth from continuing.

"It's at the Jones Mark Hotel near the airport on Executive Road just south of the Airport Highway. You can just take State Road 75 to I-74, and then I-74 to I-465, and I-465 south to the Airport Highway, and then to Executive Road," said Jack.

"Mom, *can I have some more—*" Brittany repeated.

"Eva hired a catering service and the justice of the peace in Marion County. I just hope the wedding will be a good one and that Eva and Peter Norman will have a good time together," said Aunt Mary, ignoring her daughter.

"I also hope Erin likes her stepfather," said Uncle Frank.

"*Mom, can I have some more water?*" asked Cousin Brittany, having tried two times before.

"Now, Peter Norman—"

"Are you deaf?" asked Uncle Frank.

"Deaf? Why of course I'm not deaf. But why did you interrupt me?" asked Aunt Mary.

"Well, if you aren't deaf, then you must have heard your daughter try to get your attention," said Uncle Frank.

"Yes, I did," said Aunt Mary.

"Well, then, why didn't you answer her question?" asked Uncle Frank.

"Because we were talking. And she was interrupting us," said Aunt Mary.

"Actually, *you* were interrupting *her,*" said Uncle Frank.

"Frank, my children know that when two adults are talking, they will not be paid attention to until we're done with our—"

Brittany began to choke.

"But you seemed to be done talking until you changed the subject," said Uncle Frank, who immediately shoved his own water glass into Brittany's hand.

"Why did you do that?" asked Aunt Mary.

"Your daughter was choking. And remember, it's just as impolite to interrupt a child as it is an adult," said Uncle Frank.

"No, *you're* wrong. It's appropriate to interrupt a child to show them who's boss." said Aunt Mary.

"But I'm sure you didn't like it when you were a child? I

know I didn't, and that's why I preach that children should come first. After all, those children will *become* adults and keep the family going. They are the most important part of society," said Uncle Frank.

"Stop it, Frank! You're not a parent! You don't understand! If you want to be nice to children, go hire a woman to give you some kids! Then you'll find out what they're really like," Aunt Mary sneered.

Frank knew he was getting nowhere and that he had just been insulted, but he knew a way to outsmart Aunt Mary.

"Mary, you preach that adults have total authority over children, right?" asked Uncle Frank.

"It's the truth," said Aunt Mary.

"Well, then, I am an adult, and therefore I have that power, right?" asked Uncle Frank.

"Yes, you do," said Aunt Mary, realizing her goose had been cooked.

"Then, I am going to ask that these children's questions get answered," said Uncle Frank. "And I'd like to take Jack, Bobby, and Brittany to the park alone after dinner. There's still enough light left."

"Okay, but remember, Bobby and Jack are banned from interaction, so don't let them play with each other. And you have to force Jack to play with Brittany because Jack hates going to the park. Be prepared for him to act like a brat," said Aunt Mary.

"Okay, Mary. But if they are banned, why are they sitting together at this restaurant?" asked Uncle Frank.

"The reason why is because we want to sit together and not have separate tables. And besides, they aren't talking to each other. And that's what counts," said Aunt Mary. She didn't like being talked back to.

Just then the waiter returned with their orders.

"Enjoy your meal," he said, but no one answered.

Why didn't someone say thank you? Jack wondered as everyone began to eat in silence.

Chapter 8

After dinner, Uncle Frank took all the cousins to the park. It had stopped raining, and most of the water was gone. The kids already knew where the park was, but they still pretended that Uncle Frank was leading them to a magical place they didn't know existed. Even Jack, who didn't know how to pretend, because of his autism, pretended that he was pretending, in order to fit in.

Frank led them west on State Road 26 and turned left on a side road called Liberty Street. Then they walked west on Liberty Street and saw the sign that said SWORDSMAN PARK.

"Why is it called Swordsman Park?" asked Jack.

"Because legend has it that an environmentalist had to stab numerous people to death in the 1800s to turn this park into a nature preserve, which eventually became a city park," Uncle Frank said, then winked. "All of those people would be dead now anyway, but because of that brave man, at least the trees survived."

Bobby and Brittany burst out laughing, which threw Jack into a big confusion. What part of the story was funny?

"Now go along and play," said Uncle Frank kindly.

Jack went to the swings by himself, and just swung back and forth. Realizing what was going on, Uncle Frank went to Jack and said, "Can I talk to you?"

"I guess you can," said Jack.

"Now Jack, I'm not going to force you to play with anyone," said Uncle Frank.

"I figured you wouldn't," said Jack.

"I came to talk to you about your family," said Uncle Frank.

"They don't like me," said Jack. "I don't belong."

"Children aren't property. No, you don't belong to anyone except yourself. But I don't like the way any of you are treated. You're not lab animals either."

"Aunt Mary thinks we are. She thinks children are born to

serve their parents."

"That's not true. And they should know that. After all, the whole reason why Nature wants you to live is for you to raise and nurture children. Not boss them around. Those children are entitled to grow up with love and have children of their own. Keep the family going. Unfortunately, like me, some children don't have children of their own when they are adults. Even in the natural world, not everyone has kids," said Uncle Frank.

"I also know that my aunt and uncle won't change," said Jack. "Why don't you have kids?"

"I am not meant to. Very few people believe what I believe in, for the truth is, what your Aunt Mary believes in is a very common belief. Also, I knew that my siblings would be angry at me for raising children according to *my* beliefs, and I didn't want my children to be subjected to that. And also, all of the women I tried to marry were so freaked out by my family that I felt this was God's way of saying that I should live alone. So I am content with the life I lead as a children's author. At least I can see kids that way, to compensate. Hans Christian Andersen, after all, one of the most famous children's writers of all time, had no kids of his own." Uncle Frank added. "But Jack, I want to get Bobby and Brittany with us so I can tell them what I told you."

Then he called out, "BOBBY! BRITTANY!"

They stopped playing and ran to the swings where Frank and Jack were.

"I want you to sit down. There's something I want to tell you," said Uncle Frank.

"What is it?" asked Cousin Bobby.

"I've seen how your parents treat you. I know you may not think this, but your parents are not very nice to you. It's wrong for them to yell at you for little things. Why, they yell as if one of you just murdered fifty people with a rifle," said Uncle Frank.

"Well, at times, I think it's unfair, like when I got a time-out because I whined after accidentally hitting my knee on the chair. It's like—I didn't mean to hurt myself, so why punish me?" asked Cousin Brittany.

"And the time I turned off a light switch and accidentally

turned off the computer, even though no one told me that the computer was connected to the outlet that was connected to the switch. I was yelled at for that," said Cousin Bobby.

"You probably know that your grandparents weren't very nice to your father or your mother. They weren't nice to me either," said Uncle Frank. "But something else happened."

"What is it?" asked Cousin Bobby.

"Your mother Mary has a brother and a sister, Parker and Jill. They are your aunt and uncle. You do know that Aunt Jill died two years ago. But why did she die?" asked Uncle Frank.

"She died because she was run over by a car," said Cousin Brittany.

"No. She died because of human malice," said Uncle Frank. "My sister-in-law Jill may not have seen the car that hit her, but the car did not kill her. Jill had two daughters named Ruth and Brenda. They are your cousins, and they are both grown-up, as they were born nineteen years before Bobby was born.

"Ruth was walking with her mother Jill when the car hit her. Ruth instantly called 911, and then called her sister Brenda to tell her what had happened. The ambulance rushed her to the nearest hospital. But since no one in the family could afford to have Jill stay in the hospital, Jill's daughter Brenda was willing to take care of her.

"Brenda did this not to help her mother, but she knew this was her golden opportunity to hurt her. She had always hated her mother since her mother never loved her as a child. She never paid attention to her and never praised her for anything. So Brenda realized she had this power, and she used it. In several weeks, she had starved her mother to death.

"Brenda also had another motive. Her husband had lost his job and he had flown to New York City to look for a new one. Her mother had four hundred grand that she had saved up for her retirement during her career as a successful Realtor, and she was saving it for herself. Brenda knew that she and her husband could use that money until he got a new job. She had already asked her mother to give her some money, not a hundred grand, but just some money to help her until her husband could make more money.

"And her mother refused. Brenda kept asking her, but her mother kept replying, "It is your husband's responsibility to support you, not mine." When Jill was half-starved, Brenda got her to sign a new will saying that she got all of the money, then she and her husband moved to New York and bought a town house."

"My cousin is a murderer?" asked Cousin Brittany.

"Not exactly, but sort of. If only Jill had been a little nicer to Brenda, she wouldn't have died. And that's why I hate the way your parents treat you. I'm sure you know better than to kill your parents when you grow up, but it still shows that what they are doing is wrong."

"But why didn't anybody tell us?" asked Cousin Bobby.

"When we learned about what had happened, we decided that we didn't want to subject you to the story. That it would shock you just as much as it shocked us. So your parents and everyone who knew was sworn to secrecy," Uncle Frank replied.

"But then why did you tell us now?" asked Cousin Bobby.

"I've been wanting to tell you for a long time," Uncle Frank replied. "But I didn't think you were old enough until now."

"My parents didn't give me anything to drink so I wouldn't have to pee," Jack said.

"That's terrible. What happened?"

"I had to pee anyway."

"I know that I can't stop your parents from doing that to you. But remember that I feel sorry for you. And so I wanted you to come here so that you could talk about the problems you have with your parents," said Uncle Frank. "Jack, do you want to continue?"

"Okay," said Jack.

"Okay. And I'd like everyone to listen," said Uncle Frank. "And Jack, if you can't understand something when other people are talking, let me know."

Uncle Frank knew a lot about autism, especially the kind that Jack had, the invisible kind that everyone mislabeled as naughtiness, Bad Seed Syndrome, etc., when it really was a whole bunch of perceptual and comprehension problems.

"Well, one time my parents asked me to call up our local gymnasium to ask when they had Open Gym time. Open Gym time is when families can come and use the gym for whatever they want to use it for. I called up and the woman on the telephone said that it was from six-thirty to eight-thirty p.m. on that day. So we went to the gym at six-thirty, and they told us that it was not from six-thirty to eight-thirty, but from seven to nine p.m. I was yelled at when it truly was not my fault, as the woman on the phone gave me false information," said Jack.

"Hasn't that ever happened to you?" Uncle Frank asked Bobby and Brittany. "After all, Jack wanted to obey his parents, and because of some false information, he was yelled at and falsely accused of lying."

"That has happened to me once," said Cousin Bobby. "You probably know how Jack and I are banned from interaction, right? Well, my parents throughout my whole life have promoted interaction between cousins. So when I played with Cousin Jack, I wanted to show my parents how much I liked him and that I liked to play with him. So when he gave me a map for a gift, I got interested in it, but because they thought I was acting like him when studying it, my mother thought that I was getting a bad example from Jack when all I was doing was trying to be nice to him. Then when he started teaching me state capitals, my dad was afraid I was becoming autistic, because HE was never interested in state capitals when HE was a boy, so I couldn't be his son and like state capitals. I feel angry at my father and I want to fight back, but I know it's hopeless. That's just the way it is with my parents: you try to please them and they yell at you, and when you aren't trying to please them, they still yell at you."

"Well, I think that that is wrong. All you were trying to do was be nice to Jack. And Jack didn't mean for you to get punished in such a horrible way," said Uncle Frank. "Now, Brittany, do you have anything to say about something that happened to you?"

"Yes, but this happened at school, not at home," said Cousin Brittany. "One time, we were walking back to our classroom from art, and our goal is for us to be quiet in the hallways. The teacher, during the trip, announced that we would get a reward if we were quiet. So I tried to be quiet. When we got to the classroom, a child nearby made a loud noise by clapping his hands. Because it was near me, the teacher thought I made the noise, and I was punished. As a result, I lost a week of recess and no matter how many times I tried to tell the teacher, I was innocent, the teacher claimed the reason why I was saying I was innocent was because I was actually guilty, and 'innocent people are willing to do anything it takes to be proven innocent, not beg innocence,' even though I have seen innocent people beg innocence in movies."

"That must have been horrible," said Uncle Frank. "It just shows you how wrong it actually is to force kids who don't know each other to be together six hours a day, five days a week, and force them to interact even though none of them want to be there. School is an unnecessary part of life to be endured—a waste of time, and it does not need to be endured. It is important to get an education, but you get a better education being out in the world. You can learn what you'd learn at school without getting hurt by other children. And since education is forced, school does not teach you how to learn, but how not to learn. Or that learning is only compulsory in a certain building at a certain time.

"Not many parents know or want to know that—after all, school is just baby-sitting so that during the day, parents can get their freedom back after five years.

"Teachers are also part of the problem. If teachers understood that some students hated each other and accepted their desire not to interact, some bad things wouldn't happen. If teachers were aware that children were being bullied and supported them, those children would be happier. If teachers understood that everyone tries their best to learn, they would praise you for what you've done, not for what you haven't done. But today, teachers are always putting you down and are unaware that you tried your best.

"Well, you can now go back and play, but remember, I am on

your side. I just wanted to get you together to talk about it," said Uncle Frank.

So Cousin Bobby and Brittany went off together to continue playing, and Jack went back on his swing, enjoying his solitude. Uncle Frank didn't bother him or the cousins, as he understood Jack's desire to be alone, so he just stayed and watched them to make sure they wouldn't go into harm's way.

Jack thought over what was said, things he had already thought a thousand times. But what was different this time was, for a brief period, he had actually felt comfortable with other people, as if he was an accepted member of a group. Even Brittany wasn't openly mean to him.

Of all the people who *should* have been a parent in their family, it should have been Uncle Frank, not all the other unloved rage-a-holics, murderers, and behaviorists. This was further evidence against the existence of a kind and benevolent God. A really nice God would have struck all those parents with diseases that made them sterile and married Frank off to have a dozen children.

In forty minutes, when it was very dark, they headed back to the house.

When they got home, it was bedtime. Aunt Mary yelled and screamed about how irresponsible her brother-in-law was to keep the children out so late.

"YOU DON'T KNOW WHAT IT IS LIKE TO BE A PARENT!" she bellowed. "YOU DON'T KNOW THE IMPORTANCE OF RULES!!"

Jack was going to sleep on the bottom bunk in Cousin Brittany's bunk bed, even though Cousin Brittany did not want him sleeping in her bed because he was a boy. But she had to say yes, since if she did not, Jack would have to sleep in Bobby's lower bunk, which broke house rules.

Chapter 9

The next day, everyone was up and at the breakfast table eating cereal by 9:00 a.m. Everyone except Jack. He was sitting there, but was not eating. His mother had forgotten to bring along the gluten-free cereal that he hated so much.

Although it was a Sunday, Uncle Hayes and Aunt Mary did not go to church with their kids. They were atheists and they did not believe in God.

This actually hurt the children, since many of Cousin Brittany and Cousin Bobby's friends were jealous that they didn't have to go to church and they lost some friends this way.

"Aunt Eva is coming at nine-thirty a.m. with Erin," said Uncle Hayes. "I'd like us to please be ready to leave the house, as she will be taking us to the zoo."

"Finally I get to see Erin!" said Cousin Brittany happily. "She's a lot nicer than the cone-headed boys in this house."

"Remember, Aunt Eva's been busy preparing for the wedding, so please, don't bombard her with questions when she comes here," said Uncle Hayes.

Everyone finished breakfast in silence. When they were done, it was 9:30 a.m.

Ding-dong!

The doorbell rang. Jack automatically covered his ears. No one else moved.

"I'll get it," said Aunt Mary finally. However, before she got there, the door flew open. Aunt Eva and Cousin Erin came in. Jack peeked over and noticed that Erin had neglected to close the door. He covered his ears more tightly, waiting for Aunt Mary to start screaming, but then he became very confused when she smiled warmly.

Cousin Erin was holding her coat with her left hand, and was wearing a pink dress that stopped just below her knees, with white socks and black shoes. Although she looked pretty, Jack knew the truth about her. Aunt Eva, as always, was bundled up in a black fur coat that went down to her ankles. She obviously had no compassion for the animals who died for that coat.

Then, as if they were slobs, Aunt Eva and Cousin Erin just dropped their coats on the floor. Still no one was yelling at them. Jack was shocked in disbelief.

"Hello, Eva!" said Uncle Hayes. "How nice to see you! It's been a while."

"Since yesterday," Aunt Eva reminded him.

"Jack, could you please hang up our coats and close the door," said Cousin Erin.

"No."

"How rude," said Aunt Mary.

"I didn't put the coats down, so I won't pick them up."

Jack's mother, who had gotten up from the table, shook her head. "It's the autism," she told everyone, as if Jack weren't there. "They have such strange logic."

"Jack, be nice to your cousin," said Jack's father. "She's just entered the house."

"Jack, please. I'm getting cold," said Cousin Erin, pointing toward the door.

"No," said Jack.

"Please?" asked Cousin Erin. Then she flittered her eyelashes to make her look like a helpless young lady.

"CLOSE THE DOOR, JACK!" Aunt Mary bellowed.

"You should be nice to your cousin. We pamper *you* all the time," said Jack's mother.

Actually, Jack didn't mind picking up the coats and closing the door. He was only worried about doing it wrong and getting yelled at more.

Finally Jack took Erin's coat and hung it up. Then he closed the door.

"Okay, now hang up my mother's coat," said Cousin Erin, batting her eyelashes again. Her father came from a family of Southern plantation owners. The ability to order slaves around was in her blood.

Jack realized he had to, and that no one had yelled at him, so he hung up Aunt Eva's coat, too.

"Now Jack, I want to look my best, so could you please go to the back and see if my hair bow is on straight?" asked Cousin Erin.

He went behind her to find out that her red hair bow was on completely straight.

"It's fine," said Jack.

"Now, it just so happens that my shoe got untied. Will you please tie my shoe?" asked Cousin Erin.

Cousin Erin had purposely untied her shoe when he was getting the door.

"I'm not very good at it…"

"No, you're fine. You make a *wonderful* slave. I'd love it if I had *you* for a brother! You're so willing to serve me!" said Cousin Erin.

Jack sat down by her foot, then after several attempts managed to make bunny ears and tie them together.

"Now, please bring me the telephone so I can make a call," said Cousin Erin.

"Can't you get it yourself?" asked Jack.

"Jack, I like it better when you serve me. And remember, you hate it when I'm mean to you, and I won't be mean to you if I'm happy. And the only way I'll be happy is if you give me the telephone," said Cousin Erin.

So Jack went to get Erin the phone.

"Jack, what are you doing?" asked Jack's mother.

"I'm getting the phone for Erin," said Jack.

"JACK, SHE'S WALKING ALL OVER YOU! SHE JUST WANTS TO USE YOU! NOTHING WILL MAKE HER HAPPY, SO JUST SAY NO! YOU'RE HOPELESS, JACK! WHY CAN'T YOU STAND UP FOR YOURSELF! WHY DIDN'T YOU SAY NO IN THE FIRST PLACE?" screamed Jack's mother.

Jack wanted to say to his mother, "I didn't say no because she was nice to me," but decided to keep his mouth shut about that.

Instead, he said, "Okay. I won't get the phone!"

"Why do you always ruin everything, Aunt Susan?" asked Cousin Erin.

"All I asked him to do was get the phone. And you did say Jack should be nice to sweet Cousin Erin. So could you please let him get the phone for me?"

"Oh, Jack, just get the phone for your Cousin Erin," said Jack's mother.

Jack reluctantly got the phone, not knowing who he should obey. Because of his autism, he could only obey one rule or request at a time. It turned out that Erin had forgotten the number she wanted to call.

"Okay, so now that that's done, let's go to the zoo!" said Aunt Eva.

So they all got ready to go to the zoo.

The van held nine people (three rows of three people), and there were nine people that were *in* the van. Aunt Mary drove the van, Jack's mother and Jack's father sat next to her in the first row, Cousins Bobby and Brittany sat in the second row with Aunt Eva, and Jack and Cousin Erin sat in the third row with Uncle Hayes.

"Now, remember, the adult sitting in your row is in charge. I don't want any fighting," said Aunt Mary. "And no loud voices."

They began to drive west on State Road 26. Then Cousin Erin said to Jack, "Jack, I want to listen to my new album. Could you get it for me out of my backpack?"

"No. I won't. Go get it yourself," said Jack.

"But I want to hear my album," said Cousin Erin.

"No," said Jack.

"I can't believe you're saying no to a beautiful, sweet little lady like me. It's *so* improper," said Cousin Erin.

"Jack, just do it for her. She only sees you once a year!" said Uncle Hayes.

"Well then, I guess it's time to open up *Amos and Andy*," said Aunt Mary from the front.

"What's *Amos and Andy?*" asked Jack.

"It's a disciplining tool. In the car, I'm driving, so I can't scold you. So I put a child in charge. Whenever there's a fight, I give someone the *Amos and Andy* wand and they order the one who started fighting to do something and that person has to do it. If that person refuses, then he doesn't eat dinner that night. My children are so conditioned that whenever I bring the wand up, they are quick to obey any commands," said Aunt Mary.

Then Aunt Mary gave Aunt Eva a long and narrow wooden figure that looked like a wand with the words *AMOS & ANDY* carved on it. Jack remembered that Amos and Andy were famous fictional black characters, and he wondered whether this wand had originally been used to beat them.

"I appoint Cousin Erin use of this wand," said Aunt Mary.

Cousin Erin was given the wand. At that moment, Aunt Mary turned right onto State Road 29.

Cousin Erin pointed the wand at Jack and said, "Jack, I hereby *command* you to take my album out of my backpack or else you don't eat dinner."

Jack did as he was told, as he didn't want to not eat dinner. He was already starving from no breakfast.

"See, I told you. It's a very efficient system of discipline," said Aunt Mary.

"By the way, they're having the Lions & Tigers & Bears, Oh My! Exhibit at the zoo. It's where they show you the three strongest jungle giants together. Usually, those animals aren't in this zoo," said Aunt Eva.

Then they put Cousin Erin's album into the CD player in the car and continued down State Road 29, which became U.S. Highway 421. It was some horrible rap music that hurt Jack's ears.

* * * *

They parked their van and went to the front gate of the zoo. The sign read: WELCOME TO THE INDIANAPOLIS ZOO.

Then the sign said below in fine print: *This park is subsidized by local, county, state, and federal taxes.*

"Welcome. Please remember to pick up a zoo map when entering the gate," said the gatekeeper.

They entered the zoo. There was a fountain around them with a path going around the circle. Five paths came into the circle. Everyone got a map, so Jack learned that those five paths went around the zoo. One path went to the reptile house and the restaurant. The second path went to the lions, tigers, and bears. The third path went to the birds. The fourth path went to the aquatic animals. And the fifth path went to the marsupials.

"Now, remember, these paths only lead to the South Side of the zoo. The North Side also has five main paths with another fountain," said Aunt Mary.

"Let's go to the lions, tigers, and bears exhibit. Then we can go to the reptile house," said Uncle Hayes.

So they went on the path to the lions, tigers, and bears exhibit. Since the theme resembled a scene from the *Wizard Of Oz*, when they entered the exhibit, the path became a "yellow brick road." They saw four lions, two on one side, and two on the other side with a fence to block the lions from coming onto the path. There was a sign on the fence.

"Jack, will you please read the fence signs for us?" asked Cousin Erin. "You're such a *great* reader."

Jack read:

LIONS

A member of the carnivorous cat family, lions are often called the King of the Jungle. This is a misconception, however, for lions do not live in jungles. They actually live in savannahs. They are called King of the Jungle for other reasons: Like humans, lions are on top of the food chain, and they will eat any animal that they can catch. It is very easy to recognize males from females, as male lions have a mane and female lions don't. Also, female lions stay together in one pride, and male lions wander around and may live in more than one pride in their lifetime. There are many types of lions, but the four shown here are the Angola lion, the Asiatic lion, the Barbary lion, and the Cape Lion. Lions can be found in Africa and Asia, and female lions are better hunters than males.

"Thank you, Jack," Erin said like she was dismissing a servant.

"You did a good job reading that," said Jack's mother.

"Look at the mother lion!" exclaimed Jack's father. "She's nursing her cubs!"

"Zoos really show you how animals live in the wild," said Aunt Mary. "In fact, there are some animals that you see here that are now extinct. You *have* to go to the zoo in order to see them."

"Lions are carnivorous, and can be man-eaters," Uncle Hayes said. "They hunt their prey."

"How are the lions fed?" asked Jack. "Do they throw men in there, that the lions kill?"

Erin and Brittany burst out laughing.

"No, Jack," said Uncle Hayes. "That would be murder."

They spent ten more minutes looking at the lions and then they walked to the tigers. Like the lions, there were four tigers, two on both sides.

"Now, please read this for us, Jack," said Cousin Erin.

"Okay," said Jack.

"That's the thing I like about you. You're so easy to manipulate," said Cousin Erin.

And Jack began to read:

TIGERS

A carnivorous feline mammal that originally lived in Asia, the tiger is now an endangered species. Numerous tigers are killed every year via poaching, and some species of tigers only exist now in zoos. These mammals are ferocious beasts, and sometimes eat humans if they feel threatened or are starving. Males and females can be recognized by the color of their coat. Female tigers usually have a darker coat than male tigers. Shown here are the Siberian, Sumatran, Indochinese, and Bengal tigers.

"Are any of these tigers extinct in the wild?" asked Cousin Brittany.

"Not completely, but there are less than a thousand left in Asia, which is their native country," said Uncle Hayes.

"The tigers over here are eating!" said Jack's father.

And indeed, they were eating, but Jack was too afraid to ask what they were fed.

The family spent ten more minutes looking at the tigers.

"I want to go to the Reptile House now!" said Cousin Erin. "I'm sick of stupid old endangered animals."

"Calm down, Erin," said Aunt Eva. "If those animals truly became extinct, there wouldn't be any more fur for coats." Then she said to everyone else, "My daughter wants to go to the reptile house, so I am taking her. Who else wants to go?"

Just to be nice, Jack said yes, though he was confused. If Jack had asked to do something like that, which contradicted a schedule, he would be yelled at. Bobby said yes too. But because they were banned from interaction and being together, Aunt Mary decided to take Cousin Bobby separately, using a different entrance.

Meanwhile, Cousin Brittany stayed with Jack's parents and Uncle Hayes.

So Aunt Eva walked to the reptile house with Jack, and then Aunt Mary followed behind with Bobby and Erin. When they got there, the sign above the entryway to a green-painted cement building welcomed them, saying: WELCOME TO THE REPTILE HOUSE, A HOME OF ANCIENT BEASTS.

They entered the building via the electronic doors. A sign said:

THIS REPTILE HOUSE IS HEATED FOR THE COMFORT OF OUR COLD-BLOODED RESIDENTS.

"I have to go to the bathroom," Jack said.

"Oh, all right, but be quick about it," said Aunt Eva.

Jack turned left into the hallway leading into the restrooms, and passed cages of alligators, turtles, and crocodiles. On his way he saw Cousin Bobby. Apparently, Bobby was going to the restroom too, but his mother obviously didn't know the two boys might meet.

Both Bobby and Jack entered the restroom, and Jack went into a stall for privacy, thinking that he would talk to Bobby when he came out. However, when he came out of the stall, Bobby was gone.

While Jack was washing his hands, the lights above him turned off. Then they turned back on. And then they turned back off again. Jack became terrified in the utter blackness. His heart began pounding.

Then a person announced over the P.A., "May I have your attention, please? There is a power outage in this building. It is recommended that everyone leave the building; in five minutes, the electronic doors will stop working and you could be locked inside."

Jack felt his way to the bathroom door, then opened it. At the end of the building, in the natural light coming through the outside glass doors, Jack saw Cousins Bobby and Erin leaving with Aunt Mary. Aunt Eva was nowhere in sight. Then Jack saw her. And by the way she looked, she was angry.

Chapter 10

"Well, well, well," said Aunt Eva. "If there's one thing that I must tell you, it's that you are in deep, deep trouble."

"What did I do?" asked Jack.

She grabbed him by the arm and dragged him out the exit, where Aunt Mary and the cousins were waiting for him.

"HOW COULD YOU THINK OF CAUSING A BLACKOUT!" roared Aunt Mary. "DIDN'T YOU KNOW IT WAS WRONG?"

"I don't know what's going on here," said Jack. "I'm in the bathroom, and suddenly the lights go off..."

"OF COURSE THEY SUDDENLY GO OFF! WHEN YOU SHUT OFF THE CIRCUIT BREAKERS OF ANY BUILDING, THE LIGHTS SUDDENLY GO OFF! GOD, I CAN'T BELIEVE YOU!" boomed Aunt Mary.

"But I a-am innocent!" said Jack. "I was washing my hands when the power went out!" he gasped, trying to find a way to get Aunt Mary to stop yelling at him.

"DO YOU EXPECT ME TO BELIEVE SUCH LIES? BOBBY DOESN'T CAUSE BLACKOUTS! YOU DO! REMEMBER FIVE YEARS AGO? YOU TURNED OFF OUR CIRCUIT BREAKER AND YOU CLAIMED IT WAS BECAUSE OF YOUR OBSESSION WITH LIGHTS! BESIDES, THERE'S NO EVIDENCE THAT BOBBY DID IT! WE LIVE IN AMERICA, AND IN AMERICA YOU'RE INNOCENT UNTIL PROVEN GUILTY!" shouted Aunt Mary.

Jack suddenly laughed. "If you're innocent until proven guilty in America, why are you blaming me? All you just did today was walk up and yell at me! You have no evidence to support your case."

"THAT'S DIFFERENT! YOU HAVE A RECORD OF DOING BAD THINGS! BUT BOBBY'S MY PERFECT ANGEL! HE NEVER DOES ANYTHING BAD, UNLIKE

YOU, WHO HAVE BEEN MISBEHAVING YOUR WHOLE LIFE TRYING TO GET ATTENTION! YOU'RE SPOILED AND YOU DON'T KNOW IT!"

"But there's no evidence," said Jack.

"NO MORE EXCUSES! IT'S WRONG TO SHUT OFF THE POWER OF A BUILDING!"

"All right, all right. I did shut the power off in this building," lied Jack, realizing it was the only way to get her to stop screaming at him.

"Finally. As for your punishment, you won't be able to eat dinner tonight. Let the discomfort of hunger show you the way," said Aunt Mary. "And you also will be unable to see the reptile house. You're going back to your parents."

So they returned to the Oz-like exhibit and saw Cousin Brittany with Jack's parents and Uncle Hayes. Aunt Mary had returned with Erin and Bobby.

"Did something happen?" asked Jack's father.

"Susan, your son is uncontrollable. He asked to use the bathroom and then he walked down into the basement and shut the power off in the reptile house," said Aunt Eva.

"But Bobby—"

"HOW COULD YOU DO SUCH A THING? DON'T YOU KNOW IT'S INAPPROPRIATE TO SHUT THE POWER OFF WHEN YOU ENTER A BUILDING!" screamed Jack's mother.

"I didn't…"

"STOP MAKING EXCUSES, JACK! YOU'RE ELEVEN YEARS OLD! YOU SHOULD KNOW BETTER! AND BESIDES, YOU'VE BEEN CAUGHT RED-HANDED! WHY DO YOU ALWAYS DENY WHAT YOU'VE DONE?" roared Jack's father.

"I saw…"

"I DON'T CARE WHAT YOU SAW! I KNOW YOU DID IT. I *KNOW* YOU, JACK! YOU'RE OBSESSED WITH LIGHTS, AND YOU SHUT THE POWER OFF AT HAYES AND MARY'S HOUSE FIVE YEARS AGO!"

"Actually, I've already punished him, Susan," said Aunt Mary.

"He will not be given dinner tonight."

"And let this be a lesson to you, Jack," said Uncle Hayes. "In a civilized society, adults always find out. They always win."

Uncle Hayes looked around for Erin, Bobby, and Brittany, but they were nowhere in sight. Then he found them all sitting on a bench. They looked terrified. It made sense—they had just observed adult family members yelling and screaming.

"What's going on?" asked Uncle Hayes.

"Why were you screaming at Cousin Jack?" asked Cousin Erin, secretly pleased that she wasn't the victim.

"Don't worry about it. Well, we're done now, so it's time for us to head on out to the marsupial exhibit," said Uncle Hayes.

"All right. I'm happy it's done. But I'm so angry at Jack for holding us up again, the way he does every time he comes. I wish he was dead. He ruins everything," said Cousin Brittany.

So they all went to the marsupial exhibit. Jack was silent for the rest of the time spent at the zoo, because he had realized he would get nowhere, and besides, he wouldn't get in trouble if he kept his mouth shut. And that would make all the adults happier. What he didn't understand was why autistic kids got sent to speech therapy to learn how to talk, when no one wanted to listen to them.

Jack was still thinking, though. It was important for him to find evidence to support the fact that he was innocent. But how could he? And how could he get his parents to accept it?

Still, it was his mission. Because the person who did cause the blackout could do it again, and again, and again.

Chapter 11

The zoo closed at 4:30 p.m., and everyone started heading home.

In the car, while they were driving up I-65, everyone except Jack was talking about how much they enjoyed going to the zoo. Jack felt sad. After all, he hated going to the zoo, the way he hated everything that he was forced to do with his family.

Then he realized something. His parents weren't the only people in history who had misunderstood other people merely because of a disability or a difference. Since the dawn of humanity, even before recorded history, human beings had killed and wiped out entire tribes and groups because of their differences. Americans might think they live in a country with the most tolerance, but in truth, white men are no angels. This is a country that extended voting rights to black people and Native Americans only 47 years ago. Although slavery was outlawed 147 years ago, it took 100 years after that to give civil rights to African-Americans.

And it's only been 81 years since women have been able to vote.

So then, Jack thought, is this civilization? Are we truly civilized?

Even today, discrimination exists. For example, let's say two nice children go to a school. They both know the same amount of knowledge. But because one is ugly and fat, and the other is skinny and handsome, the ugly and fat child is teased and has no friends. Dr. Martin Luther King, Jr. said that he dreamt that his children could live in a world where people didn't discriminate against them because of skin color, but because of character. But people are still being judged by appearance.

Jack realized, too, that he would have to accept his lot in life as the misunderstood individual wherever he went. So he was silent for the rest of the trip home.

When they pulled into the driveway, he left the car like anyone else. Everyone walked into the house, and then Aunt

Mary announced that she was going to start cooking dinner.

Jack instantly went onto the computer in the office, and he stayed there happily. If he wasn't eating anything, there was no reason for him to be sitting at the dinner table.

"AAAAAAAAAAAAAAAAAAAAAAAAAHHHHHHHHHH HHHHHHH!"

A shrill scream suddenly pierced the silence. It was faint because Jack had closed the door to the office, and it didn't scare him.

"What? Is someone hurt?" asked Aunt Mary.

"Someone stole my book on electricity!" wailed Cousin Brittany.

"Someone did?" said Aunt Mary. "Well, I believe you, since you keep your room clean, unlike your brother!"

Then Jack overheard frantic footsteps, which soon stopped. There was silence for a couple more minutes until...

"Well," said Aunt Mary, who was obviously in Brittany's room, "you are right. It was stolen. But who stole it?"

"I don't know," said Cousin Brittany. "I walked in and it was gone. I saw it before we went to the zoo."

Hmm, Jack thought. The power was turned off at the zoo, and that involves electricity. If someone had stolen Brittany's book on electricity, then that person could have stolen it to learn how to shut the power off! And therefore it must have been a family member, since family members are the only ones who live in the house and would have access to such a book. On the other hand, maybe Brittany was just pretending it was stolen, to mislead people into thinking she was innocent.

Realizing that he should make the most of the time on the computer, he went on to his favorite website about a TV show that he liked. He was enjoying himself for quite some time until suddenly Aunt Mary announced, "Dinner's ready!"

Everyone ran down the hallway past where the office was. But it didn't matter to Jack, since he couldn't eat.

"Dinner's ready!" said Aunt Mary again. Jack automatically expected to hear more footsteps out in the hall, but there were none.

Out in the dining area, everyone was restless and hungry.

"Why can't we start dinner? Everyone is here," said Uncle Hayes, who had been tapping his foot while sitting at the head of the table.

"Someone's missing," said Aunt Mary.

"Who?" the kids said in unison.

"Jack," said Aunt Mary. "Jack! It's time for dinner!" she called out.

"But Jack isn't eating dinner," said Erin. "He's being punished."

"The rule in this house is that no one eats until EVERYONE is present at the table, whether they're being punished or not."

"Jack!" his mother called out.

Jack came out of the office and into the dining room.

"Why should I come to dinner if I'm not allowed to eat anything?" said Jack.

"What a foolish question! Just because you can't eat doesn't mean you have the right to break the mandatory dinner attendance rule in this house," said Aunt Mary.

"I don't have to follow the rules concerning your table in your house," Jack said. Instantly there was a hushed shock that filled the room.

"Are you questioning my divine authority?" asked Aunt Mary.

"Mary, don't forget. You're not the only adult here. It's *our* authority," said Jack's mother.

"All right, all right, Susan. Are you questioning *our* divine authority?" asked Aunt Mary. "You aren't following the rules, so yes, you are questioning our divine authority."

"Divine authority? What divine authority do *you* have? School has already taught me that my parents and other adults are just ordinary human beings like me and not God," said Jack.

"Jack, why do you have to fight with everyone?" asked Jack's father. "It is dinnertime."

"Well, I'm not going to eat, so it must not be dinnertime for me," said Jack.

"Wait a minute right there. Didn't Aunt Mary just tell you to come sit down? Why are you such a difficult person? In my day, kids obeyed without asking," said Aunt Eva.

"Well, I guess we've found a generation gap. My generation, unlike yours, thinks for itself," said Jack.

"Jack, that's not true. If you observe any other household in the whole world, you will see that children are obedient," said Jack's father.

Jack realized that it was hopeless. Everyone was against him. And although his cousins, since they were also children, had no true authority, they were angry at him too, since they were hungry. And according to their rules, he was holding up dinner.

"Jack, I'm hungry," said Cousin Brittany.

"So am I," he said.

"That's different," she said.

So Jack went to the table and sat down.

"Okay," said Jack's father. "Since I am the oldest person here, I would like to pray."

Everyone stopped talking.

"Dear God, O Heavenly Father," said Jack's father. "We are thankful for the food and bread that you have put on our table..."

Meanwhile, Jack had to sneeze, but tried to hold it in.

"...We are also thankful..."

Jack tried his best to hold it in, but couldn't.

"...that we are gathered here safely at the dinner table..."

It was coming out.

"...and we thank you for our family and may you..."

Achoo! Achoo! Achoo!

"...may you always bless us and, as the Bible says, lead us not into temptation, but deliver us from evil. Amen."

Jack's father looked sternly at his son.

"Jack, what is going on with your behavior? First you start a blackout at the zoo, then you fight us when we want you to go to the dinner table, and now you've shown disrespect for the Lord our God by sneezing during a prayer. Have you no shame?"

"It isn't my fault I have to sneeze. It just comes. And people can't hold sneezes in," said Jack.

"Well, I can. And if I have the potential, then that means that you do too. Therefore, I have the right to blame you for what you've done," said Jack's father.

"But I'm not old enough to hold sneezes in yet," said Jack.

"You interrupted the prayer and you shouldn't have," said Jack's mother.

"Honey, I'm hungry," said Jack's father. "I don't want this fight resulting in seven other hungry people."

"You're right, Marvin," said Jack's mother, admitting defeat where her son was concerned. "Let's eat."

Jack just sat there, watching everyone enjoy their meal. Actually, he wouldn't have enjoyed it. It was a Chinese-style meal with fried rice, sautéed tofu with vegetables, and shrimp with broccoli. Jack hated Chinese food. So he was happy that at least he didn't have to eat it.

Everyone seemed to just eat, but then someone decided to start talking.

"I don't understand why Jack is so picky about foods," said Jack's mother, as if she had just read his mind. "He's a human just like us."

"And the excuses he gives are so lame," said Aunt Mary. "He says, *"I can't eat because I don't like this food. It will make me throw up and it stinks."* And he also says, *"The food also looks horrible."*

Everyone laughed like crazy except Jack. They didn't seem to notice that he was there.

"Just because he hates it doesn't mean he has to *say* he hates it. My mother Martha always said that, " said Jack's mother. "In my day, we ate what was placed in front of us. We didn't refuse it. If we did, we didn't get anything to eat for the next meal."

She continued, "When we all went to see Marvin's parents, Millicent and Brutus, Jack had a big fit since they didn't serve any food he liked. We asked him whether he wanted to starve or eat the food that was being served. Jack chose to starve. Realizing it was only fair, as I had given him that choice, I let him starve. And he continued starving, and he did that for one week, the whole time we were there."

"I feel so sorry for you," said Aunt Eva. "Everyone else is so normal in this family. How come Jack turned out that way?"

"Well, there *is* Frank. He's pretty weird."

Everyone laughed again except Jack. He glanced up to see if his cousins Bobby and Brittany were laughing. After all, they had had that good talk with Uncle Frank. But they were laughing just as hard as the adults.

"I still don't know why Jack is such a hard kid," Aunt Eva said. "Everyone must obey some of the time, but your kid never obeys without questioning. Your son truly is spoiled."

"The doctor said it was because of his autism," said Jack's father. "Disobedience is part of the disability."

Everyone laughed except Jack.

"Don't believe doctors. There's *nothing* wrong with Jack. He's just a very willful boy," said Aunt Mary. "Still, I don't know how you can tolerate him. I would have yelled at him until he listened."

If *they* had listened, however, they would have heard that Jack was crying.

Chapter 12

Jack awoke the next morning after having cried himself to sleep. He made sure nobody heard him, though, because autistic children were not supposed to have the feelings that would let them cry, and he was afraid he'd be accused of pretending.

It was 9:00 a.m. and Cousin Brittany had already gotten up. So Jack got up and went to the breakfast table. Although the family ate dinner in the dining room, they ate breakfast in the kitchen.

On this Monday morning, it rained again. There was a horrible storm outside. When Jack got to the table, nobody had eaten. Uncle Hayes, Jack's parents, Bobby, Brittany, Aunt Mary, and Erin were there. But strangely, Aunt Eva wasn't there.

"I got special permission to go to work late today so I can attend the final wedding arrangements," said Uncle Hayes.

Usually, though, Hayes would be gone by now. He left home at seven o'clock. Hayes worked as a lawyer in a law firm.

Jack was happy that it was raining, because that meant that no one could do much but stay inside. Bobby and Brittany weren't going to school because of their strange schedule.

"Good morning, Jack," said Jack's mother. "You may sit here."

"Where's Aunt Eva?" asked Jack, despite the fact that he didn't want to know where she was.

"Eva is off getting our breakfast from McDonald's. We ordered you a Big Breakfast with pancakes without butter. You should eat it up, and be thankful that Eva drove off in this horrible storm to get you and everybody else food," said Jack's mother.

Although Jack usually hated eggs, he somehow liked them at McDonald's. He didn't know why, but he assumed that it was because McDonald's eggs were fake and his body didn't react to them like real eggs.

Then the side door that led into the kitchen opened, and in

came Aunt Eva with a big bag.

"Okay, I have the food," said Eva. She put the bag in the center of the table and gave everyone what they had ordered. True to his mother's word, Jack got a Big Breakfast with plain pancakes. He was so hungry, he forgot that he was allergic to gluten.

Aunt Eva sat down and said to everyone, "After breakfast, I have an appointment at the Jones Mark Hotel to make the final arrangements for the wedding. The hotel decided to give us a room for the children to play in. Since Mary and Hayes had no choice, Bobby has been granted special one-day permission to play with Jack. We must be there by ten a.m."

Realizing that they were in a time pressure, everyone began to eat. Everyone except Bobby.

"Mom," said Bobby, "I'm not hungry now. I don't want to eat."

Mary glared at her son, then studied his face, as if looking for signs of developing autism.

"Bobby, if you don't eat now, you're going to starve until lunch. I won't cook food especially for you because of your hunger," said Aunt Mary.

"I won't eat then," said Bobby.

"Fine. But if you complain about hunger, I won't feed you," said Aunt Mary.

Jack ate his breakfast in silence, and it tasted wonderful. This was the only food he liked that came from a fast-food restaurant. He tried to eat slowly to delay their departure, but the inevitable came—in thirty minutes, everyone else had finished so reluctantly he ate the final bite.

Then everyone put on their shoes and coats and got ready to leave.

"Mom, I'm hungry," Bobby complained.

"Thirty minutes ago you turned down the breakfast that your aunt got for you," said Aunt Mary. "You chose to starve, and therefore must learn the logical consequences of your actions."

"But I'm hungry!" said Bobby.

"That's *one*," Aunt Mary said, and Bobby fell silent.

* * * *

They took State Road 26 down to State Road 29 and turned left. State Road 29 became U.S. Highway 421 and they took U.S. Highway 421 a long time until they hit I-465. They went west on I-465, and Jack noticed signs that told drivers to stay on this road to reach the airport. Then he saw a tall building ahead of him. He counted the floors to see how big it actually was. There were fourteen. He thought they were passing it but then he saw the words **JONES MARK HOTEL** on the top and realized that this was where they were going. He wondered something else: did the hotel really need all that room? Most likely, it didn't.

The van pulled into the parking lot of the hotel and parked. Everyone got out and Aunt Mary organized them into a single-file line. They walked into the hotel, led by Aunt Eva, with Aunt Mary, Uncle Hayes, Jack's parents, Erin, Bobby, Brittany, and Jack at the back of the line. Jack didn't care since he liked being at the back. Why? Because of his poor depth perception, he often would involuntarily cut in line, making everyone else angry. (This usually was because he was walking slower than someone else and someone passed him.) At the back, no one would or could pass him.

They walked into the hotel.

"Hayes, I need you to take everyone to the lounge while I go to the front desk," said Aunt Eva.

Uncle Hayes said, "Everyone, come with me," and Aunt Eva went to the front desk while everyone else went with Uncle Hayes to the lounge. "Now please find a chair, and no talking."

"How may I help you?" asked the woman at the front desk.

"Hello. My name is Eva Martock and I'm here for my appointment to look over my wedding arrangements," said Eva.

"Okay, Mrs. Martock. You've been assigned to go to the Arkham Room. Mr. Jones and Mr. Jackson will be waiting for you. Mr. Norman and Mr. Thoms are already there," said the woman.

"Mr. Thoms? What's he doing here?" Eva asked.

Then Aunt Eva went to the lounge and said, "I'm ready.

Mary, Marvin, and Susan, please come with me. Hayes, you may take the children to the playroom."

After Aunt Eva left, Uncle Hayes said, "Now that she's gone, I'm going to take you to the two rooms that we've rented for playtime—rooms 1010 and 1012. There is a door from room to room so that everyone can play together. And remember, I won't be there to supervise, so you're on your honor to play properly."

Uncle Hayes led everyone to the elevator. Jack realized that he was walking slower than everyone else, so he walked faster until he caught up. But it didn't work. So he walked faster and faster and faster until...

BUMP!

"Ow!" said Cousin Brittany. "You did that on purpose."

"I didn't!" said Jack. "I tried to not get left behind and so I walked faster. I guess I must have..."

"You guess you must have what?" said Uncle Hayes meanly. "You see, I'm sure there's something you should have done, but you didn't know. Inexcusable, Jack. Any *other* eleven-year-old would. SO WHY DON'T YOU!"

"I ONLY TRIED TO NOT GET LEFT BEHIND!" shrieked Jack, realizing that he had to tell the truth.

"ENOUGH EXCUSES! I KNOW YOU, JACK! YOU'RE *ALWAYS* BUMPING INTO PEOPLE IN LINES! AND YOU ALSO CUT IN LINE! WHY CAN'T YOU UNDERSTAND AND ACCEPT THE CONCEPT OF LINES WITHOUT RUINING IT FOR OTHERS THAT DO UNDERSTAND IT? YOU CAN'T BLAME IT ON YOUR DEPTH PERCEPTION PROBLEMS, SINCE YOU DON'T HAVE THEM. THAT'S JUST A LIE YOUR MOTHER TOLD YOU TO KEEP YOU FROM BECOMING NORMAL!"

"Yeah, Jack. It's just a lie. There's nothing wrong with you. But why do you have to bump into me and cut into everyone else? It's so inappropriate," said Cousin Brittany.

"WELL, YOU'VE SAID ENOUGH!" Uncle Hayes cut in, yelling so he would be heard. "I'm sure you all want to go to the rooms to play. So let's go on. And Jack, please walk slower so you don't bump into anyone."

So Jack walked slower and finally decided not to care if it seemed as if he was being left behind, since no one else cared. They walked into a hallway with entrances to guest rooms on both sides, and then they turned right into another hallway. Jack fell farther behind to make sure that he wasn't going to hurt someone. He saw them turn right into another hallway and heard sounds of an elevator. But when he got to the elevator, the doors were shut. Apparently they had forgotten about him, and he had walked so slowly that he had missed the elevator.

Now he was all alone. He enjoyed the feeling. Then he realized that if he stood there thinking, he would also get in trouble. This put him in a "damned if you do, damned if you don't" place. So he pressed the UP button on the elevator and the elevator opened. It was empty. Jack had thought that someone would be in there trying to look for him, but no one was. He got in and rode up to the 10th floor. When he got out, he saw a sign saying:

← Rooms 1001 – 1040
Rooms 1041 – 1080 →

This was pleasing to him, the predictability of numbers in a series.

He turned left, and then the hallway ended. He saw another sign at the junction:

← Rooms 1001 – 1020
Rooms 1021 – 1040 →

Jack felt warm and safe inside. More soothing numbers.

So he turned left and then saw rooms 1010 and 1012 on his right. The doors were open, and he walked into room 1010.

"There you are, Jack!" said Uncle Hayes. "We were worried about you."

"Dad, isn't this the time you should be *yelling* at him?" said Cousin Brittany.

No, not again, thought Jack. He didn't feel warm anymore.

"You're right, Brittany. JACK! WHY DIDN'T YOU COME INTO THE ELEVATOR LIKE EVERYONE ELSE?" screamed Uncle Hayes.

"I was just walking slower like you told me to," said Jack.

"I SAID THAT, BUT I DIDN'T TELL YOU TO MISS THE ELEVATOR!" roared Uncle Hayes.

"I was just trying…"

"I JUST CAN'T HEAR ANY MORE OF YOUR EXCUSES, JACK! HOW COULD YOU BE SO STUPID?"

"It was just a mistake," said Jack.

"MISTAKE! WHAT MAKES YOU THINK IT WAS A MISTAKE? YOU THINK THAT PURPOSELY NOT GOING ON AN ELEVATOR WAS RIGHT! WELL, LET ME TELL YOU SOMETHING, MISTER! IT IS NOT RIGHT TO NOT FOLLOW THE LEADER OF A GROUP! JACK, PLEASE LISTEN TO ME! DO NOT PLAY WITH BOBBY WHEN I'M GONE! AND DO NOT LEAVE THE HOTEL ROOMS!" screamed Uncle Hayes.

"Okay, Uncle Hayes. I won't," said Jack.

"And I hope this time you're true to your word, even though you've lied to us every other time. You must watch him carefully, Brittany and Erin. To make sure he doesn't misbehave, here's the *Amos and Andy* wand," Hayes said, then threw it on the floor. "You can boss him around legally. Now I must go."

Uncle Hayes departed, leaving Jack vulnerable to the horrors that would soon be inflicted upon him by his cousins.

Chapter 13

Cousin Erin picked up the *Amos and Andy* wand.

"As the one who holds the wand, I am going to assign everyone their status in the game we are about to play. My father came from a family that owned plantations in the South. In a plantation, there was a plantation wife, a plantation husband, an overseer, and a house slave. I will be the plantation wife. Bobby will play my husband. Brittany will play the overseer. And Jack will be the house slave. Everyone I talked to this morning at seven-thirty a.m. accepted their part," said Cousin Erin.

"Wait a minute!" said Jack. "I didn't agree! I wasn't up at seven-thirty!"

"But my plantation is not a democracy," Erin declared. "You are going to play the slave, Jack, and if you don't, you will not get dinner tonight."

"Who gave YOU the authority to take away my dinner?" Jack replied.

In response, Erin twirled the wand a few times, as if it were a whip.

Jack felt a surge of anger. *You have to fight them. You have to show them that you have courage to not give up,* said the voice of Jack's anger. Even if that meant no dinner—again.

"Okay, Erin. For years, slaves have fought for their freedom. So I will fight you. I am not a person who can be pushed around. DO YOU HEAR ME, ERIN! I WILL FIGHT BACK UNTIL I AM UNDERSTOOD!" screamed Jack.

"Well, well, it looks like a slave is thinking for himself," said Erin menacingly. "We are now playing Plantation, and on a real plantation, slaves were beaten for thinking. My dutiful overseer Brittany, slap the slave until he submits!" said Erin, pointing the *Amos and Andy* wand at her.

Brittany ran to Jack and shoved him to the ground. Then she slapped his cheeks and started pounding his back. She kept hitting him and hitting him and hitting him. But Jack knew something that Brittany didn't. When Brittany was hitting Jack, Brittany was not defending her own safety. And he was in a position where he could hurt her the way she was hurting him.

Jack, however, unlike his cousins, was not a violent person. He had never physically hurt anyone in his life. It was the autistic code of honor. He usually just let people hurt him, since he did not believe in hurting others. He was reminded of school, where the bullies pounded him during their riots.

But this time was different. Eleven years of anger suddenly spread throughout his body. The only way he could stop Brittany was to hurt her. After all, what Erin didn't bring up was that in history, slaves rebelled and sometimes killed plantation owners, even though they themselves got tortured or killed as punishment.

Jack made a hard fist and punched Brittany in the stomach.

Brittany, in shock, stopped hitting him. She sat still for a moment. Then she started to cry. And she cried and she cried and she cried.

And Jack also, realizing what he had just done, started to cry. He had just hurt another human, even though that human had been hurting him.

"Look what you've done to my overseer, Jack the slave!" cried Erin. "You've hurt her! You've made her cry! You are a bad slave and must be punished! On plantations, slaves who rebelled were given more work. So, my sweet husband Bobby, what is the punishment?"

"Well," said Bobby, who secretly wanted no part of this, "I think you should decide. You are in charge of the slaves."

"Very well, my darling, the slave shall have no food or water for a week."

Jack relaxed. None of the adults in the family would really carry this out.

"Do you have any first orders for slave Jack?" said Erin.

"Yes," said Bobby. "I want him to take this money and buy me a Sprite."

"Jack, please take this money and get your master and mistress a can of pop," said Erin.

Then Erin gave Jack two dollar bills and said, "Now buy us two Sprites, please, Mr. Slave."

"*Cer*-tain-*ly*," said Jack, so that Erin could clearly hear his sarcasm.

Jack walked out of the room and turned left and soon found signs directing him to the vending machines on the 10th floor.

He returned with two cans of Sprite.

"Now, please untie my shoes, Mr. Slave," said Bobby.

Jack untied Bobby's shoes. He hoped that he wouldn't be asked to retie anyone's shoes and be further humiliated.

"Now untie my wife's shoes, Mr. Slave," said Bobby.

"I don't want to fight you, but just be aware that you're breaking the rules by playing the same game with me," said Jack.

"Slave Jack," said Brittany, "my father gave us special permission to play with you as long as we kept you in your place and treated you as an inferior."

"That's not true," Jack said.

Bobby said sadly, "Do you think I want to play stupid games like this? Do you think I want to hurt you?"

"Why don't you stand up for yourself? You're not autistic," said Jack.

"No, I'm not. But I still don't have the power to—"

"Honey, what are you waiting for?" asked Erin. "Make him untie my shoes."

Jack untied Erin's shoes.

"And now, Jack, I seem to be needing some more to drink. Please buy me another Sprite," said Erin. "Here's another dollar."

"But you haven't even started drinking your first one."

"I am the wife of the plantation owner. I am entitled to have much more than I need. Don't be unruly, or I'll have the overseer hit you again."

So Jack went back to the vending machines, bought the Sprite, and returned to the room, where Erin was lying on the bed, sobbing. Bobby and Brittany were gone.

"What has happened here?" asked Jack.

Pages torn from the phone book were wadded up and strewn around on the floor. As Jack bent down to clean up the paper,

Uncle Hayes, Bobby, and Brittany stepped into the room.

"Well, well, well," said Uncle Hayes. "What have we here? Jack, I thought you had gotten over your obsession with tearing paper! How could you do this again?"

"I don't know what's going on!" said Jack. "All I did was go to the vending machine to get Erin a drink and the room was trashed!"

"OF COURSE YOU KNEW WHAT WAS GOING ON! YOU DID IT! AND BE THANKFUL YOU HAD A PURPOSE WHEN YOU LEFT THE ROOM, SINCE IF YOU DIDN'T, YOU WOULD GET YELLED AT FOR THAT! BUT JACK, HOW COULD YOU THINK OF RIPPING UP A PHONE BOOK!" yelled Uncle Hayes.

"This is unconstitutional!" said Jack.

"AND HOW IS THAT?" screamed Uncle Hayes.

"There's no evidence to support your accusation," Jack declared.

"Well, listen to him talk!" Uncle Hayes said sarcastically. "The evidence is that you tore up an entire phone book when you were five. That's called a prior conviction. None of your cousins has ever ripped up a phone book before! There is nothing to gain from such a silly action."

"You're right," said Jack. "There *is* nothing to gain. I never purposely do things wrong. I just do them involuntarily."

"INVOLUNTARILY? NO ONE RIPS UP A BOOK AND CLAIMS THEY DID IT INVOLUNTARILY!

"I am also very angry that you punched my daughter."

"But she hit me first!"

"Jack, she was only playing the game. She was your overseer, and overseers beat up slaves in the plantations. There was no historical reason for you to fight back," said Uncle Hayes. "And also, since it was just a game, I'm sure she didn't hurt you much. It was just your misperception."

In one way, Uncle Hayes was right. Jack did experience touch differently. But still, when Brittany was hitting him, she was doing it as hard as she could.

"You're right, Father," said Cousin Brittany. "I was only patting him. Do you think that I would ever hurt my poor, defenseless, autistic Cousin Jack? It was only a game."

"LIAR!"

"Jack, Brittany is not a liar. You are. Why can't you understand when something is make-believe?" said Uncle Hayes. "You have to be punished. No dinner again tonight."

Jack decided not to complain. In fact, he was already starting to get a headache because of the pancakes he had that morning. He would be in pain and unable to eat for the next twelve hours anyway.

"I must return to help with the wedding arrangements. Someone else will supervise," said Uncle Hayes.

And the moment he walked out, another adult did come to supervise.

Chapter 14

Uncle Frank walked into the room.

"Hi, children," said Uncle Frank.

"Uncle Frank!" said Jack. "How come you're here? You weren't with us this morning!"

"I came from my house. I am staying at this hotel for the next week to attend the wedding," said Uncle Frank. "Next week I'll be working at the law firm where your Uncle Hayes works. I'm going to be teaching the lawyers how to write good English."

"But why didn't you tell anyone you were coming?" said Jack.

"Oh, I'm sorry, Jack. I must have forgotten," said Uncle Frank. "But by the look of your face, I'm sure you're very happy I've come."

"Oh, yes. I'm always happy when you come. But why did you come? I thought you hated Aunt Eva!" said Jack.

"Jack, stop it. I don't hate Eva. It's wrong to hate other people. I just don't like what she and my brother Hayes do.

"What have you been doing this morning?" asked Uncle Frank.

Erin, Brittany, Bobby and Jack explained the plantation game.

"Let's play!" said Cousin Brittany.

"Now, Brittany, I think you should be punished," said Uncle Frank.

"What?" asked Cousin Brittany in shock.

"Because you beat up your Cousin Jack. It's not right to beat people up, even if it is a game," said Uncle Frank.

"Well, he hit me in the stomach," said Brittany.

"He only did that in self-defense. Jack is not an aggressive person. But he is going to be punished anyway, and I believe it is unfair," said Uncle Frank.

"My father only did that because Jack ripped up the phone book."

"I did not! I wasn't even in the room!" Jack screamed.

"If there's one thing I want to tell you, it's that Jack never lies. Whenever he does, he always tells the truth later," said Uncle Frank.

"Jack always lies," said Brittany. "He's always trying to get out of punishment by saying that he didn't do things when he actually did them."

"Why don't you ask him whether he's telling the truth, Brittany? I believe him when he says that he wasn't in the room when the phone book was ripped up. Didn't YOU see what happened?"

"I didn't see anything. Can we play now?" asked Cousin Brittany.

"Okay, Brittany," said Uncle Frank. "You can all play with each other—but I require that everyone treat each other with kindness and respect. And no one is going to be forced to do anything they don't want to do when I'm around."

"So I guess that means we can't play plantation?" asked Cousin Erin.

"Only if everyone agrees, and can choose their own parts."

"Okay," said Erin in a tone so everyone knew she was defeated, "does anyone have anything against the game? Please let there be no one, since it was a wonderful game before Uncle Frank ruined everything."

Jack, realizing that Uncle Frank was on his side and that the tables had turned, spoke out. "I have something to say. Every time I play with you, Erin, you've always given me a part where I am humiliated. When I resist, I am hurt. When we played Hotel Lobby, I was the bellhop. When we played King and Queen, I was the food-taster who ate the poison tart and died a horrible death. When we played Mansion, I was the illegal alien who cleaned the swimming pool. And now I'm the house slave. I would like you to see me as a human being for once."

"Okay, then. Uncle Frank is forcing me to accept your opinion, so I'm going to give you a higher rank. You can play a serf," said Erin.

"Erin, a serf has no higher authority than a slave," said Uncle Frank.

"Of course he does. Serfs, unlike slaves, could not be bought or sold, and they could own land, unlike slaves," said Erin.

"That's not the point! What gives you the right to always be in charge? You're no better than your cousins."

Jack felt a surge of energy. At last, someone was on his side. He said, "Yes, what gives YOU the right to boss everyone around? Why can't you think of someone besides yourself?"

Erin batted her eyes a few times, then peeked to see whether that had had an effect on her uncle. It hadn't. "I WAS thinking of you when I asked whether you wanted to play a serf rather than a slave, wasn't I? Jack, every person has their own place, and until you accept yours, you're on the way to a lifetime of failure. And so I refuse to answer your questions. They are beyond the intellect of an eleven-year-old girl," said Erin.

"Cut the crap, Erin," Uncle Frank said. "If you're old enough to know how to hurt someone, you're old enough to know better."

"It's all ready!" said a voice from somewhere outside the room. Aunt Eva walked in.

"Mommy," Erin cried, sniffling. "I'm so glad you're here! Uncle Frank and Jack were bullying me. They're awful."

"Don't listen to your Uncle Frank," Aunt Eva said, glaring at him. "He is crazy, and like Jack, he has no feelings. Whenever he's around, he causes trouble. You aren't even a parent, Frank, yet you lecture all of the other parents in your family. You know nothing!"

"I know that your daughter Erin ordered Brittany to beat up Jack! How can you tolerate hitting in your household?" said Uncle Frank.

"I'm sure it was for a punishment. Jack is a known troublemaker and so the hitting was justified. Frank, I want you to leave. You have disturbed enough people's lives. Everyone, we're going home. Uncle Hayes, Aunt Mary, and everyone else are waiting in the car," said Aunt Eva.

"You're wrong, Eva! Frank is the nicest man alive!" said Jack.

"How dare you talk back to an adult! Because of your cheek, you will be grounded. At twelve noon today to midnight on Friday, you cannot leave the house. What have you got to say for yourself?"

"Nothing. No one listens," mumbled Jack to himself.

"Fine. Everybody get ready now—we're going," said Aunt Eva.

And they left, with Jack feeling total confusion. Autistic people always got social things wrong and reversed, but somehow he just couldn't believe that his Uncle Frank was the crazy one.

Chapter 15

In the car, Jack suddenly was overcome with happiness. He was grounded for the rest of the day and for four more days—and during that time, no one was going to force him to interact or use appropriate social skills, and no one was going to force him to go anywhere! He could do anything he wanted at home without being interrupted, except maybe for the meals he wasn't banned from. Jack realized that he had to take advantage of this time.

When he got home, the first thing he decided to do was rest. While resting, he thought about what had happened. Yesterday he was framed for causing a blackout at a zoo. And today he was framed for tearing out the pages of a phone book in a hotel room. Anyone could have shut the power off at the zoo, but he suspected it was one of his cousins. *Someone was out to get him.*

It was more obvious that one of his cousins had ripped up the phone book, since they were the only ones in the room. Someone was definitely out to get him.

Jack decided to look inside the rooms of the three suspects—Bobby, Brittany, and Erin. Because Erin was only staying here until the night of the wedding, that meant Jack had to look through her suitcase and overnight case. Before he could do any of this, he had to plan how to do it. If he was caught, who could imagine the punishment that would happen to him?

He decided to go into Bobby's room first and look inside Erin's suitcase, which Jack assumed was there, since Erin was sleeping there. He could also look at Bobby's things, and take care of looking at two people's things in one trip.

But Jack risked more yelling at if caught, since he was not sleeping in Bobby's room and there was no acceptable reason for him to be there. Also, since Bobby and Jack were banned from interaction, he was breaking the strict rule of the house.

Despite the threat of yelling and punishment, he walked into the hallway and stopped at the entrance of Bobby's room. The door was slightly open. Peeking in, he could see that Bobby, Erin, and Brittany were playing. The only thing he could do now was wait and listen to their conversation, possibly hearing when he could come in to snoop. They were talking. Jack had trouble recognizing people's voices, but that didn't mean he couldn't hear what they were saying:

"I challenge you to...a duel!"

Apparently they were playing duel. This was the game that Bobby liked best.

"I accept the challenge, Bobbius."

Then Jack heard sounds of toy swords hitting each other. This continued for five minutes until...

"I have won! I beat Britannius! I am the victor!"

"So, Bobbius, you proved that you were triumphant over Brittanius. But you must defeat me, Erinnius, in order for you to have dominion over this castle. So I challenge you to a duel. Do you accept the challenge?"

"I do, and I hope that you take the form of a ghost by the end of the duel!"

"We shall see about that, Bobbius."

"Everyone, get ready! We're going to visit Uncle Parker!" said Aunt Eva.

Realizing that his cousins were about to leave the room, Jack quickly ran into the nearby closet in the hallway.

Being unable to see anything, he decided to listen to what people were saying as a clue to when the coast was clear.

"I can't believe we're going to see Uncle Parker!"

"And it'll be just us too. No Jack."

Be my guest, thought Jack.

"Come on. We're leaving, so put on your socks and shoes and get in the car. And don't put them on the other way you did six months ago, Bobby. This time I remembered not to say 'shoes and socks,' even though the *other* kids understand. But hurry up!"

"All right, Aunt Eva!"

Then Jack heard pounding noises, evidently the sounds of people running to the living room. When the pounding noises stopped, Jack opened the door a little bit and saw that everyone had left. He walked into the hallway and into Bobby's room.

The room was a complete mess. Everything was strewn around everywhere, and there was no place where you could see carpet, as it was all covered by things that were on the floor, except for several areas that Bobby must have made clear for trails through his room. One of the good things about this wss that at least he could see everything that was in the room by looking down, and if he trashed the room even more, no one would be able to tell (unless he trashed the trails). The bad news was that he had to watch his step or else he'd walk on something that was important to Bobby.

To his right, he saw a suitcase. It was open and strangely, everything in the suitcase was still there. So Erin must be very organized unlike Bobby, who seemed to be very messy.

Jack carefully walked up the trail, which led to the suitcase. Then he lowered the top and saw a big sign taped on to it saying:

This suitcase belongs to Erin Milne Martock.

He opened it up again and looking closely, saw two piles. One contained clothes, and the other contained numerous things, such as toys and paper. He decided to look at the pile with the toys and paper. He saw a box of crayons, a box of markers, a toy shield, and paper stapled together.

He dug down deeper and saw a notebook. Then he saw two computer disks, four music CDs, and a large, torn sheet of paper at the bottom. There was something different about this sheet of paper, though.

Jack picked it up and turned it around and he was shocked. It was the cover of a phone book. He saw the names of 25 neighboring cities that the phone book offered information for. Was it the cover of the phone book at the hotel? It could be. Did that mean that Erin was the one who ripped up the phone book?

Jack thought that now he had evidence to support his innocence. But looking again, he realized that he didn't. The cover was dated 1995-96. Why would Erin keep something that was six years old? This was an important clue.

Jack decided to watch Erin, to see whether she enjoyed tearing up paper or chewing pencils or twirling pens. He recalled being blamed for chewing on the antenna of Uncle Hayes's new $250 two-line portable phone, although he was convinced that Erin had done it during the yearly family gathering.

It was time to look for more evidence. So Jack looked through the mess on the floor—comic books, schoolbooks, crumpled sheets of paper, shirts, sweaters, jeans, and other items. He didn't find much information. Then he found a small book titled

ELECTRICITY: From the Plant to Your Home.

Jack gasped. After all, this book may have provided a guide to shutting the power off at the zoo. However, the only way he could be sure was to open the book and find out. He did, and found the Table of Contents. There were six chapters in the book, and the inside cover of the book said:

THIS BOOK IS THE PROPERTY OF:
Brittany Thatcher

Jack knew that it was a schoolbook. The first chapter introduced electricity, the second chapter talked about sources of electricity, the third chapter talked about the dangers of electricity, the fourth chapter talked about the origins of electricity, the fifth chapter talked about light switches, and the sixth chapter talked about what to do in an electrical emergency. Apparently, there was nothing in there about shutting down a circuit breaker. So Jack put the book down. Nevertheless, he wondered why Brittany's missing book happened to be on Bobby's floor.

Then something happened so suddenly that Jack shook in fright.

"Bobby, where are you?" someone called out. "We've been waiting for you to get ready to go to Uncle Parker's for twenty minutes! I am so angry at you!"

Jack's heart began to pound. The person who was looking for Bobby was most likely going to search for him in the most logical place—his room. Realizing he had to hide, Jack turned off the light in the room to make it look like no one was in there, then ran into the closet and closed the door. There was nothing in there but an empty clothesline and a big box with the word BRITTANY on it. Jack crawled into the box and curled up, using his hands to close the top and cover himself.

Now Jack was on full alert. Any noise he heard terrified him.

"Are you in here, Bobby?" asked Aunt Mary, whose footsteps could be heard in Bobby's room.

Chapter 16

"I hope you're not in the closet, because if you are…"

Then she opened the door of the closet and listened for any sound.

"Don't hide from me," said Aunt Mary. "Because if you are hiding, you're in for the biggest punishment of your life."

Aunt Mary walked around the closet, her footsteps pounding on the floor and terrifying Jack each time. Jack was trying to hold his breath and to make no sounds. "I guess you're not here, Bobby. But I'm going to find you."

Jack felt a sigh of relief as she walked out of the room. He decided to stay there until he did not hear a sound for a couple more minutes.

"Did you find Bobby?" asked Uncle Hayes.

"No, I haven't," said Aunt Mary. "I'm going to look in the basement."

"Are you looking for me?" asked Bobby.

"Bobby! There you are! Where were you?" asked Aunt Mary.

"I was in the kitchen waiting to go to Uncle Parker's," said Bobby. "Where were you?"

"I came looking for you since you weren't in the car!" said Aunt Mary.

Realizing that Bobby was found and they were going to Uncle Parker's house, Jack decided that the coast was clear. He opened the flaps of the box and stepped out of it. He opened the closet door and saw Bobby's room, as messy as always.

Then he continued looking for clues. For a half hour he looked and saw toys and wrinkled papers and books, but found nothing else related to electricity or phone books.

Suddenly another idea came to Jack. Could Bobby have ripped the phone book up and strewn it around the same way his room was messed up?

Jack left the room and decided to do things that he enjoyed doing—playing computer games, reading books by his favorite author, Ivan Hert, and taking a nap to refresh his mind. The first thing he did was to go in his room and continue reading a book he liked.

For the next two days, Jack pretty much enjoyed himself, feeling sad for his cousins who had to go to the arcade on one day and to the mall the next day. But then he thought that maybe he shouldn't feel sad for them. After all, only he hated outings—they didn't. He was in heaven, being able to do anything he wanted (provided he remembered that 12:00 p.m. and 6:00 p.m. were mealtimes).

After those two days, Jack woke up feeling sudden terror. This would be his last day of pleasure. The next day, he would be forced to interact again—and what's worse, he would have to do it at the hotel room during the wedding rehearsal.

Since he did not have much time, he decided to make the most of it. He finished his book by lunch, played a computer game after lunch, and then took a nap.

But when dinnertime came, Jack felt that the world was going to come to an end. His fun was over, and he knew that he would be expected to do what he was expected to do.

At dinner, Jack reluctantly sat down with everyone else. At least they were serving chicken Parmesan—a dish that he liked.

"I have an announcement to make," said Jack's mother. "Before we begin dinner, I must talk about what is happening tomorrow. On Saturday, your Aunt Eva is going to marry Peter. Before all weddings, there is a rehearsal, followed by a special dinner. Everyone who is part of the wedding is going to attend. Peter's nephew will be the ring bearer, Brittany will be the flower girl, and Peter's brothers will be ushers."

Jack was very happy that none of this involved him.

"Being the sister of the bride, I will be the matron of honor. There will be two other bridesmaids. One of them will be Mary Thatcher, a bride matron. The other one will be my cousin Penny, a bridesmaid."

"What about me?" Erin protested.

"You can be a junior bridesmaid."

Brittany and Aunt Mary stood up. Everyone clapped for them.

"Everyone will learn what to do at the rehearsal tomorrow," said Aunt Eva. "And I must also tell you that in order for you to get to know her, my fifty-seven-year-old cousin Penny is coming at eight p.m. She will be spending the night here and will be here until the wedding is over. Now, let's begin eating."

Jack was afraid again. He was looking forward to his last evening alone, and now it had to be ruined by being forced to interact with some distant cousin he didn't even know. (She was a distant second cousin to him, but not to his mother or his Aunt Eva.) And because she was an adult, she would soon be yelling at him for his mistakes.

Every bite he ate of his chicken brought him closer to the meeting. He realized that he had reason to be terrified even if he wasn't autistic. He hadn't met Penny before, and he wouldn't even know Penny existed (except for seeing her name on a family tree). Wouldn't *anyone* be terrified at first meeting a stranger, even if it was a distant blood relative?

Jack was positive he would have to do something social with her. He decided to stop thinking about it and enjoy his meal of chicken. He recalled his father always telling him to "be here now" and yelling at him—since the age of six—when he was caught thinking about the future. Jack was thankful that at least the meal they served was not a bad one. Usually he was served food that resembled broken pencil tips, fried insects, or authentic swamp water, as he experienced it.

"It's been fifteen years since I've seen her," said Jack's mother. "I still feel sad for her ever since her father died in that plane crash fifteen years ago."

"Well, I'm sure Penny will be happy to see you," said Aunt Eva. "The main reason why I asked her to be involved in the wedding was so that we could see her again. I'm sorry I forgot to tell you earlier."

"What does Penny act like? Is she stern or caring?" asked Cousin Brittany.

"Well, that is a hard question," said Jack's mother, eating a chunk of chicken, "because I watched a movie once about a stern but caring nanny. Normally Penny is a nice person but there are some things that she will just not talk about. As a child, she treasured her one and only doll just like you treasure the antique doll your great-aunt gave you when you were a newborn. You'll have that in common. But one thing you should not mention is the death of her father. She loved him so much, and always gets touchy whenever someone mentions him. He was such an honest man. And Penny's mother was struck with depression when he died. Every day, Penny would get a telephone call at work from her mother about the crying spells she would have when remembering him. To answer your question, though, she's more caring than stern."

They finished dinner in silence, and Jack knew that he would be expected to be on his best behavior.

But what was best behavior? Jack always tried to be on his best behavior and he was always criticized for doing something wrong. According to them, he was not behaving the way other boys his age did. Why did everyone assume that he should act one way because of his age? Jack's age meant nothing to him. He had felt the same whether he was four, seven, or ten. To him, what was the big deal? It was a big deal to them, though.

Hoping that nothing would go wrong, Jack pretended that he wasn't terrified. At eight o'clock, though, Penny wasn't there. Jack realized that she might be a little late for a reason— according to his mother, it was a rule of hospitality for guests to be fashionably late. At five minutes past eight, Penny arrived. Everyone was in the living room waiting for her.

"Hi, everyone," said Penny as she came in the door.

Penny walked into the room. She was wearing a black coat like Aunt Eva's, but it did not seem to be made out of fur. She had black-and-white hair, and was a person you would call middle-aged—not a young beauty, but not an old hag either.

"Hi, Penny," said Jack's mother. "I'd like to introduce you to my son, Jack."

"Hello, Jack," said Penny.

"Hi," said Jack very softly and very fast so that he could get it done quickly.

"Jack, say it louder," said Jack's mother. "I'm sure Penny didn't hear you."

"Hi," said Jack louder. Apparently, his mother was satisfied, so he sat down and kept quiet.

"Your son is very shy," said Penny. Jack was shy because that was the only way he wouldn't be yelled at. Penny had already met the spouses of Jack's mother, Hayes, and Eva fifteen years ago.

"I'd like to introduce my son, Bobby, and my daughter, Brittany," said Uncle Hayes.

"Hello," Bobby and Brittany said in unison.

"And I'd like to introduce my daughter Erin," said Aunt Eva.

"Hello," said Erin.

"Well, it's nice seeing everyone," said Penny. "I have some news for all of you. I just spoke to Peter. It seems that his nephew Charles, who was going to be the ring bearer, suddenly came down with the flu this morning. He won't be able to take part in the wedding.

"What are we going to do?" asked Aunt Mary. "What about Bobby?"

"I talked about it for a while with Peter. Bobby is too tall."

"Then—" Jack's mother began, though Jack felt his throat go dry.

"There's only one choice," Cousin Penny said. "Because he is small for his age, we have decided that the ring bearer will be Jack Lack."

Chapter 17

"WHA-AT?"

The way it had worked so many other times was the way it worked now. He was told one thing, which his nerves relied on, then at the last moment, the adults around him made some horrific change, which meant that he had been living under false pretenses.

All of Jack's nerves froze in horror and betrayal.

Not only did he have to attend a wedding he didn't want to attend, but now he would have to play a part where millions of eyes would be staring at him and watching his every move. If he screwed up, everyone would laugh at him, even if what he did was not his fault, like the time he tripped over an invisible wire that was stretched over the floor.

Jack also suffered from back problems related to his autism. In previous experiences, if he carried things using his arms and his back, he would drop them. One time he had to carry a glass of juice and he slipped on something on the floor and the juice spilled all over his clothes.

At the wedding, if he made a mistake, he would be seen and laughed at by the ruthless eyes that were connected to the minds of ruthless people, who would not understand his disability. If he tried to explain it was a mistake, they would assume that he had tripped on purpose to get attention, or to get people angry, the way adolescents do things just to defy people. The idea of breaking a rule on purpose was totally absurd to him.

Being scared that he would ruin the wedding because of a mistake—that was not absurd. His body. His entire system. His very essence was in turmoil.

"We were intending to call you tomorrow afternoon, but when Eva called me and asked me to come over tonight, I decided to deliver the message personally," said Penny.

"But…but why me? I thought ring bearers were always young children, and I'm eleven years old. Why can't Bobby be the ring bearer?" said Jack.

"Bobby is too tall," said Aunt Mary. "Even though he is only ten, he's taller than you, Jack."

"But doesn't Peter have any other nephews from his five brothers?" asked Jack.

"He does, but they are all too old," said Penny. "Besides, one of his brothers is taking his family on vacation for the weekend, so they won't be able to attend. His other nephew…"

"What inconsistency!" said Jack. "Those kids are excused because they're too old, but I'm not…"

"As I was saying, the other nephews are very tall for their age. You are the perfect candidate," said Penny. "Why aren't you proud? *I would be proud if I was a ring bearer.* "

"Can't we change the subject?" asked Uncle Hayes. "We haven't seen Penny for fifteen years, yet we're griping about a trivial detail in a wedding. We should be thankful we have a ring bearer! Some weddings don't have them."

"But they should," said Penny. "I despise the ones that don't."

"Would you like some tea?" asked Aunt Eva, who walked into the living room from the hallway.

"Oh, yes, of course," said Penny. "Remember, we may live in America, but our ancestors lived in Britain, and the British drink tea every day. Since I believe in preserving cultural heritage, drinking tea is part of it. I'll still take it, even though the British drink tea at four p.m., not at eight-twenty, the way it is now. But I'll still take it."

"Are your ancestors from England?" Erin asked.

"Yes," Penny replied. "They came in the 1700s during colonization. All except my Great-Great-Great-Great-Great-Great-Uncle John. They left him behind because he was crazy."

Jack's ears perked up. Whenever anyone talked about family misfits, he felt an instant kinship and wanted the details.

"As John got older, his abnormal behavior grew worse. He would stare at the wallpaper of the bathroom in his house, as well as letters and numbers on signs, for hours. He had no friends and would reject anyone who came his way. They took him to a doctor who was shocked at his unusual behavior and told them that there were children that just were different, and the only way to cure him was to punish him if he performed those behaviors, and if he continued performing them, they should just punish him even more, making the punishments even harsher, and if he talks back, threaten to make the punishment twice as bad, and soon he'll shape up. When he went to school, he was beaten up by the school bullies by the end of the first week. And he always made lame excuses whenever he did something bad as if it wasn't his fault. But we all knew—"

"Could you tell us about your grandparents?" asked Aunt Mary. "It seems as if you're rattling on about your crazy ancestor!"

Jack stopped listening suddenly and realized something. All those behaviors he had just listened to—hostility toward strangers, only safe in one's own home, beaten up by bullies in school, people thinking that excuses are lame when they aren't— all resembled Jack's behaviors in the family. So therefore, Jack wasn't all at fault for his autism—there apparently *was* some autism running in the family. And his grandmother Martha, who was related back to crazy John, was weird all her life too. But then, since the term "autism" didn't exist a hundred years ago, there was no way of knowing whether or not it was real autism.

"All right, all right," said Penny. "Well, let me just tell you that there is a technical term for that behavior today. It's called autism, and that doctor was right about everything back then as doctors are today. Back to my grandparents. My grandmother came from the Smith family, because her ancestors were blacksmiths. Her father was well-known as the best maker of horseshoes where they lived. When my grandmother was fifteen, she was given a horse that had horseshoes made by her father. To this day, it was the best moment of her life.

"Her ancestors were also Puritans, and they fought in the American Revolution, so my mother and I could join the club called the Daughters of the American Revolution. But my mom and I never did.

"All of the children that my grandparents and great-grandparents had were normal, so I won't be talking a lot about them." said Penny. "Do you have any questions?"

No one said anything.

"So," said Penny, "does anyone want to play a game? How about we play an old game my mother gave me—Pick Up Sticks. I brought the game with me."

"That's fine," said Aunt Mary. "But remember, Jack's still grounded, so he won't be able to play. But you can play without him."

The other kids began to play Pick Up Sticks with Penny, and Jack went off to his room to read a book.

Chapter 18

The next day, Jack got up and went to the breakfast table, only to find that again there was nothing for him to eat. Oh well, it didn't bother him that much. At least he was spared having to force down the flaxseed cereal he hated. Everyone was sitting around dressed in fancy clothes, as if they were eating in an expensive restaurant.

"Well, Jack," his mother said, "it's time for you to get dressed up."

Jack just stood there, not knowing what to do. Normal clothes meant pain, and he could only imagine what dress clothes would mean. His parents were always so embarrassed about his behavior that they never took him to formal occasions, where he would have to look nice and know unwritten rules of conduct that weren't a part of daily life. Not that he knew the rules of daily life either. But at least he didn't have to wear fancy clothes like the ones people were in at the breakfast table.

"No," he said. After all, people are born with an instinct to not put themselves into pain.

"No is not an option," said Uncle Hayes, dressed up in black and white.

Jack looked down at his feet. It would be impossible to reason with the adults once more. Adults were horrible—just horrible—when it came to understanding other people. Strangely, he was mocked for not being able to understand others—but he understood others just fine. No one seemed to understand him. Nor did anyone seem to understand the juvenile delinquents in his school classroom, as year after year, they weren't getting better.

Life was full of suffering, and Jack lived from pain to pain. The Buddha was right, and may have been autistic himself—he lived in an age when people didn't know about special needs. If the life expectancy of humans was seventy years, then Jack would suffer for seventy years until he went to heaven, unless he went to hell for not being subservient to his parents. According to his parents, not being subservient was a sin in God's eyes, since God wanted children brought up to obey their parents. This was still more evidence that whoever lived up there was a jerk, not kind and loving.

Realizing he had no choice but to suffer, he said, "But I don't know where those clothes are. How can I put them on?"

"Marvin, he's—"

"Hayes, he is not lying this time. We didn't tell him about those clothes, so he truly doesn't know. We didn't want him to worry for three weeks," Jack's mother said.

Jack looked at his mother suspiciously. *She knew about this? So maybe there is no Charles with the flu?*

"You knew about—"

"Come on, Jack, don't cause trouble. Come with me, and I will show you where they are so you can put them on."

Jack went with his mother to Brittany's room, and Jack's mother took out a white shirt with embroidery and a pair of black pants with belt loops. Then she showed him a belt that looked a medieval instrument of torture.

"Now put these on," said Jack's mother.

"But why today? Isn't the wedding tomorrow?"

"We're doing a dress rehearsal. With pictures afterwards."

"But that's not how they do it in the movies. Nobody dresses up for the rehearsal."

"This isn't the movies. This is real life, and we can do whatever we want."

Jack looked at this mother, and was confused. That was one of the stupidest lies his mother had ever told him.

"But the wedding rehearsal isn't until five p.m. Why do I have to put the clothes on now?" asked Jack.

"Don't talk back to me! Everyone else put on their clothes without going crazy! And besides, if everyone has their clothes on now, we don't have to worry about it later!" said Jack's mother.

"You mean I have to wear this stuff all day?"

"That's right. Your cousins think it's fun to be dressed up."

So Jack put on the white shirt, the black pants, and the belt.

When he did, his legs instantly felt horrible itching pains. He scratched his itches, which helped a little, but a minute later they came back. Realizing there was no way he was going to win, he just decided to scratch the itches to get rid of the horrible pains that the ruthless adults in his world forced him to suffer.

Then the embroidery started making tiny cuts in his chest. He couldn't scratch them because they hurt so much.

He walked back to the breakfast table and sat down, thankful there wasn't anything for him to eat, since he wouldn't have been able to concentrate on food in the middle of such pain.

"Now Jack has put on decent clothes," said Uncle Hayes while Jack was scratching his legs everywhere. "When we get to the hotel—Jack, why are you scratching yourself every minute?"

Jack could not take any more of this. He suddenly began to cry and instantly felt relieved.

"Why are you crying?" said Uncle Hayes. "Surely you're happy that you're a ring bearer."

"No," sobbed Jack. "I have been treated horribly. I have to wear these painful c-clothes, and I h-have to suffer for someone I hate and for someone I don't even know."

"Eva is your aunt!" said Uncle Hayes. "She is related to you by blood."

"B-but she is mean to me! Y-you are mean to me! E-everyone is mean to me!"

"Jack, stop it this minute. Why do you always have to fight authority?"

"I am not fighting authority! I am just saying that I am in pain!" said Jack.

"How can you be in pain by wearing dress clothes? None of us are," said Uncle Hayes.

"But I am," said Jack.

"You can't be. I forbid you to have pain. It's not allowed in this house," said Uncle Hayes.

"I am not you. And you are not in my body. You can't just say I'm not suffering because you are not suffering," said Jack.

"Oh yes, I can. I am in charge here. You are not suffering because I say so," said Uncle Hayes.

"What authority do you have to rule my body?" asked Jack.

"You're right, Jack, I cannot control your body. That's your business. But I can control your behavior. If you don't stop scratching this instant, you'll have no dinner tonight."

"Does that mean I can take off these clothes and starve by myself?" Jack asked hopefully.

For the next seven hours (nine o'clock to four o'clock), Jack stayed away from the family as much as possible. This was so he could scratch his itchy legs without embarrassing someone. The only time he was forced to spend time with his family was when Cousin Brittany returned at ten o'clock and showed everyone her flower girl outfit. But for the rest of the time he was in his room trying to read with his itchy legs. He looked at his legs and they had red spots everywhere from where he had scratched them.

At four o'clock, everyone was called into the living room so that they could start getting ready for the rehearsal. Jack didn't really think that it would take that long for everyone to get ready, but by four-thirty, Jack realized that it did. They were combing their hair, washing their hands, making sure that there were no wrinkles on their clothes. Jack just sat and thought how crazy people were. His family was obsessed over little marks on clothes—yet everyone yelled at him when he obsessed over things like marks on his paper.

Needing to get out of a house so full of nasty spirits, he went outside in the afternoon and found a hose to play with. His parents always insisted that he water the grass, not the driveway, but when water soaked into the grass, it disappeared. When it fell on the cement, it made wonderful patterns and rivers that twisted and turned like a shipping canal system. It was one of his calming mechanisms, way too complicated for his parents to understand.

Forgetting that he was wearing dress clothes for a moment, Jack turned on the front hose full force and squirted the driveway. Instantly his nerves calmed down. He was just about to put the hose straight up in the air to make rain when Aunt Mary came out of the house shrieking.

"NEVER TOUCH MY HOSE AGAIN!!" she screamed. "NOT EVER!! DO YOU UNDERSTAND?"

"What if there's—"

"THERE ARE NO EXCEPTIONS! NONE!" she shrieked. "IS THAT CLEAR?"

"Yes," Jack mumbled.

"Now get in the house and stay there. If you wrecked your clothes, I'm sure your father would beat you."

Jack scratched his legs as he went back into the house. Maybe a beating would stop the itching.

* * * *

"This is where the wedding will take place tomorrow."

Aunt Eva led everyone into a huge room at the Jones Mark Hotel with dozens of chandeliers on the ceiling and rows of chairs throughout the room. Everyone was there, including Uncle Frank and Peter, the groom-to-be.

There was an aisle in the middle of the chair rows, dividing the chairs into two sections. In the front of the room in one corner, there was an organ. There also were two large signs hanging from the ceiling in the middle of the chair sections. The sign to the left read BRIDE. The sign to the right read GROOM. Those signs indicated where the bride's family and friends sat and where the groom's family and friends sat. In the front row of the GROOM section, all of the chairs were reserved for Peter's family. At the end of the aisle in the front was an altar.

Aunt Eva asked everyone to sit down when they had walked to the front row of the chairs in the BRIDE section.

A man walked in from a side entrance wearing a suit and tie with a whistle around his neck and came over to Aunt Eva. She got up and said to everyone, "I'd like you to meet the justice of the peace in Marion County. He has agreed to officiate at our wedding."

Peter walked over to Aunt Eva and the justice of the peace.

"Nice introduction," said the justice of the peace. "If you want to know my name, it's Jacques Gunne-Wedden. But you can call me Mr. Gunne-Wedden.

"Before we begin, I need to know the roles that are going to be played in this wedding," said Mr. Gunne-Wedden.

"The matron of honor will be my sister, Susan Lack," said Aunt Eva. Jack's mother stood up.

"There will also be another bride matron and two bridesmaids. The bride matron will be my sister-in-law Mary Thatcher. And the bridesmaids will be my cousin Penny Milne and my daughter Erin," said Aunt Eva.

Penny, Erin, and Aunt Mary stood up.

"The flower girl will be my niece Brittany, daughter of the bride matron. And finally, I must inform you that the ring bearer, a nephew of Peter's, grew ill yesterday, and will be replaced by my nephew Jack Lack," said Aunt Eva.

Brittany and Jack stood up. No one noticed that Jack was shaking.

Then Peter said, "There will be three ushers and a best man. The three ushers will be three of my brothers: Chester Norman, Evan Norman, and Robert Norman. And the best man is my brother Arthur."

"Thank you," said Mr. Gunne-Wedden. "Now I am going to talk you through the wedding. Then we'll rehearse it twice."

"After that," Aunt Eva cut in, "a catered dinner will be served to everyone in a private banquet room."

Step by step, the justice of the peace explained the wedding while Jack's legs itched and his chest hurt so badly that, for a while, he didn't pay attention to the feeling of being strangled by the belt. But eventually, he felt as if he were being cut in two. He dreaded having to do his part as ring bearer. He didn't think he would be able to do it.

Chapter 19

"Now that we're at a breaking point, can I go to the bathroom?" asked Cousin Erin after the justice of the peace finished his explanation and told everyone it was time to rehearse.

Realizing that she couldn't act like a disciplinarian in front of the justice of the peace, Aunt Mary said, "Yes, you may."

They waited until Erin returned. When she did, Mr. Gunne-Wedden spoke again.

"At the beginning of the wedding, the three ushers are seating the guests. Ushers, please come up and pretend to seat guests. At this time, the groom and the best man will be at the northeast corner of the room. I should like to ask the groom and the best man to position themselves there.

"The flower girl and ring bearer are positioned in the hallway at the main entrance of the room. It will be open tomorrow, but since it is closed today, I would like the flower girl and ring bearer to stand right next to the door. The bride matron, bridesmaids, matron of honor, and bride shall leave the room at the main entrance and position themselves anywhere in the hallway and will not walk down the aisle until after the flower girl and ring bearer have entered. Will the bride, matron of honor, bridesmaids, flower girl, and ring bearer please leave the room?"

Penny, Jack's mother, Mary, Eva, Erin, Brittany, and Jack left the room. Jack stood as far away from everyone as possible, so that no one would know that he could hardly stand on his feet.

"And now, let the music begin!"

One of the ushers went over to a tape recorder, and pressed the PLAY button.

"Oh, I must tell you something. If there are any mistakes during the rehearsal, I will blow my whistle and everything must stop," said Mr. Gunne-Wedden.

The music seemed to go on for a long time while everybody waited, and then the justice of the peace gave the cue for the flower girl to enter the room.

Brittany walked inside the room and started to throw out the flower petals she was carrying in a basket. Jack tried to block her out, so he wouldn't miss his signal.

But he had misunderstood the long speech and didn't know that he was supposed to count to ten by himself and then enter on his own. There would be no signal.

Suddenly a piercing blast of shrill sound shook the atmosphere, like a fire alarm during a fire drill. When Jack looked around, he saw that none of the fire alarms were going off. He sank to the ground in tears, crying, wishing he could go home in his agony, when suddenly the sharp, piercing blast of Mr. Gunne-Wedden's whistle came again.

Jack knew that it had to be that whistle, and the reason why the whistle was going off was because he had broken a rule already—that the cue given to Brittany was his cue to start counting, and now he was being punished for not understanding something. He just sat there, crying when he heard voices:

"Stop whistling! It's not working!"

"Where's Jack?"

"He's disobeying his instructions!"

"I can't believe this kid!"

"It's not his fault. He has—"

"We've heard enough, Marvin, we already know—"

Then Jack held his hands over his ears as the pounding of frantic running came closer and closer and closer and a shrill, piercing sound shattered his dying nerves again, except this time it was a person screaming...

"Jack! Get up!" called Jack's mother.

"Susan, you're too nice to him. Let me do it," said Aunt Mary. Then she yelled into his left ear, "JACK! YOU GET UP THIS INSTANT OR ELSE I'M GOING TO LIFT YOU UP! IF YOU DON'T LET ME LIFT YOU UP, NO FOOD OR DRINK FOR TWO DAYS!"

Jack cried and cried, and then felt the arms of a person surround him, and he cried again, the feeling of the arms hurting him too. Realizing the only way to get out of the misery was to get up himself, he did. But he didn't look anyone in the eye. He just had to be alone. His body had just gone through four shocks.

"JACK! WHY DON'T YOU OBEY ORDERS THE WAY OTHERS DO?" shrieked Aunt Mary.

Five shocks.

"WHY DIDN'T YOU COME IN WITH COUSIN BRITTANY WHEN MR. GUNNE-WEDDEN GAVE THE CUE?" roared Uncle Hayes.

Six.

Then a soothing voice said, "Stop yelling at him. He obviously didn't understand his instructions, and the whistle must have terrified him," said Uncle Frank. "This isn't the army." He gave a look at Hayes when he said that.

"HOW DARE YOU CRITICIZE ME? YOU ARE ONE OF THE CRAZIEST MEN I HAVE EVER MET, AND THEREFORE YOU ARE NOT AUTHORIZED TO CRITICIZE ME BECAUSE ALL I AM DOING IS PUNISHING—"

"Calm down, Hayes," said Uncle Frank.

"DISOBEY MR. GUNNE-WEDDEN?" boomed Jack's father.

"Get r-rid of the sound!" cried Jack.

"WHY DIDN'T YOU WALK IN WHEN THE WHISTLE WAS BLOWN? HE WAS TRYING TO GET YOU TO REMEMBER! WAS THAT THE SOUND?" barked Jack's mother.

"The s-sound...."

"You better stop complaining or there will be a lot more sounds in this room."

Jack was struck dumb. He didn't always understand figures of speech and other non-literal language, so he instantly imagined sounds flying around the room like bomber planes, aiming their missiles right into his ears.

"Stop yelling! He didn't mean it!" said Uncle Frank.

"Shut up, Frank," said Hayes. "How dare you interfere with our discipline?"

"I will shut up. But before I do, I must tell you one thing. I do not see discipline taking place here," said Uncle Frank.

Jack just stood there, crying and crying and crying, his tears soaking his white shirt.

"Oh, no," said Jack's mother, noticing the stains. "Stop crying this instant, or you'll ruin your shirt. Okay, I'll try to be calm. Jack, why didn't you come in when Mr. Gunne-Wedden told you to?"

"I-I didn't know," sobbed Jack.

"HOW COULD YOU NOT KNOW?" screamed Aunt Mary. "How can you be so stupid?"

"Could we please get ourselves organized here?!" said Mr. Gunne-Wedden. "*You're* holding up the rehearsal—by yelling at an innocent child!"

"Now pull yourself together, Jack," Aunt Mary continued. "You heard what the man said—you're holding everything up because we had to yell at you. Repeat after me: I will enter the room and carry the ring when asked."

"I...will...enter...the...room...and...carry...the...ring... when... asked," Jack echoed slowly, not able to comprehend a word by now.

But he knew he had to do the right thing the next time, or he'd be tortured with another blast of the whistle.

They began again. Brittany started walking, then when his mother nodded at him, Jack started walking. He was doing his best not to fall over from the stress when Mr. Gunne-Wedden shouted, "Stop!"

"Why?" said Aunt Eva.

"Where's the pillow with the ring?" he asked.

"It's over here," she said, then walked over to the chair where she had set down her black fur coat.

"Uh-oh!" she cried.

"What happened? Is everything okay?" Aunt Mary called.

"The pillow is here," Aunt Eva called back, "but the ring—*it's gone!*"

Chapter 20

The justice of the peace asked everyone to stay in the room while he went to the front desk to report the missing ring. When he left, Aunt Eva said, "Jack, where did you put the ring?"

"I-I never saw it."

"You do not have to yell at Jack, Miss Martock," said Mr. Gunne-Wedden, who returned. "I have another ring that I keep in my car in the event of such a mishap."

"All right then, but Jack, you will still get punished since it is an offense to steal," said Aunt Eva. "I'll confer with your parents to find out the most suitable punishment to teach you a lesson."

This was ridiculous. Jack didn't steal the ring. It was another setup to get him in trouble. This time he decided that no matter what happened, he would keep searching for evidence. He would fight back. He was innocent, and all of the readers reading this book know that. But no one would believe him.

Even if he did find a decent clue, he wouldn't be able to get anyone to believe him right away. It was hopeless for the moment. For now, he would have to get through this wedding, and he would have to listen to everyone, since if he didn't, the whistle and the screaming of everyone would hurt him more.

"Now that everything is settled," said Aunt Eva, "here is the pillow, Jack."

Jack was given the ring and pillow. "Now, we are going to begin again. Places, everyone!" said Mr. Gunne-Wedden.

Jack walked to the outside of the room again.

The recorded music began playing, and the ushers began to pantomime their roles. Suddenly, the music was stopped, and Mr. Gunne-Wedden gave the cue. The ushers sat down and Jack, trembling and shaking, walked with the ring and pillow step by step, down the aisle. Jack remembered that it could always be worse. After all, they could be laughing at him for walking like a zombie in his "preyed animal" state, ignoring the flowers that were flying above his head, thrown by his cousin Brittany, who seemed to be as happy as could be. Mr. Gunne-Wedden gave the cue for the groom and the best man to walk to the altar. When Jack and Brittany got to the end of the aisle, flowers were strewn throughout the room, and the justice of the peace called, "Stop!"

The music stopped, and so did everyone else.

"You have done very well. Jack and Brittany were excellent as the ring bearer and flower girl. And the ushers were terrific. For the next part of the wedding, the ring bearer shall take the ring and give it to the best man, who gives it to me. Then the bride, the bridesmaids, and matron of honor will enter the aisle in this order. The matron of honor will enter first, the bridesmaids will enter second, all carrying flowers, and the bride will enter last on her brother's arm. These five women and Hayes shall leave the room until I give them the cue. Start the music again!" said Mr. Gunne-Wedden.

Marvin hit the PLAY button, and Jack gave the pillow to the best man, and was happy to be able to finally put his arms down. When the music changed, the matron of honor, the bridesmaids, the bride matron, and Eva the bride entered on Hayes's arm. Jack thought that Eva looked funny on the arm of her brother.

They went to the end of the aisle, and Eva found Peter and they held hands.

"Perfect!" said Mr. Gunne-Wedden. "Now the ceremony begins."

"We are gathered here today," said Mr. Gunne-Wedden, "to wed Mr. Peter Norman and Miss Eva Martock in holy matrimony, which is an honorable estate created of God, signifying unto us the union that is between Christ and the Church; which holy estate Christ made beautiful with his presence. He is to be honored among all men and not be used to satisfy temptation but to honor, and to use in God considering the reasons for Holy Matrimony.

"Reason 1: It was created for raising children to be brought up in the way of the Lord and to praise his name.

"Reason 2: It was created as a remedy against sins of the flesh.

"Reason 3: It was created for the society, help, and comfort one shall have of the other, both in happiness and sadness, into which estate these two people shall be joined.

"If there is any reason why Peter Norman and Eva Martock should not legally be joined together, please speak now or eternally hold your peace."

Jack felt an uncontrollable urge to shout something, like in the movies. He'd seen a bunch of movies where people yelled "Stop!" at this point in a wedding. Against his will, the thought started demanding release. He stuffed it into the cattle chute where he confined such thoughts. But like a raging bull, it demanded release. He put his hand over his mouth and tried to swallow it down. Soon he was retching. In another second it would have to come out.

"Uuuu-nnn-ggg-hhh," he groaned.

Everyone turned and glared at him. Brittany took her pointed dress shoe and kicked him hard in the leg.

"Owwww!" he screamed.

Jack's mother jumped up, raced over to him, and grabbed him by the collar. She whispered in his ear, "You utter another sound and I'll make you wear those pants for a month."

Jack withdrew into himself and checked out the mental cattle chute. It was empty. No more raging yells bursting to come out.

The justice of the peace was silent for a minute, then began speaking again.

"Do you, Eva Martock, take this man to be your lawfully wedded husband, to have and to hold, to love and to cherish, for richer or poorer, in sickness and health, 'til death do you part?" asked Mr. Gunne-Wedden.

"I do," said Aunt Eva.

"Do you, Peter Norman, take this woman to be your lawfully wedded wife, to have and to hold, to love and to cherish, for richer or poorer, in sickness and health, 'til death do you part?" asked Mr. Gunne-Wedden.

"I don't," said Peter.

"WHAT?" asked Aunt Eva. "You don't take me as your wife?"

"I'm sorry, I was just curious to see everyone's response. In reality, I do," said Peter.

That got Jack's attention. It was something an autistic person might do—not to be weird or hurtful but as an experiment, to be able to witness another person's reaction.

"Who gives this woman to be married to this man?"

"I, Hayes Albertus Thatcher, give my sister Eva Thatcher Martock to wed Peter Angus Norman," said Uncle Hayes.

"By the power vested in me by the state of Indiana, and Marion County, I now pronounce you husband and wife. You may kiss the bride," said Mr. Gunne-Wedden.

And then Eva and Peter, even though it was not their wedding day, kissed.

"That was excellent!" said Mr. Gunne-Wedden. "But Peter, you only have to say, 'I do,' rather than what you said."

"Now, we are going to re-enact it without any breaking points after I get more flowers for Brittany," said Mr. Gunne-Wedden.

Mr. Gunne-Wedden left the room and returned ten minutes later with another bouquet of flowers and said, "Everyone return to their places at the beginning."

The tape recorder continued playing. Jack and Brittany left the room and the ushers returned to pretending to seat people. The bride and her bridesmaids and bride matrons left the room. And the groom with the best man returned to a corner inside the room. The justice of the peace stayed at the altar.

They rehearsed again. This time Jack didn't feel the impulse to shout "Stop." Once something was out of his system it was out forever, and Peter didn't clown around either. Maybe it was out of his system too.

After the rehearsal, Mr. Gunne-Wedden led the party of thirty people (Eva, Eva's sister and brothers, Jack's father, Aunt Mary, the children of Eva's sister and brothers, Peter and his parents, Peter's four brothers, the four wives of the four brothers, and the children of Peter's four brothers) to the hallway and turned right. He took them to a doorway, and they walked into another very big room, possibly twice the size as the wedding room. There were two rows of tables to the left, each of which had serving plates full of food and ten rows of tables for people to sit.

"Now, everyone, take a table and start to eat!" said Mr. Gunne-Wedden.

Everybody sat down at a table, but before anyone got to eat, a bell rang, so everyone stopped.

"Before we have the rehearsal dinner," announced Peter Norman, "I must introduce you to the people that are making this wedding possible. My bride Eva hired the justice of the peace and chose the location for our wedding with her brother Hayes and sister Susan. Let us give a round of applause for my parents, who paid the money to make this wedding possible and arranged the rehearsal, Homer and Agnes Norman!"

Homer and Agnes Norman got up, and everyone looked at them, clapping and cheering.

"And let us give a round of applause to the bride, who will be my wife by tomorrow night, Eva Thatcher Martock!" announced Peter.

Aunt Eva got up from her table, and everyone looked at her, clapping and cheering.

"And let us give a round of applause to my future brother-in-law and sister-in-law Hayes Thatcher and Susan Lack, who are also helping to make the wedding possible!" announced Peter.

Jack's mother got up from Jack's table, and Uncle Hayes got up from his table, and everyone cheered and clapped while looking at them.

"That's all I have to say now. Dinner is served!" announced Peter.

Everyone went to the food tables, including the bride and groom, and got things to eat. Jack was happy that they served chicken with Alfredo sauce, his favorite dish, so he wouldn't have to go hungry again.

Jack was also happy the rehearsal was done. All he had to do now was think about having a meal of food that he liked. And he didn't have to scratch himself anymore—his legs had been scratched so much that they felt numb.

Chapter 21

The next day, Jack was walking down the hallway of the Jones Mark Hotel when suddenly Aunt Eva popped out with a great big dragon. Jack was terrified. He didn't think dragons existed.

"Where have you been? The wedding has just started a minute ago, and the justice of the peace, Mr. Gunne-Dragon, has been waiting for you!" snarled Aunt Eva.

"Any more mistakes," said the dragon, "and I will burn you up." He breathed a flame to demonstrate.

"Now get moving!" said Eva.

He walked into the wedding room and everyone was laughing at him, because he was dressed in sweat pants and a T-shirt. Then he dropped the ring along with the pillow, and the dragon came up to him and said, "You made a mistake, so I will burn you!"

Orange flames burst out of the dragon's mouth, and Jack was in the worst pain ever until...

He looked up. The flames were gone, and all he saw was a dark room. He was in a bed, terrified as can be. He did not know where he was and could only see that he was in someone's bedroom. He heard the sound of someone breathing and thought that it was the sleeping dragon. But if he had been burned, wouldn't he be dead? Wouldn't he be going to heaven?

He thought now that he was in the dragon's lair, and was sleeping on a bottom bunk, the dragon on top.

He turned to his left and saw a clock with the time: 7:02. Then he looked around and saw that this room was not heaven, nor the dragon's lair. It was Brittany's room, and he was lying in the bottom bunk of the bed. The wedding had not taken place, nor did a dragon burn him to a crisp. It was just a horrible, horrible—

DREAM!

Jack was terrified again. That terror was just a dream! Now he would really have to go through the wedding that was going to happen today in real life! He could not escape the way he could from a dream. He wanted to go back to sleep, hoping he would never wake up again, because a day of utter misery was ahead.

He tried to get back to sleep, but he couldn't. He was just too terrified to sleep. So he got up, dressed in his usual attire, and went to the dining room.

When he got there, everyone was already up and eating breakfast except Brittany, and at least this time, no one was dressed up. They were wearing what they usually wore. "Hello, Jack. Excited about being the ring bearer?" said Uncle Hayes.

"Yes, I am," Jack lied, since adults were never interested in the truth.

"The wedding's at one o'clock," said Aunt Mary. "But we'll have to be there at noon."

"I found my electricity book," said Brittany, who walked into the dining room.

"Where did you find it?" asked Aunt Mary.

"I found it in Bobby's room. And it was opened to a page titled *How to Shut the Power Off in a Building.* I don't know why Bobby wanted to steal the book, though," said Brittany, showing the book to Aunt Mary. "We all know who did it."

"Bobby may not have stolen it. Erin also sleeps in that room," said Penny.

"But why would the book be open to that section?" asked Brittany, looking at Jack.

"I assume it was a coincidence," said Uncle Hayes.

Suddenly, rage surged into Jack's body. How could everybody be so stupid? Someone was plotting in their family.

But what was there to be gained by shutting the power off at a reptile house at a zoo? And was that crime related to the mysterious disappearance of the ring yesterday at the rehearsal?

Sooner or later, Jack knew he would find out the truth.

At ten o'clock, Aunt Eva called out, "It's time to get ready!"

They all ran to their rooms, even Jack, who reluctantly put on his white shirt and black dress pants. When he walked to the living room, Aunt Eva, Uncle Hayes, Aunt Mary, Penny, and Jack's mother were not in their wedding clothes.

"If you want to know why we're not dressed up," said Aunt

Eva, "it's because our wedding clothes are at the hotel. We're going to dress there."

At 10:30, they all put on their shoes, and they were on the road by 10:45. It took them one hour to get to the Jones Mark Hotel, and when they entered the hotel, there was a sign saying: Today's Events: THE WEDDING OF EVA MARTOCK AND PETER NORMAN—*Martin Ballroom, 1:00 p.m.*

In the lobby, they met Uncle Frank. Then a man walked up to Eva and said, "The groom has already arrived. The women's clothes are in the Stanton Suite, number 105; Mr. Thatcher's clothes are in room 106, across the hall."

The man led everyone to rooms adjacent to the ballroom.

"Okay then, Frank, Marvin, please stay here and take care of the children. Penny, Susan, Mary, come with me. Our clothes are in this room." said Aunt Eva. "Hayes, your clothes are in 106."

Eva and the other women went into room 105. They seemed to be gone for ages until Aunt Eva walked out wearing her beige wedding dress and veil. Because it was her second wedding, she could not wear white.

"How do I look?" asked Aunt Eva.

"You…look wonderful," said Uncle Frank.

Then Jack's mother, Penny, and Aunt Mary walked out of the room, all three wearing their pink formal dresses. Penny and Aunt Mary held flowers in their right hands.

"How do we look?" asked Jack's mother.

"You look wonderful," said Jack's father.

And then, Uncle Hayes walked out, dressed in a tuxedo.

"So, I guess we are all ready. Let us go to the ball room," said Uncle Hayes.

They walked across the hall to the wedding room. The room looked exactly the same as yesterday, except there were white streamers taped to the ceiling and on the wedding aisle. They kept the door open until Eva's long wedding train was in the room.

Mr. Gunne-Wedden had not yet come to the room. On one side of the room was a computer and a projector. On the wall near the altar was a projected version of what was on the computer, and the organ was gone. The computer screen read:

Welcome To
Microsoft®
WEDDING
Version 1.2

From the Makers of Microsoft®
DIVORCE

Press any key to continue . . .

"What is going on here?" Aunt Eva demanded. "Where is Mr. Gunne-Wedden?"

"I don't know. We were wondering ourselves," said Peter, who walked up to greet Eva.

Jack looked to the right and saw that Peter's family had already come and were in the front row of the GROOM section.

"I'm sorry to inconvenience you," said a woman's voice.

Everyone looked to the door of the room and saw a middle-aged woman wearing a yellow dress.

"I have some bad news. I am Zelda Gunne-Wedden, the wife of Jacques Gunne-Wedden. My husband was throwing up everywhere this morning, and he can't come. I called the hotel to supply you with this computer, which contains the current state-of-the-art wedding program. It will tell you how to use it. I have to go to the beauty parlor, but I hope you have a good wedding. The computer can play synthesized organ music, so you don't need your own tape player," said the wife of Mr. Gunne-Wedden.

"Thank you for telling us," said Aunt Eva, in shock.

"Bye then," said Mrs. Gunne-Wedden, and she left.

"Well, what are we going to do?" asked Aunt Eva.

"Let's press any key to continue!" said Uncle Hayes. He strolled to the computer and pressed a key.

"Are you serious?" cried Jack's mother, looking around the room for support.

"Hey, don't look at us," said Peter's mother defensively. "We don't want to have anything to do with it."

Suddenly, a man's voice was heard, and apparently it was coming from the computer.

"WELCOME TO MICROSOFT WEDDING. TO START YOUR WEDDING, PLEASE SELECT YOUR WEDDING STYLE. TO CHANGE THE VOICE, PLEASE PRESS 0."

The computer showed the following list:

Microsoft® WEDDING: LIST OF WEDDINGS

0. Change Voice
1. American Wedding
2. Jewish Wedding
3. Buddhist Wedding
4. Christian Wedding
5. Muslim Wedding
6. Hindu Wedding
7. Pagan Wedding
8. Shotgun Wedding
9. Your Own Wedding

"Well, then," said Uncle Hayes, who was at the computer. "Do you want to change the voice?"

Aunt Eva looked at him blankly. "Are we really going to have some dumb machine officiate at my wedding? I mean, is it even legal?"

"Does that matter? It's a Microsoft product. I'm sure they have some sort of licensing agreement. Besides, do we have a choice?"

"I guess I don't. But please, change that voice," said Eva.

"It appears to be God's will," said Peter's brother Chester.

Hayes pressed 0.

"YOU HAVE DECIDED TO CHANGE THE VOICE. PLEASE CHOOSE YOUR VOICE."

Another list popped up:

Microsoft® WEDDING: LIST OF VOICES

1. MAN
2. WOMAN
3. SPANISH ACCENT
4. BLACK ACCENT
   (Indicate educated or soul talk)
5. BRITISH ACCENT
   (Indicate what class)
6. FRENCH ACCENT
7. IRISH ACCENT
8. CHINESE ACCENT
9. INDIAN ACCENT
   (Indicate Asian or Native American)
F1. NEW YORK ACCENT
0. RETURN TO WEDDING LIST

"Well, I don't want to be absolutely traditional, but I don't want to be fancy either, so how about a woman's voice. Hayes, put in a woman's voice," said Aunt Eva.

"Okay," he said, and pressed 2.

"YOU HAVE SELECTED A WOMAN'S VOICE. PLEASE PRESS 0 TO RETURN TO THE WEDDING LIST," said a very high female voice.

Hayes pressed 0.

"So, shall we start the wedding?" asked Uncle Hayes.

"Okay then," said Aunt Eva.

"Which one do you want? We have weddings from cultures other than American," said Uncle Hayes.

"We're pressed for time, so let's say American," said Aunt Eva.

Hayes pressed 1 for American, and the computer said:

"YOU'VE DECIDED TO HAVE AN AMERICAN, AN AMERICAN, AN AMERICAN, AN AMERICAN, AN AMERICAN..."

"What's going on?" asked Aunt Eva. "Why is it repeating "AN AMERICAN? Is the computer unstable?"

Hayes tried to press keys to get it to work again, but it didn't. It just kept repeating those two words. "I don't know! It didn't say that it would crash with the American wedding!" he said.

"Well, you're a man, so you should be able to figure it out. In my opinion, men naturally know how to use computers." Aunt Eva said. Next to the computer she picked up a big book that had about 1,500 pages and gave it to Uncle Hayes.

"Read this. It's called *Microsoft WEDDING for Dummies*. It'll teach you everything," said Aunt Eva.

"All right, but I don't need this. I am going to reboot the machine," said Uncle Hayes. He pressed Ctrl, Alt, Del but it didn't work. He tried again and it still didn't work.

Grumbling, he opened up the book and went to page 512, which was listed in the Contents as the page that tells you what to do when the computer crashes.

The book said:

If Microsoft WEDDING crashes at any time, please reboot the machine by pressing Ctrl, Alt, Del.

He wasn't getting anywhere, so he put the book down.

Then he illegally shut the computer down by flipping the power switch, waited 5 seconds, and restarted the machine. It loaded Windows 2000, and he started Microsoft WEDDING. He pressed any key to continue. The computer said:

"WELCOME TO MICROSOFT WEDDING. TO START YOUR WEDDING, PLEASE SELECT THE WEDDING STYLE. TO CHANGE THE VOICE, PLEASE PRESS 0," said the high voice of a woman.

"Well, at least it remembered what voice we wanted," said Uncle Hayes. He pressed 1 for American Wedding.

"YOU'VE DECIDED TO HAVE AN AMERICAN WEDDING. HOW MUCH TIME WOULD YOU LIKE ORGAN MUSIC TO PLAY BEFORE THE WEDDING BEGINS? PLEASE TYPE IN A NUMBER AND PRESS ENTER TO CONTINUE."

The words appeared on the screen and on the projector:

ORGAN PLAYING TIME: ___ MINUTES

Since the current time was 12:20, Uncle Hayes decided to put in 45 minutes of organ time. So he put in the number 45 in the blank space and pressed Enter.

Suddenly the room was filled with organ music. Uncle Hayes got up from the computer. The computer screen showed:

THE WEDDING WILL BEGIN IN
45:00

And it started counting down.

"Success!" said Uncle Hayes. "However, during the wedding, since I will be escorting the bride down the aisle, Marvin will have to operate the computer. Can you do that?"

"Yes, I will," said Jack's father, who was a programmer.

For twenty minutes, everyone sat down in the waiting room and waited for guests to come in. The first guests began to arrive, and the three ushers walked up to seat them.

Aunt Eva gave Jack the pillow with a new replacement ring, and Brittany her stack of flowers. Peter the groom, Arthur the best man, Jack the ring bearer, who was terrified as can be, Brittany the flower girl, Susan the matron of honor, Mary the bride matron, Penny and Erin the bridesmaids, and Eva the bride all got into position. For twenty-five more minutes, guests were seated by the ushers.

Then Jack's father got up from the computer and stood at the microphone at five minutes until the wedding.

"Thank you for coming to the wedding. You probably are wondering why there is no minister here. Well, the justice of the peace, Mr. Jacques Gunne-Wedden, came down with a sudden illness this morning, so we are using a computer with the state-of-the-art wedding program, *Microsoft WEDDING*. Everything that you see projected on the wall will be read out loud by the computer," said Jack' father as he pointed to the projection on the wall, "so you can follow along. And to make sure nothing goes wrong, I will be controlling the computer."

Three more minutes passed, and then the organ music changed and the computer read:

THE WEDDING BEGINS

Press any key to continue . . .

The computer said in its female voice, "THE WEDDING BEGINS."

Jack stood there, now terrified. Even though a machine could not yell at him for making a mistake, people could. Horrible terror rushed via a tremor through his entire body.

"Come on," said Brittany. "It's time to walk down the aisle!"

Chapter 22

This was the moment he had been fearing. The moment he had been dreading. It had finally come.

Now Jack would have to present himself holding a ring on a pillow, with no one knowing or caring about the terror, the pain he suffered when holding the pillow, or the terror that at any minute, he would be hurt.

Jack was all alone.

But he still walked, slowly, and if anyone saw him, you would assume that he was a walking zombie. Right behind the flower girl, he walked into the aisle, all the hundreds of eyes staring at him and laughing at him for acting like a zombie…it was horrible.

Realizing that at any minute he could trip over something, he watched to see where Brittany's flowers were falling. He wanted to cry, but he knew that if he cried, he would be laughed at even more. He just kept walking.

He knew that it could happen—he knew that it might happen, and if it happened, he would be the laughingstock of the wedding. Everyone's eyes were now glued on him, evil eyes staring at his every move. They all knew that something was wrong, but didn't know why he was acting so strangely.

Then what he feared happened. First he was walking in terror, and suddenly he had fallen to the ground, having tripped on something. He got up and realized that this was the wrong time to trip. Everyone had seen him. And by the looks of his family, they had seen him too. And they were furious.

"Ow!" said a woman nearby.

The floor, however, which was made of painted wood, did not seem hard when he fell. He looked down and saw a flower that had been squashed by the weight of his body. Then he saw that he was stepping on someone's fur coat, which he obviously had tripped on. He also had bounced off his pillow.

Hearing laughter in the distance, Jack saw the pillow on the floor, and that the woman wearing the fur coat had made the

"Ow!" previously, as if her coat had been hurt. Brittany was right next to him, laughing away at his mistake. Jack wanted to cry, since he was now full of rage at all of the heartless people that were at the wedding, but he couldn't.

The wedding had been stopped. The organ music had stopped, too. On the computer screen and the wall, it said:

WEDDING PAUSED - Press F2 to resume

Jack looked down. The pillow was there, but where…where was the ring? He looked and could not find it. Then he saw it.

He looked at his family, in the front row, and they were furious. They knew better than to yell at him in front of everyone, because even though they were tyrannical parents, Jack was sure they wouldn't want to reveal themselves as tyrannical parents—or would they?

Jack knew what he had to do. He saw the ring in the aisle, so he picked it up, and carried the pillow and ring to the end of the aisle, where Brittany was waiting. The groom and the best man started coming down the aisle. Jack's father pressed F2 on the computer, and the wedding continued. The organ music started, and Jack dutifully gave the ring to the best man and sat down. Brittany put the empty flower basket on the floor and sat down.

While sitting, Jack realized what he had done. He had, in the eyes of the heartless guests and family, committed a serious crime. He had failed his duty—a duty he had not known existed until two days before the wedding, because of the illness of Peter's nephew.

Thoughts such as, *Why couldn't someone else do it? Why did Peter's nephew have to get sick? Couldn't Bobby have done it?* raced through his mind.

Even though he knew he would get in trouble, he started to cry. He couldn't take it anymore. He had bungled his duties, and Jack knew that he would pay. In some form, he would pay.

Why did everyone have to hurt him? Why can't people tolerate differences? thought Jack, crying. Jack never hurt people on account of differences.

Before he had time to think, the wedding hymn began and in came Jack's mother, followed by Aunt Mary, Cousin Penny, and Erin, all in their pink dresses. All of them held flowers. When the bride walked in, everyone stood up to honor her. On the computer screen and wall, it said:

PLEASE RISE

The bridesmaids walked down the aisle, and then came Aunt Eva, on the arm of Uncle Hayes, in her beige wedding dress, with her very long wedding train.

They walked to the altar, and when the groom and bride found each other and held hands, Jack's father pressed a key on the computer. Everyone sat down. There were two blank spaces (for the names of the bride and groom), and Jack's father filled in the names of the bride and groom. Then he pressed a key, and the female computer voice said exactly what was on the computer screen while the organ music still played softly.

PLEASE SIT DOWN. DEARLY BELOVED, WE ARE GATHERED HERE TO WED MR. PETER NORMAN AND MISS EVA MARTOCK IN HOLY MATRIMONY, WHICH IS AN HONORABLE ESTATE CREATED OF GOD IN THE TIME BEFORE SHAME, SIGNIFYING UNTO US THE UNION THAT IS BETWEEN CHRIST AND THE CHURCH, WHICH HOLY ESTATE CHRIST MAKES BEAUTIFUL WITH HIS PRESENCE.

Jack's father pressed another key and the screen changed, continuing the wedding.

HE IS TO BE HONORED AMONG ALL MEN AND SHALL NOT BE USED TO SATISFY

MEN'S DESIRES BUT QUIETLY, AND IN GOD CONSIDERING THE REASONS FOR HOLY MATRIMONY.

Jack's father pressed a key, and the screen changed. Since no blank spaces needed to be filled in, the computer continued:

REASON 1: IT WAS CREATED FOR THE RAISING OF CHILDREN, TO BE BROUGHT UP IN THE LORD, AND TO PRAISE HIS HOLY NAME. REASON 2: IT WAS CREATED FOR A REMEDY AGAINST SINS. REASON 3: IT WAS CREATED FOR THE SOCIETY, HELP, AND COMFORT ONE SHOULD HAVE OF THE OTHER, BOTH IN PROSPERITY AND ADVERSITY. INTO WHICH ESTATE THESE TWO PEOPLE SHALL BE JOINED.

Reaching the bottom of the screen, Jack's father pressed another key and the computer continued:

THEREFORE, IF THERE IS ANY PERSON WHO HAS ANY REASON WHY PETER NORMAN OR EVA MARTOCK SHOULD NOT BE LEGALLY JOINED TOGETHER, LET THEM SPEAK OR FOREVER HOLD THEIR PEACE.

The computer was silent for a minute, and then Jack's father pressed another key. The computer talked again:

DO YOU, EVA MARTOCK, TAKE PETER NORMAN TO BE YOUR LAWFULLY-WEDDED HUSBAND, TO OBEY, SERVE, LOVE,

CHERISH, HONOR, AND KEEP HIM IN SICKNESS AND HEALTH, FOR RICHER OR POORER, AND KEEP ONLY TO HIM 'TIL DEATH DO YOU PART?

"I do," said Aunt Eva.

Jack's father pressed another key, and the screen changed again. The computer then said:

DO YOU, PETER NORMAN, TAKE EVA MARTOCK TO BE YOUR LAWFULLY-WEDDED WIFE, TO OBEY, SERVE, LOVE, CHERISH, HONOR, AND KEEP HER IN SICKNESS AND HEALTH, FOR RICHER OR POORER, AND KEEP ONLY TO HER 'TIL DEATH DO YOU PART?"

"I do," said Peter Norman.

The screen changed again. The computer said:

WHO GIVES THIS WOMAN TO BE MARRIED TO THIS MAN?

"I do," said Uncle Hayes.

The screen changed again. The computer said:

BY THE POWER VESTED IN ME BY BILL GATES AND THE MICROSOFT® CORPORATION, I NOW PRONOUNCE YOU HUSBAND AND WIFE. YOU MAY KISS THE BRIDE.

Aunt Eva raised her veil, and they kissed.

Aunt Eva then took her bouquet of flowers and threw them across the room. When that was done, Jack's father pressed another key.

ON BEHALF OF THE MICROSOFT® CORPORATION, GOOD LUCK IN YOUR NEW LIFE. THANK YOU FOR CHOOSING Microsoft® WEDDING. WOULD YOU LIKE ANOTHER WEDDING?

Jack was so happy. Everyone stood up, and the bride and groom walked down the aisle. Jack got up and was led by his father with his family to the reception room.

The reception room was not at all like the way it looked the day before. There were three long tables against the wall, filled with sandwiches, small tacos, strawberries, cakes, and then there was the biggest cake Jack had ever seen—the wedding cake. Smaller tables were set in the middle of the room, and in one section of the room, the carpet had been removed to create a wooden dance floor. On one side of the dance floor was a stage where a band was playing.

Aunt Eva and Peter were at the entrance.

"Come this way," said Aunt Eva. "I want everyone to be with me in the receiving line."

Uncle Hayes, Aunt Mary, and Uncle Frank all went to what was called the "receiving line," with Brittany, Bobby, and Erin. Jack stayed behind, hoping to become invisible.

"Susan, Marvin, come to the line!" said Aunt Eva.

"Jack, come with me to the line!" said Jack's mother.

Jack was too terrified to reply.

"The receiving line! That's where the bride and the groom's family welcomes everyone that attended the wedding," said Jack's mother. "You're part of Aunt Eva's family, so you must come."

Even though Jack was only eleven, he could foresee the stupidity of making him be in the line. How could he possibly know how to behave?

Jack followed his parents to their place in the receiving line, and then the groom's family was called. A long line was formed, and Jack knew that all the people who had secretly laughed at him during the wedding would now be able to laugh at him face to face.

Chapter 23

"Now, Jack, since you're just the nephew of the bride, just smile, and don't talk unless you're spoken to," said Jack's mother.

The first person spoke in the line.

"Congratulations on your marriage," the woman said, "and best wishes for all."

"Thank you, Joyce," said Aunt Eva, and they hugged. Then the woman called Joyce left.

The second person came up. "Good luck in your new life, Peter," said a man. "Your brothers did a good job as ushers."

"Thanks, George," said Peter, and they hugged.

The third in line, a husband and wife, came up and said, "Surprise, Peter!"

"You came! I thought you were on vacation!" said Peter.

"I couldn't miss my brother's wedding! After all, it only happens once in a lifetime!" said the husband.

"What about your children? Where are they?" asked Peter.

"They're still on vacation. No one wanted to leave, so we decided to come alone," said Peter's brother. "Sorry, pal."

"But you're here, that's what's important," said Peter.

"And I hope you and your wife have the best of luck," said Peter's brother.

"Now, you see that?" asked Jack's mother. "That woman did not talk at all, and no one cared. One thing you must know about life is that you have to keep your mouth shut unless you're spoken to. My mother once said to me when I was a girl, 'One thing that I've learned since I got married to your father, which you'll have to do when you grow up, is to keep your mouth shut. You'll receive more respect letting your husband do all the talking. That happened to me. Your father's family hated me until I stopped talking, and now they love me. If a woman wants to talk, she should not get married.'"

"But I'm a child!" Jack complained, unable to see how the rules applied to him.

"It's the same thing," Jack's mother said. "The rules apply to all second-class citizens."

The fourth person came up. "Good work on your wedding! Your husband seems to be a wonderful person!" said a woman.

"That's very nice, Willa," said Aunt Eva. They hugged.

As people came up to see the bride and groom, Jack realized that nobody was paying attention to him or his family, or any of the bride and groom's siblings. So why were they there? Why was he suffering all that anxiety for no reason?

Jack may have thought he wasn't needed, but then his question was answered. A very old man and a very old woman walked up, both walking with canes, and they hugged Eva. "We had to see your wedding, Eva. You look wonderful in that dress. I never thought I'd ever see my niece in a wedding dress again after you married Abraham years ago," said the old man, who obviously was Eva's uncle.

"You're doing well for your age, Uncle Rollo," said Eva. "I hope that you are taking good care of yourself and that you are happy and content."

"Sixty-one years of marital bliss, to be exact. We married in 1940," said Uncle Rollo.

"Since we haven't seen you for a long time, I'd like to say hello to everyone in your family," said Eva's aunt.

"Well, Aunt Jamie," said Aunt Eva, "right next to me is my daughter, Erin, who is your grandniece. She's getting along *so* well with Peter."

"Hello," said Erin.

"And here is your nephew, Hayes, with his wife Mary, and their children, Bobby and Brittany," said Aunt Eva.

"Hello," said Bobby, Brittany, Uncle Hayes, and Aunt Mary in unison.

"Nice to meet you all," said Aunt Jamie.

"And here is your niece Susan, her husband Marvin, and their son Jack. He was the ring bearer," said Aunt Eva.

"Hello," said Jack's mother.

"Hi," said Jack's father.

Everyone turned their attention to Jack, waiting for him to

say something. He looked down, trying to remember what he was supposed to say. What did people say? His mind was a complete blank. In fact, he had forgotten how to talk.

"A shy one, huh? Well, he seems a little old to be a ring bearer," said Aunt Jamie.

"The real ring bearer caught the flu. Jack had to take his place," said Aunt Eva.

"Hmm, no choice then, eh?"

"And here's your nephew Frank," said Aunt Eva.

"Not married yet, huh?" asked Aunt Jamie.

"Well," said Uncle Frank, "there is no generation in any family that does not include one person who remains single."

"We'd like to see Peter's family," said Uncle Rollo.

"Well then, Peter can introduce you," said Aunt Eva. Then she said to Peter, "Honey, could you introduce my uncle and aunt to your family?"

"Certainly," said Peter.

The next person to come was another old woman, who was dressed in a suit and tie, unlike the other women who were wearing dresses of various colors, or a shirt and skirt combo. Jack was still struggling to remember what it was that people said in greeting. This often happens to autistic children under severe stress—they lose the ability to retrieve any information at all.

"Why, you came!" said Aunt Eva. "I never thought you would come!"

"Well, I just had to see my daughter Penny be a bridesmaid. After all, I'll never let her be a bride, so now she's got weddings out of her system," said the old woman, who was obviously Penny's mother. "I'd love to see everyone," she continued. "And I'd like to see Penny."

"Well, Penny's right here," said Aunt Eva. She called Penny, and she came back to find her mother.

"Mother!" shrieked Penny. "You came!"

"You look wonderful in that pink dress," said Penny's mother. "Now, your cousin Eva is going to show me her family."

"Well," said Eva. "Right here is my daughter Erin."

"Hello," said Erin.

"And here is my brother Hayes and his wife Mary, parents of Bobby and Brittany. Brittany was the flower girl," said Aunt Eva.

"Hello," they all said in unison.

Jack was breathing heavily. His ability to generate speech was completely gone now. In his mind, he saw a large red STOP sign. It was his mind's visual way of formulating a thought.

Then, "And this is my sister Susan and her husband Marvin, parents of Jack," said Aunt Eva. "Jack was the ring bearer."

They all said "Hello" together, fortunately, so no one knew that Jack hadn't joined in.

"We came here a week ago to help with the wedding," said Jack's mother.

"Oh? Did you drive from East Germantown?" Penny's mother lived in McCordsville, a town about thirty minutes away from the city of Indianapolis, where the Jones Mark Hotel was located. "How long did it take?"

"I'd say about two hours. We got here at noon."

Jack suddenly found his voice. That was because his mother had just committed hypocrisy. His mother had told a *lie* in front of her aunt. And for years he had been told never to tell a lie. They did not get there at noon—they got there at 12:05. So why didn't his mother say so? Jack was so angry, he decided that if she wouldn't say so, he would.

"No, we got here at 12:05, not noon," Jack corrected her.

Everyone looked at Jack disapprovingly.

"JACK! Why did you say that?" Jack's mother said.

Then she said to Jack's father, "I want you to take him to a table, but don't yell at him until I have finished here. I cannot have him embarrass me again."

"Come with me, Jack," said Jack's father, and they walked to a table. Jack was happy to not have to be with his family, but he knew that his father would not be nice to him. Which showed that his parents were hypocrites by telling Jack to always tell the truth when they didn't.

Jack sat down with his father, aware of all the possible terrors that could happen to him. He still couldn't understand why his mother would lie like that.

They sat silently together for about thirty minutes. Jack didn't mind. Sitting with his father was about the same as sitting alone, and Jack enjoyed solitude.

Then a bell rang.

"We shall now announce the special people who have made this event possible," said Peter's father, who stood up from his table. "To begin, let us give a toast...to the bride and groom!"

"To the bride and groom!" everyone said after him. Jack did not say anything, since he seldom was yelled at for keeping his mouth shut.

"A toast...to the parents of the groom!" said Peter's father.

"To the parents of the groom!" echoed the guests.

"A toast...to the best man!" said Peter's father.

"To the best man!" said the guests.

"A toast...to the ushers!" said Peter's father.

"To the ushers!" said the guests.

"Sadly, the parents of the bride have both passed away. But that does not mean that the bride's two brothers and one sister have not worked hard to help organize the wedding. They all have been busy supporting her. So let's have a toast...to the bridesmaid!" said Peter's father.

"To the bridesmaid!" said the guests.

"A toast...to the bride matron!" said Peter's father.

"To the bride matron!" said the guests.

"A toast...to the matron of honor!" said Peter's father.

"To the matron of honor!" said the guests.

"And finally, a toast to everyone that has been invited to the wedding," said Peter's father.

"To everyone that has been invited to the wedding," said the guests.

"And now, let the reception begin!" said Peter's father.

Jack's mother walked back to the table.

"Even though you may think that you get a day where you are honored as a ring bearer, think again. I'm sure you are aware that you have committed several crimes today, and therefore as your mother, I must punish you. No wedding cake for you."

Jack decided not to remind her that he was allergic to it.

Chapter 24

"Attention, everyone," said a voice on the P.A. system. Jack did not know who it was. "The wedding dance will now begin."

Jack looked at the wedding floor and saw that Aunt Eva and Peter were on the dance floor waiting to start when the music began. The music did begin, and they started dancing.

Five minutes later, Jack's mother got up and said, "I'm going to dance with your father, so Frank will watch over you."

His parents got up and went to the dance floor, yet they did not dance until the next song started playing.

Then Uncle Frank walked up to the table and sat across the table from Jack.

Realizing that Uncle Frank would understand, Jack started to cry.

"What's wrong?" asked Uncle Frank.

"I-I've failed," Jack cried.

"No, you haven't," said Uncle Frank. "Every child, even a normal one, makes mistakes."

"But I *have* failed," Jack cried.

"No, you haven't. I know the entire story. My cousin Penny told you the day before that you had to be the ring bearer, and believe me, she was wrong to do that, since Peter has a very young second cousin who could have done it instead. It was stupid to put you through that."

"Was the original ring bearer actually sick?" asked Jack.

"Yes, he was. When I heard the story, I went to his house to talk to the brother about a possible substitute ring bearer. Therefore, I saw him, and yes, he was sick," said Uncle Frank. "But why they chose you, I do not know.

"When I was growing up, Jack, I was always put down. Just like you. Your Aunt Eva was the favorite child. Whenever there was only one piece of candy left or some other toy or food, she always got it. And Hayes would beat me up during his games. Your mother would set me up in situations where I was blamed for something I did not do. And now they're doing the same thing to you."

"But I did do something wrong! I tripped over a woman's fur coat!" said Jack.

"That is not a mistake. The fur coat was not involved in the tripping. I witnessed the entire thing. Brittany purposely threw a bunch of flowers in your path. You tripped over one of the flowers, and because the fur coat was lying there, you fell on it, making everyone assume that you tripped over the coat and not the flower. When I tried to tell your mother during the wedding, she wouldn't listen to me. Your parents are always assuming that you're misbehaving to get attention. But I know you don't want attention. All you want is to be left alone," said Uncle Frank.

"But I messed up walking down the aisle!" said Jack.

"It wasn't your fault."

"But I talked back to an adult!" said Jack.

"Only in the line of truth. You did the right thing. No matter what they try to tell you, remember that you did nothing wrong. Believe in yourself. And I also believe that you should never force someone to do something you have not experienced yourself," said Uncle Frank.

"But how can I believe in myself if I'm being hurt all the time?"

"I know that it is hard. But I know you can do it. Throughout your life, nobody's reaction has made sense to you. There is always a decent explanation for your actions that your parents cannot figure out. In that regard, they are the dumbest people that I know. But whenever I hear the stories that my sister tells me, I always know why you did it, and I always think that my sister is crazier each time she tells me these things. I have given up the approval of my family, my credibility, and my popularity for what I believe in. It is wrong to give up your ways for others, if you know in your heart that you are right," said Uncle Frank.

"Can't you do something, though?" said Jack.

"Yes, I can. Remember at dinner one week ago when I forced your parents to answer your cousins' questions?"

"Yes," said Jack. "You were great."

"Well, I hope I can help you. That extreme punishment that they gave you is wrong. I know that you are an innocent victim. I will try my best to stop your punishment—but there are no guarantees," said Uncle Frank.

"Well, all right. Just don't get me in more trouble," said Jack.

"Okay. And also, let's remember that there is a reception prepared for us. Let's get some food, and make sure you get what you want, Jack," said Uncle Frank.

They both got up from the table and each returned with a plate of food. At the reception were various sandwiches, fruit, three cut cakes, cubed cheese, and vegetables. Jack liked fruit and cheese, so he filled his plate with that and returned to the table.

Uncle Frank returned five minutes later.

"You are the nicest man I have ever known in my life," said Jack. "If you were my father, you'd yell at me for not putting cake on my plate. I'm allergic to cake. It gives me a headache. But because the headache happens two days later, my father says I'm making it up to get attention."

"I believe that children should be respected even more than adults. No one is born with the ability to love. Parents must give their child love, and when those children become parents, if they were given love as children, they can transfer it to their children. If children are not loved, they cannot love their own children. Your mother was not loved. Nor were her siblings," said Uncle Frank.

"If you weren't loved, why are you such a nice person?" asked Jack.

"Because I was affected differently. Not all people are affected the same when they are hurt, Jack. I vowed never to act like my parents," said Uncle Frank. "My punishment was, well, I never learned how to have a successful relationship. But don't worry about me; it's time to eat."

They ate in silence for a few minutes, Jack as happy as could be that he wasn't being yelled at as song after song kept playing for the dancers.

Thirty minutes later, Jack's parents walked back to the table.

"I hope he hasn't been filling your head with crazy ideas,

Jack," Jack's mother said. "Uncle Frank has a lot of problems; that's why he never married."

"AAAAAHHHH!"

A scream was heard at the side of the room. Jack looked and saw that Aunt Eva had screamed.

"What happened?" asked Jack's mother and ran over to Eva.

"The cake...someone cut a piece from the wedding cake!" said Aunt Mary. "It's ruined."

"Where's Jack?" Eva demanded, and they all turned furious faces in his direction.

Chapter 25

"Susan and Marvin, I have had enough of your son. He is a disgrace to the entire family," said Uncle Hayes. "Why can't you discipline him better? He'd NEVER survive in the army."

"I yell at him just like you do," Jack's mother said in defense.

"But Susan, why doesn't it work? You don't discipline him enough. I've yelled at my children for years, and they are the most perfect children I have ever seen," said Aunt Mary.

"I completely agree. But I don't know what to do. I have punished Jack for years and he still misbehaves. Can't he get the message, or do we have to punish him even more severely?" said Jack's father.

"It's not just his fault this time. It's Frank's fault. He is the craziest man alive, and I would murder him if he weren't my brother," said Aunt Eva.

They all walked to the table where Jack and Uncle Frank were sitting.

"JACK! I AM SICK OF YOUR MISBEHAVIOR! YOU HAVE RUINED MY WEDDING WITH YOUR VERY PRESENCE…" said Aunt Eva.

"Oh, I get it. You think that because something happens, it's Jack's fault," said Uncle Frank. "Jack has been sitting at this table and only left to get food; I was watching him the entire time. Jack doesn't even know how to use a knife to cut a wedding cake!"

"Besides, I'm allergic to—"

"Cut the crap, Jack," said Marvin, who came up to them.

"HOW DARE YOU CONTRADICT ME?" Eva shrieked. "I'M WARNING YOU, FRANK, IF YOU OPEN THAT CRAZY MOUTH OF YOURS ONE MORE TIME, I'M GOING TO EXCOMMUNICATE YOU FROM OUR FAMILY. YOU WON'T BE ABLE TO TALK TO YOUR BROTHERS, YOUR COUSINS, OR YOUR NIECES AND NEPHEWS FOR THE REST OF YOUR LIFE!"

"All right, I'll shut my mouth. But not until you—"

"Frank, *that's one,*" said Aunt Mary.

"What lunacy! Now you're treating ME like a lab rat?"

"Frank, *that's two,*" said Uncle Hayes.

Frank kept quiet. This was hopeless.

"Well, now that we have dealt with that, let's get down to business," said Aunt Mary. "WHY ARE YOU SO DIFFICULT JACK? WHY CAN'T YOU GO TO A SOCIAL OCCASION WITHOUT ALWAYS RUINING IT FOR EVERYONE EXCEPT YOURSELF? AND WHY DO YOU ALWAYS THINK THAT EVERYTHING PREPARED ON A TABLE IS FOR YOU? THAT CAKE WAS FOR US TO CUT, NOT YOU!"

"THIS IS INEXCUSABLE, JACK!" Jack's mother chimed in. "DON'T YOU KNOW BETTER THAN TO EAT YOUR AUNT'S WEDDING CAKE! ONLY YOUR AUNT AND UNCLE CAN CUT IT. STOP TRYING TO DENY THAT WHAT YOU'VE DONE IS WRONG! WHAT DO YOU HAVE TO SAY FOR YOURSELF?"

"I am innocent..."

"We have evidence! When you were five, you blew out Bobby's candles even though it was *his* birthday! You have always been obsessed with other people's cakes. That's the proof."

"It wasn't the cake. I was obsessed with the candles. The flickering light hurt my eyes, so I had to blow them out."

"You are lying again, Jack," said Jack's mother, "and I won't stand for it! Jack, *that's one.*"

"I will not be silent until I speak my mind!" said Jack.

"Jack, *that's two.*"

"You are only hurting yourself!" said Jack.

"Jack, *that's three.* Now you are going to have to shut up or else I'm going to make you," said Uncle Hayes.

Jack was full of rage. He no longer cared about rules or laws of civilization. He didn't care that he was only eleven years old. He just had to get revenge. But how?

Just then, the caterer came over and said it was time to cut the cake. He had turned it around and repositioned the bride and groom figures on top so no one would see the gap where the piece had been cut.

* * * *

The wedding reception ended at 5:30 p.m. Eva and Peter walked out of the hotel into a "JUST MARRIED" limousine. Everyone returned to their homes.

Jack was bursting with unwept tears, but he couldn't cry because that would just get him into more trouble. Throughout the entire day, he had been lectured and screamed at. And even when nobody was talking to him, his clothes had stabbed him like tiny knives. If only he hadn't been the ring bearer.

The only good thing that happened—besides talking to Uncle Frank—was that Jack discovered a clue as to who had cut the cake. He had one chance to look at the cake, and he noticed there was a red knife next to it. Jack knew that it was not the official cake-cutting knife, since that knife was black and it was on the other side of the cake.

When he was sure he was all alone, when he heard everyone talking downstairs with no indication that anyone was coming up, Jack allowed himself to cry—out of pain and injustice. He would prove his innocence—even if his family did live in the Middle Ages.

Chapter 26

Two days later, October 15th

It came time to suffer the consequences of his actions.

His actions? Were those really his actions? Jack didn't think that they were, after all. They were actions, but that didn't mean that they were *his* actions. They were the actions of other people. A conspiracy—being pulled off to hurt him.

But who was he to complain? His cousins for years had been hurt the way he was. And Jack assumed his cousins didn't want to be hurt just like he didn't want to be. He vowed to never hurt his children the way he was hurt. He vowed to use his adult powers in good ways. And he also vowed to never send his children to school. He would educate them at home.

However, he was in the camp of the enemy. And his punishment was settled the next day. From ten to two (with a one-hour break for lunch) he would be forced to socialize. For two days after that, he would not be permitted to talk to anyone at all. And it would start in thirty minutes.

No matter what he did, the authority figures would be angry at him. This was why teenagers rebelled. They got so angry at authority's unnecessary rules that they decided that they couldn't take it anymore. They would fight until they won the battle.

Then something distracted Jack. He overheard fighting, and he walked into the hallway and saw that the fighting was in the office. He stayed in the hallway to spy on Brittany, Bobby, and Erin, who were there.

"Hey, it's our turn to go on the computer," said Erin.

"I want to play Cockroach Eater! After all, I paid for the game," said Brittany.

"No, I paid the money. And we were here first, so we have the right to kick you off the computer. You did not pay for that, after all," said Bobby.

"But I want to play it!" said Brittany.

"No, you can't. I'm sorry, but we won't let you. And I paid for it, not you," said Erin. "I brought it here from Frankfort."

"No. This is the copy *we* have," said Brittany. "And I bought the copy we have."

"You still can't play," said Bobby.

"MOM! BOBBY AND ERIN WON'T LET ME PLAY COCKROACH EATER OR GO ON THE COMPUTER!"

Realizing that he could get in trouble for spying, Jack ran back into the living room and sat as if he had always been there. He then overheard a long conversation with yelling and screaming about how Brittany should be allowed to play the game since it was *her* game.

Twenty-five minutes later, the big cuckoo clock in the living room, which had two painted figures cutting down a tree, went off. Usually everyone would ignore it because it went off quickly, but the ten cuckoos seemed extremely slow to him. He was under extreme stress, and therefore everything seemed extremely slow.

"It's time for the bad to be punished," declared Aunt Mary at the sound of the cuckoo. Then she walked into Brittany's bedroom, where Jack was. Jack realized that he shouldn't mess with Aunt Mary, because she was wearing a whistle around her neck with a sign on the tip in small letters that read:

TO CAUSE INSTANT PAIN, BLOW WHISTLE.

And Jack did not want to suffer any more "instant pain."

"Jack, it is time to come and fulfill your mandatory three-hour socializing. You can play with Cousin Bobby if he does not take your side in the game. And remember another rule: *you can't say you can't play*. Therefore, if someone walks up to you and asks you to play a game, you must say yes and stop what you are doing," said Aunt Mary.

He walked out of the room and into the hallway, and then walked into the living room. No one was there.

"That's funny. Doesn't my niece know that she has to play with my nephew?" asked Aunt Mary to herself.

"ERIN!" she suddenly screamed. "WHERE ARE YOU?"

No response was heard.

"ERIN!" she roared again. "WHERE ARE YOU?"

The entire house was silent. Then Jack remembered that he, his Aunt Mary, Bobby, Brittany, and Erin were the only ones in the house. Uncle Hayes had to go to work. He had missed several days due to the wedding. Jack's parents went shopping in downtown Indianapolis. Aunt Eva had to move to her new home with her new husband. Since they wanted to spend time alone, Erin was going to spend one additional week with Aunt Mary and Uncle Hayes. But where was Brittany? Shouldn't she be in the office playing her game? The fight had resulted in Brittany winning custody of the game.

"ERIN!" shrieked Aunt Mary. "FOR THE THIRD TIME, WHERE ARE YOU?"

As if on cue, Erin walked in the front door holding a package.

"WHERE WERE YOU?" roared Aunt Mary.

"Marsh Store on Lowell Street," said Cousin Erin.

"WHY WERE YOU THERE? DID ANYBODY GIVE YOU PERMISSION?"

"Why yes, of course, so there's no reason to be yelling, Aunt Mary," said Cousin Erin. "In fact, I was indeed given permission. My uncle asked me to go there and pick up his delivery at a quarter to ten."

"THEN WHY DID YOU NOT INSTANTLY RETURN HOME?" roared Aunt Mary. "DID YOU NOT KNOW THAT YOU HAVE A DUTY TO PLAY WITH JACK AT TEN FOR ONE WEEK? THAT WAS PART OF JACK'S PUNISHMENT!"

"The store was packed and there was a huge checkout line," said Cousin Erin.

"THAT IS INEXCUSABLE! YOU WERE AWARE OF YOUR DUTIES! WHY COULDN'T YOU TELL YOUR UNCLE YOU WOULD BE UNABLE TO GET HIS DELIVERY?" screamed Aunt Mary.

"My uncle is also an adult, and I couldn't disobey him. Besides, why do I have to play with Jack? This seems more like a punishment for *me* than a punishment for him," said Cousin Erin.

"BECAUSE I SAID SO! AND IT'S ALSO TO TEACH HIM A LESSON!" yelled Aunt Mary. "NOW GO PLAY WITH HIM AND GIVE ME THE DELIVERY!"

Erin was acting just like Jack. "No, I won't. Get your daughter to play with him," she solemnly said.

Jack was surprised. Usually Erin wanted to play with him so he could be her slave.

"NO IS NOT AN OPTION. I GAVE AN ORDER AND I EXPECT IT TO BE OBEYED!" roared Aunt Mary.

"Okay, I will play with Jack," said Erin.

"That sounds better," said Aunt Mary.

And Jack knew from that moment Erin would dump on him for being forced to interact.

Cousin Brittany walked in.

"I had to get something from the car," said Brittany.

"Erin, I guess you are excused from your duties. Brittany, now *you* must play with Cousin Jack," said Aunt Mary.

"Do I have to?" asked Cousin Brittany.

"Yes, you do. It's part of Jack's punishment."

"This seems more like a punishment for me than a punishment for him," said Cousin Brittany.

"I d*on't care*. Now start playing," said Aunt Mary.

Jack knew that Aunt Mary was wrong, as he saw the anger and rage in Brittany's eyes. He knew that Brittany would be out to get him at any minute.

"Well, I guess I am going to have to play with you because of some foolish thing you have done. Why do you have to hurt everyone, Jack? Is it because of self-pride?" asked Cousin Brittany.

Jack had no self-pride, since he was terrified all the time.

In the next minute, Jack was escorted into Bobby and Erin's room.

"So, what do you want to play? The rule is that anyone over the age of nine cannot choose the game. Because you're over nine, you'll have to play my game. And that game is Cat Burglar. You'll be the cat burglar, and I'll be the person whom you are robbing. As the Cat Burglar, you will try to steal something and then you'll be arrested and sent to the police, where you will be beaten," said Cousin Brittany.

Jack knew nothing of this game, nor was he a very good cat burglar. Cat burglars sneak around, and he knew little about sneaking around. Except for that time a couple days ago, he always failed when sneaking around. Autistic people are terrible at deception. He also knew that the rule of anybody over age nine being unable to pick the game was a fake.

"So, cat burglar, do your stuff," said Cousin Brittany.

Jack walked very softly, and realizing he had no choice, he decided to go steal something in her drawer.

The light suddenly turned off. This was part of the game. Then Brittany turned on her CD player and "The Pink Panther Theme" began to play. This was to provide spirit for the robbery. Jack walked silently, and when he started making noise, he went down and crawled. He continued until he got to the drawers. He was on total alert as if he were about to be killed, since at any moment, he could be set up and terrified by his cousin.

He was about to open the drawer . . .

Suddenly someone hit him in the back. He fell over.

"Round up the suspect!" cried Brittany.

In ran Erin, who obviously was part of the game. Jack was crying, his face drenched in tears because he was hit. "Silly boy!" said Brittany. "Look at him! All I do is rub his back and he bursts into tears!"

Brittany knew that he was easily hurt. Erin took him and grabbed his arms and dragged him through the hallway.

"I guess Jack wasn't a very good cat burglar, Brittany," said Erin.

"Where shall we take him?" said Brittany.

"Into the dungeon," said Erin. "Where he'll be tortured."

Jack actually was not taken to a dungeon. He was taken to Brittany's room.

"Well, I must continue my police duties. You may take care of the prisoner," said Erin.

Then she left.

"I hope you sit here and think about what you've done! Why

do you always get caught every time you try to rob someone! You are not a good burglar at all!" said Brittany. "I am going away so you can think."

They all left. He could not think, since he was set up. He stayed there until someone entered the room. It was Erin.

Jack assumed that Erin was there to talk to him. But she wasn't.

She walked into the room, and picked up a CD case. She picked it up so that Jack could see it. It was the case that held the game Cockroach Eater. It looked like Erin was stealing it.

Jack was silent and she left.

Then Brittany returned. "Erin has to continue fulfilling her police duties. But I must ask you: why are you always getting caught? Every time you try to rob someone, the police always arrest you! Why can't you give up your career as a thief?"

Jack knew that this was just a game, but he was full of rage anyway.

"I don't know. I'm just a bad thief," he said.

"A bad thief! Why are you such a bad thief? I hired you from Cat Burglar Incorporated! And that is an organization that trains the best thieves," said Brittany.

"I'm sorry," said Jack.

"Sorry is not enough. My mother keeps asking me when I'm going to get some valuables from you. For punishment, you are going to have to come with me to a tea party in the kitchen," said Brittany.

This was a bad punishment for Jack. He hated tea, and he also hated the cakes and cookies that came with a tea party.

He walked with Brittany to the kitchen, but then as they approached the office they heard the sounds of a computer game. Brittany stopped at the office door and looked and saw that Bobby and Erin were there.

"Hey! Why are you playing Cockroach Eater?" asked Brittany.

"Because we want to play it," said Bobby.

Jack instantly understood what was going on. Erin had "broken into" Brittany's room and taken the CD to play the game with Bobby. He was the eyewitness to this crime. But he still kept his mouth shut, since no one believed what he said.

"How did you get the CD?" asked Brittany.

"Please be quiet. We are playing a game," said Bobby.

"AUNT MARY! BRITTANY'S BOTHERING US!" said Erin.

"Wait here until this is settled," said Brittany to Jack.

Jack stood there and was silent. Aunt Mary ran into the hallway, rage showing on her face.

"Bobby! Erin! What are you doing?" she asked.

"We're playing Cockroach Eater!" said Bobby.

"The CD was in Brittany's room. Now the two of you know better than to go into Brittany's room. Brittany, did you put the CD in the office?" asked Aunt Mary.

"Of course not. I knew what could happen if I put it in the office, so I didn't," said Brittany.

"So how did you get the CD?" asked Aunt Mary, looking at Bobby and Erin.

Jack realized that he did not care what he said now, except that he had to tell them what had happened, as he knew.

"I know what happened," he said.

"This is unrelated to you, Jack. Unless you're going to tell me something related to this crisis, keep your mouth shut," said Aunt Mary.

"Yes. I know how they got the CD. I was playing with Brittany and Erin in Brittany's room, and they left. Then Erin came back in. I assumed she was going to continue playing with me, but she wasn't. She took the CD and left. I was unaware of this crisis, so I didn't know that it mattered," said Jack.

"Just because you tell me this doesn't mean I can trust you, Jack. You have a history of lying," said Aunt Mary.

"Jack's just lying," said Erin.

"I don't trust Jack, but I trust Erin. Jack, why did you just tell that lie? Do you want to see your cousin punished even though she's innocent?" asked Aunt Mary.

"I'm telling the truth. I am struck with guilt every time I lie. It is because of my autism," said Jack.

"Even if you are autistic, you still have the potential to lie," said Aunt Mary.

"I can't take this anymore!" said Bobby.

"What?" said Aunt Mary.

"I have to tell the truth," said Bobby. "Jack is telling the truth, and I can't see him suffer like this. I, uh, I *walked into Brittany's room and took the CD.* "

"I do, however, trust Bobby. And because of this evidence, Erin and Bobby are going to have to be punished. They both are going to have to be in their room for thirty minutes to think about what they did. Jack will continue playing with Brittany. And Brittany must be given back her CD. Bobby, thank you for telling the truth." said Aunt Mary.

Bobby and Erin gave the CD back to Brittany, and left for their rooms.

Then Brittany said to Jack, "Now that that's settled, let us have our tea party."

They both walked to the kitchen. "I hope you like this food, since I spent two hours preparing this tea party with my silverware," said Brittany.

Jack went to his seat. He looked at what he was being served. He was being served a brownie and a piece of toast with his cup of tea. Then he looked at his silverware. There was a fork, a spoon, and a knife with a red handle.

A knife with a red handle?

Jack looked at the knife. It was the red knife he'd seen at the wedding. *If that red knife was there and it was Brittany's, did Brittany cut the cake?*

Chapter 27

"So, how about we start drinking our tea?" asked Cousin Brittany.

Jack, realizing he had to, sipped from his cup. Although tea usually tasted horrible, this tea actually had no taste at all. He looked at the clock. It read 10:35. This meant that he had over two more hours to continue this terror.

For thirty minutes, they sat in silence eating their food and drinking their tea. Jack forgot for now about the red knife. He couldn't question Brittany because she had accused Jack like everyone else, even though there was possible evidence that Brittany had cut the wedding cake.

"Now that we are done having our tea, let us play another game. We will now play spies. It is our job to spy on Bobby and Erin," said Cousin Brittany.

They walked to Bobby and Erin's room, and as they got closer, they could overhear Erin yelling at Bobby. They could not hear what they were saying yet. When they got to the door, Brittany opened it a little bit.

"What's that sound?" asked Erin.

"It's obviously a door creak caused by the wind," said Bobby.

"All right, then. Bobby, for the tenth time, *why did you take the CD from Brittany's room?*" said Erin.

"I got it for you," said Bobby.

"But why? Didn't you know that you would get me punished?" asked Erin."

"Don't you have punishments at home?" asked Bobby.

"No, I don't. If I do, it's only once a year. But I also make sure I do not misbehave, unlike Jack, who hungers for punishment," said Erin.

"I have been punished my entire lifetime," said Bobby. "But I do not hunger for it."

Just then a very faint bell rang. It was very soft where Jack was; it was coming from Bobby and Erin's room.

Aunt Mary walked into the hallway at the moment the bell went off, as if she had heard it from miles away.

Jack hid in a nearby closet because he did not want to be seen, but he could hear everything.

"Your punishment is done," said Aunt Mary. "You may now go and play, but you must return Brittany's Cockroach Eater. In five minutes, I will be checking Brittany's room for the CD."

Then she turned and saw Brittany. "Brittany, shouldn't you be playing with Jack?"

"Yes, I am. Jack is in my room. We are playing Hide and Seek, and I am hiding here," said Brittany.

Jack did not care to correct what Brittany was saying, since at least they wouldn't get in trouble.

"Well, okay, but doesn't that seem to be an easy place for him to find?" asked Aunt Mary.

"Of course. That's the point. If he tries to find me in a hiding place, he won't expect me to be in a non-hiding place," said Brittany.

"Well, continue playing."

"You can come out now," said Brittany when Aunt Mary left.

"Thanks for the lie," said Jack, astounded that he could feel grateful to his hated cousin.

"Now that there is nothing interesting to spy on, we will continue playing burglar," said Brittany. "But we must make sure that they are in the office."

They walked to the office and saw that they were playing the game Son of Sally together, about a murderer who must kill to destroy a top-secret organization that wants to take over the world. The murderer's mother is called Sally.

They went to Brittany's room and saw that her CD had been returned, and then they went back to Bobby and Erin's room.

"Now you can try to steal something without Erin catching you, as she's on the computer," said Brittany.

Brittany closed the door, turned off the lights, and turned on the Pink Panther Theme.

Although Jack knew that Erin was playing with Bobby, he still was on alert for another set-up. He walked up to the drawer, and opened it to find something to cat-burgle. Inside were three pairs of pants, two shirts, and a ring.

What is a ring doing there? Jack thought. If this was a drawer for clothes, why was there a ring? Shouldn't the ring be placed in a ring carrier? Then Jack realized something. If there was a ring in an underwear drawer, maybe it was there because Bobby or Erin didn't want anyone to know it was there. But why would they be hiding a ring? And then he remembered the wedding ring that disappeared at the rehearsal.

Although this could have been the ring at the rehearsal, Jack had no true evidence. But he, being a burglar (or pretending to be one, at least), took the ring. He put it in his pocket and said to Brittany, "I have stolen something."

"Now we may go," said Brittany. Jack closed the drawer and they left.

"Good work, Burglar Jack," said Brittany. "You bungled your first assignment, but you were successful for this time in stealing something. What did you steal?"

"A ring," said Jack.

"A ring? What was a ring doing in Bobby's drawer?" asked Brittany.

"I do not know. It was just there," said Jack.

Jack gave Brittany the ring. Brittany put it in her back pocket.

"Ah, a ring that's all mine. Now, what shall we…"

"Excuse me, did you mention a ring?"

Aunt Mary walked into the hallway. Jack stopped breathing.

"Well, did you mention a ring or not?" asked Aunt Mary.

"Yes, I did," said Brittany.

"Why did you mention a ring?" asked Aunt Mary. "Because you both know that your Aunt Eva's wedding ring mysteriously disappeared right before the wedding, and Peter had to buy her a replacement ring."

"Jack and I are playing Cat Burglar," said Brittany.

"Cat Burglar? With Jack?" Aunt Mary laughed. "How could Jack be a burglar? He'd never get away with anything."

"Well, he did steal a ring for me."

"Let me see it," Aunt Mary said.

"All right," said Brittany. She put her hand in her front pocket. Jack knew instantly that something was going on. After all, the ring was in her back pocket, and Jack knew that if she was going to look for something in a different pocket, she must know something that her mother didn't.

Brittany took out a toy ring, which you can get for a small amount of prize tickets at an arcade. Jack knew that either Brittany made a mistake, or she was hiding the real ring from her mother. Brittany normally didn't tell lies. He would have to confront her now.

"But that isn't—"

"This is the ring," said Brittany.

Aunt Mary looked at it. "Hmm, that's just plastic. Okay, it's not the ring that got lost. If Jack 'steals' a ring of gold, though, let me know." Then she left.

Jack was now confused. Why did Brittany just lie to her mother? Why didn't she show her mother the real ring? Brittany obviously knew something that he didn't.

"Brittany, why did you…"

"Stop talking, Jack. It is none of your business what I did," said Brittany.

"Of course it is. Why did you lie? Why couldn't you show her the real ring?" asked Jack.

"I was the one carrying both rings, and therefore it is my choice to choose what ring that I wish to show my mother," said Brittany.

"But that is not the ring that you were talking about!" said Jack.

"Stop fighting with me, Jack. I chose to lie, and I'm not letting a mere child criticize the way I want to do things in my life. My mother and father are entitled to do that, but not you," said Brittany.

The more Brittany resisted the truth, the more he realized that something suspicious was going on. If Erin had put the ring in Bobby's drawer, maybe she was involved in stealing the ring during the rehearsal. But why was Brittany covering up for her? Were they both involved in a plot?

All these thoughts were confusing to Jack, as he wondered why his cousins were acting this way. Perhaps he was jumping to conclusions, the way everyone else did around him. He had no real evidence to support his suspicions except that there had been a ring in Bobby's drawer, and Brittany was hiding the ring from Aunt Mary. It didn't have to be the wedding ring. It could have been another ring. He would try to forget all this. Even if he tried to make his thoughts public, no one would listen to them.

"Now that we are done playing Cat Burglar, we are going to play a board game called Chutes and Ladders. Let me set the game up," said Brittany.

"Only if you put the ring back."

Jack and Brittany went back to Bobby's room and returned the ring.

Jack didn't say anything, but he hated Chutes and Ladders. Throughout his life, every time he landed on a space that involved a bad action, everyone made a comment that that was his fate because he was bad in real life.

The clock struck 11:00, and that meant he had one more hour until lunch break.

"Okay, we're all ready," said Brittany.

Then they sat down to play Chutes and Ladders.

"I will assign pawns by personality. Jack, you get the mule, since you are stubborn and disobedient. And I will get the dog, since I am nice and loyal," said Brittany.

"And since I am nice and loyal," she added, "I will go first."

They continued playing Chutes and Ladders, with more insults to come.

Chapter 28

Brittany rolled the dice. Four and four. Then she moved her pawn nine spaces.

Nine? Jack was wondering why she moved nine if she was supposed to move eight.

"Brittany, why did you move nine spaces if you rolled eight?" asked Jack.

"How dare you challenge my move? I rolled nine," said Brittany.

"Prove it," said Jack.

Brittany took the dice in her hands and held them so that her finger would conceal a potential fifth dot on one of them.

"See? It's nine," said Brittany. "The fifth dot is concealed under my finger."

"Show me," said Jack.

"I will not. How dare you challenge me?"

"Oh, go ahead then."

"Okay, I rolled nine, and therefore I am obliged to go up this ladder to square 31," said Brittany.

Jack then realized that if this game allowed cheating, he could cheat too. He found the six on each dice and plopped it down on the floor.

"Hey, that's cheating," Brittany complained.

"It's no different from what you did."

"You're a liar. And since you lie, I can't trust you with rolling the dice. So I will roll for you, since I *always* tell the truth," said Brittany.

She rolled four. She rolled again. Nine. She rolled again. Six. She rolled again. Four. She rolled again. Five. Then she rolled again. Two.

"Why are you rolling so many times?" asked Jack.

"Because I was not pleased with your number," said Brittany. "You got a two, Jack."

"You're not supposed to be pleased with it. It's just supposed to be luck. Why are you cheating?" asked Jack.

"The die isn't completely still, so it isn't cheating."

"I'm getting the rule sheet. There is no such rule."

"How can you prove me wrong if I am right?" asked Brittany. "But if you insist, I will read the rule myself."

She got up, got the rule sheet from the game box, and read, "A person may roll the dice again if they are not completely still and he is not satisfied with the number on the dice."

"But the original game doesn't have dice. It has a spinner. Let me see that rule."

"It's under the heading, 'What to do if you lose the spinner.' And if you take a look," she said as she showed Jack the empty game box, "the spinner is indeed gone."

Jack knew that Brittany was not lying about the missing spinner, but she was lying about the rules. "It does not say that!" he said. "You're lying!"

"How can you tell me I'm lying if you have no evidence?" said Brittany.

"Show me the rules and I'll find evidence. You're a liar."

"I am not. I am just reading the truth. But it seems as if you can't handle it," said Brittany.

"I can handle the truth. But I cannot handle liars," said Jack.

"I am not a liar," said Brittany.

"Well, who went nine spaces when they rolled eight? And who is rolling the dice on their opponent's turn? And who is rolling over and over again on their opponent's turn? Admit you've broken three rules," said Jack.

"I have not broken three rules. It is against my nature. And besides, *you* are holding up the game," said Brittany.

Jack was furious. He knew that if he complained, he would get in more trouble, since Brittany would make up a story that it was his fault.

"And now you have your number. Two," said Brittany. "And since you have just had an outburst, I am going to watch you carefully when you move your pawn."

Jack moved his pawn two spaces, knowing what was going on. She was cheating so she would win and he would lose.

Although he did not care about winning or losing, he did care when someone cheated. And with a pair of dice, two was the lowest number one could get.

He also cared about the larger picture. As an autistic child, he was always being accused of poor social skills and an inability to relate to his peers. But it was his peers who couldn't relate appropriately to him. They set him up every time; they were always out to get him, while adult observers kept writing articles and books about the hopelessness of his condition. Why didn't they write about the hopeless cruelty of the normal child?

"It's my turn." Then Brittany rolled seven (two and five), but moved five spaces.

"Why did you move five spaces if you rolled seven?" Jack asked.

"I rolled five. Take a look," said Brittany. She did the same thing she did before. She took the dice and positioned her fingers so that the die that showed five looked like it showed three.

"You're cheating," said Jack.

"It's none of your business as to whether I'm cheating or not," said Brittany.

"None of MY business? Of course it's my business. I'm playing this game. And if I can't get my voice heard, I will not play. How about you take all the turns and I will just watch?" asked Jack.

"Fine, I will. Thank you for surrendering. You rarely do that," said Brittany.

Brittany went up the ladder at her square to square 46. Then she took Jack's turn. Jack was relieved, but angry as he watched Brittany play the game, purposely making Jack go behind so she could win. But at least he didn't have to move his pawn. And she didn't want to play with him anyway, so at least they were both happy in their own way.

Finally, the game ended at 11:11. Brittany, knowing how to get places, won the game in less than ten moves. Jack was only at square 17 when the game ended. This was because she choreographed his moves so that he would be constantly riding chutes down to the beginning.

"So, what would you like to play now?" asked Brittany.

"Listen to me, Brittany. I know you don't want to play with me. That is why you're so mean to me. But look around. No one is forcing you to play with me. No mother, no father, no aunt, and no uncle. If you don't want to play with me, you don't have to. I certainly don't want to play with you," said Jack.

"I don't care. I have to play with you. My parents forced me," said Brittany. "So now we will play Hide and Seek."

Jack knew he had to agree, even though he knew Brittany would hurt him in this game as well.

"First, I am going to hide," said Brittany. "You count to twenty."

Jack decided not to count to anything. After all, he did not want to look for her, and therefore would try to delay it.

The clock read 11:15. In forty-five minutes, he would have lunch break. So he lay there, his heart pounding. Then he walked out of the room and suddenly overheard talking.

"Are you enjoying playing with Jack?"

"No. Why do I have to keep playing with him? He lies, cheats, and even steals."

"I know. It's part of autism. You don't have to play with him. You are going to take turns with Erin. Tomorrow she will play with Jack."

"We are playing Hide and Seek again. I must hide. Now, Mother, if you hear any loud noises, ignore them."

Jack just walked through the halls, looking at closets, trying to find where she could be. She was nowhere. Then he walked and walked, terrified because he knew that Brittany could be scaring him. His heart beat faster and faster. Finally he entered the living room and...

"AAAAAAAAAAAAAAAAAHHHHHHHHHHHHHHHH!"

Suddenly a loud screaming pierced the air. Jack fell to the ground, terrified. Then he started to cry.

"Why did you do that?" he sobbed.

"Why are you so sensitive to loud noises?" asked Brittany. "I was only hiding."

Jack had to cry, even though he knew his cousin felt no

sympathy for him. "Don't you know it hurts me?"

"What is going on here?" asked Aunt Mary.

"I scared him, Mother," said Brittany.

"Brittany, I am so proud of you," Aunt Mary replied. "You're growing up disciplining him the way he deserves to be disciplined and the way I do it. You're a real chip off the old block."

Jack cried and cried and cried, his tears spilling on the floor. "Why did you scare me?"

"It didn't bother anyone else," said Aunt Mary.

"Why is it that you never think that maybe someone else experiences things differently? And why is it that you can only understand things that you've experienced yourself?" asked Jack.

"Why are *you* so different from everyone else? Be thankful you're in this family, because if you were in a REAL family, you would have been beaten, spanked, and whipped a thousand times by now!" said Aunt Mary. "Now get up and continue playing! And I must also tell you that Aunt Eva called. She wants us to go see Uncle Peter today at one o'clock. So one hour of socializing has been canceled until further notice."

Jack was happy about that, but it was only 11:23. He still had thirty-seven minutes to deal with.

"Now it is my turn," said Jack.

He walked with Brittany down the hall to their room, Jack still terrified of any new noises that would come.

"So now, I will hide," said Jack.

"Fine. Hide," said Brittany.

Jack left Brittany's room and walked through the hallway of the house looking for a place to hide. He found the laundry room and hid inside the dryer. The washing machine was running.

He stayed there. There were no clothes in the dryer. Realizing that no terrors took place here, he scrunched himself up and relaxed, waiting for Brittany to find him. Then the washing machine turned off and he continued waiting.

It seemed like hours until finally the dryer door opened.

"Jack, what are you doing in here?"

It was Aunt Mary.

"I can't believe it," she said. "I try to put the laundry in the dryer and you're there. There must be a reason why you're there."

"We're playing Hide and Seek."

"Well, I'll give you five minutes before I start the dryer—whether or not you are in it."

As he waited for Brittany to find him, he thought about what was going on. What was his life? Was life just a journey from punishment to punishment? Was life being hurt, recovering, then feeling terrified that at any moment he would get hurt again? If that was life, why did people talk about wanting to live to be old? How come people weren't happy when they died? He just stayed there, thinking about the horrors of life. He also thought about his home life. For years, the reason why he did everything was because he was determined to help his parents. But his parents were always angry at him. And then he thought, why was he helping his parents? If his parents would not appreciate his help, why bother?

Jack kept thinking about the inconsistencies of his world when Aunt Mary called throughout the house, "LUNCH!"

It startled Jack as he went back to the real world from his thoughts, but he climbed out of the dryer, walked to the lunch table, and sat down.

He looked at his plate. On it was rice and beans, grilled chicken, salad, and mashed potatoes. Jack hated Aunt Mary's salad because her lettuce tasted bitter and felt weird in his mouth, but he kept his mouth shut, since he knew that his punishment was canceled and was happy about that.

He ate the rice and beans, mashed potatoes, and grilled chicken. He moved the beans and lettuce around his plate to make it seem like he had eaten some. When everyone was done eating lunch, they left the table and Aunt Mary posted a note about their plans in the event that Jack's parents and Uncle Hayes came home. Then she announced, "It's time to get ready! Put on your shoes so we can go to Uncle Peter and Aunt Eva's new home in the new development!"

His cousins instantly ran to the front door to get their shoes. Jack walked and put his shoes on slowly. Aunt Mary called, "It's time to go."

So he followed his cousins and Aunt Mary to the garage, where they all piled into the van. Aunt Mary started the van and they were on their way.

It took them twenty minutes to get to Aunt Eva's new house in Forest, Indiana. They took State Road 26 west to CR 870 W, which they took south to CR 600 N, which they took west to the town of Forest. In Forest, they took W 3rd Ave to Morrison Street, and entered a new development. This was strange because on CR 600 N, they saw cornfields on both sides, and it seemed as if cities never existed. They took Morrison Street one block west until they saw Aunt Eva's new home, and then Aunt Mary pulled into a driveway.

"Welcome to Aunt Eva's new home," Aunt Mary said.

Chapter 29

The house was a big one. It was three stories high, and there was evidence of a basement.

Aunt Mary walked to the entrance and knocked on the door.

The door was answered by Uncle Peter, whom Jack did not recognize at first since he last remembered seeing him in his tuxedo at the wedding. Peter, unlike Hayes, did not wear a moustache, and he was dressed in a casual outfit.

"Isn't my new husband nice?" asked Aunt Eva as she walked into the entryway of the new house. "We've only been married for two days, and I've learned so much about him. And I'm sure he's learned a lot about me. Let's have a warm welcome for Peter Thomas Norman."

"Shouldn't you be thinking of having a honeymoon?" asked Aunt Mary.

"Of course not. After all, Peter's still going to have to get used to me and normal life after the honeymoon, so why not get used to it now?" asked Aunt Eva.

"It seems you got a deal with this house. Three floors and a basement. Do you really need all of this room?" asked Aunt Mary.

"You do when there's potential children or guests in the future," said Aunt Eva. "By the way, my husband is very talented in many different ways. He often helps his brothers with conflict. I know already that he is the best storyteller."

"Peter, could you tell my children a story?" asked Aunt Mary.

"Well, maybe I could. It's not hard, since so many stories exist," said Uncle Peter.

"He also does a very good job sewing things together," said Aunt Eva.

"Uncle Peter, my stuffed animal is ripped. Could you sew it back together?" asked Cousin Brittany.

"I will after I am done talking," said Uncle Peter. "So Brittany, *please keep your mouth shut.*"

"And I hope you do not talk again unless you have been granted permission by your parents or another adult," said Aunt Mary.

Jack kept his mouth shut too, since he now knew that Peter was just as bad as everyone else.

"He also does a good job cleaning the house," said Aunt Eva.

"Well, maybe I can get you to clean my house," said Aunt Mary. "Ours is a mess."

"Before I am asked to do any favors," said Uncle Peter. "I would like to get to know some things about you. For example, since it is one-thirty, I assume that everyone has eaten lunch by now. Is that correct?"

"Yes, it is," said Aunt Mary.

"Now, since I have been requested to, I am going to tell all the children a story in the attic," said Uncle Peter.

Then the phone rang.

"Don't worry. I'll get it. Go be with the children," said Aunt Eva.

She walked out. "Come with me," said Uncle Peter.

Jack followed him with Bobby, Brittany, and Erin up the stairs to the second floor, and then up another flight to the third floor.

"Welcome to the third floor," said Uncle Peter. "Now, we have only lived here for a couple days so the entire room is empty. We can all sit down in this room and listen to a story. Although I have no books, I have a lot of stories in my memory. And I'm sure you know a lot of them."

"Can we choose a story?" asked Bobby.

"No, of course not. After all, you are not me, and therefore you do not know the stories that I know," said Peter. "But they will be entertaining. Before we begin, does anyone have to go to the bathroom?"

"Yes," said Jack.

"Well, everyone should go since they will have to be listening to me for a long time," said Peter. "It is just down the stairs."

So everyone, even Jack, went and then returned in ten minutes.

"Now we can begin the story. *Once upon a time, in a faraway land, there was a dry forest. It rained one day in the forest and all the plants were competing to get more rain. Ray, one of the trees, bragged and boasted at how much rain he could get. This angered the neighboring tree, May, who said that everyone needed rain and that you should only get what you need. But Ray was determined to get all the rain he could get. He even stopped one of the small trees nearby, which was born from one of his seeds, from getting rain. This angered the smaller tree, who was not getting enough water because of Ray, yet Ray was the tree's father. This went on until it stopped raining. May was furious at Ray by the end of the day, and decided that she would have to teach Ray a lesson.*

"*The next time it rained in the forest, May and the other trees decided to teach Ray a lesson. They drank up all the water with roots, so Ray could not get any water, nor did Ray's offspring. At the end of the day, two woodsmen came and cut down Ray and the tree that had been sprouted from his seed because they were dry and would make good firewood. May and all of the other trees were so happy that they were gone that they all rejoiced. The moral of the story is to respect everyone in your community, to treat everyone equally, and to share, because if you don't, you may get punished.*"

"Am I interrupting something?" a voice said from nowhere. The door opened, and in walked Aunt Mary and Aunt Eva.

"Come in. We were done with our story," said Uncle Peter.

"I didn't mean to interrupt your get-together," said Aunt Eva, "but the person on the phone was your brother Lenny. He asked whether you wanted to go see the magic show today at the carnival in Thorntown with him. It starts in fifty minutes."

"This is very short notice. Is he still on the phone?" asked Uncle Peter.

"Yes. I put him on hold. Do you want to take everyone there or not?" asked Aunt Eva.

"I think we should go. It's not very often that the kids get to see a magician."

"Okay then, we'll just get ready," said Aunt Eva, and both aunts left.

"Did you hear that, everyone? We're going to a magic show!" said Uncle Peter.

This made all the kids except Jack happy. It was bad enough

he had to visit Eva and Peter, but now a magic show? And Peter was just another hypocrite, telling stories about treating everyone equally while treating kids like second-class citizens.

Suddenly everyone heard a piercing scream.

"What happened?" shouted Uncle Peter.

"There's a flood in the bathroom!" Aunt Mary called out.

Peter ran to the bathroom. Everyone followed him.

He pushed open the door to find Aunt Mary on the floor in a puddle of water and unmentionable other things.

"Oh my God! What's been going on here?" asked Peter.

"The toilet overflowed," said Aunt Mary. "I came in here and slipped."

"Who was the last person to use the bathroom?"

The three cousins looked at each other and said in unison, "JACK!"

"I did not!" Jack protested.

"Of course you did," said Aunt Eva. Then she said to everyone as if he weren't there, "Jack's always been stuffing wads of toilet paper into toilets. He also flushes empty toilets," said Aunt Mary.

"That was when I was eighteen months old."

"But it is more inexcusable today. JACK, WHY DID YOU DO THIS?"

"I just went to the bathroom. I did not stuff—"

"THE TOILET JUST OVERFLOWED! DO YOU DENY IT?" roared Aunt Eva.

"No, I don't deny—"

"There! You heard him, everyone! He admitted it." screamed Aunt Eva. "YOU SHOULD NOT MAKE TOILETS OVERFLOW! AND DON'T TELL ME YOU'RE INNOCENT BECAUSE THERE'S EVIDENCE RIGHT HERE THAT THE TOILET DID OVERFLOW! WHAT IS THERE TO GAIN BY LYING? YOU MUST KNOW! ANY SENSIBLE PERSON WOULD KNOW! BUT WHY DOES HE ALWAYS HAVE TO DENY THE THING THAT HE HAS DONE WRONG! WHY CAN'T HE ACCEPT THE FACT THAT HE HAS DONE SOMETHING WRONG?"

roared Aunt Mary.

"Is he really this bad?" asked Uncle Peter.

"Peter, he is worse. I do not know why he has turned out this way—it must be those faulty Lack genes—and I do not know why my sister puts up with it," said Aunt Eva. "If I were his mother, he would be whipped so many times he'd want to behave."

"Are you sure he's guilty this time? Because I do not want to yell at an innocent boy," said Uncle Peter.

"He is far from innocent," said Aunt Eva. "Go ahead. Yell. Children are put on earth to listen and obey, as my mother always said."

"All right. I guess I'm going to need practice for my own kids. JACK, WHY DID YOU MAKE MY TOILET OVERFLOW? HAVEN'T YOU LEARNED ANY RULES OF RESPECT?" roared Uncle Peter. "I GUESS YOU HAVEN'T, SO I AM GOING TO PUNISH YOU, JACK! YOU WILL NOT BE ALLOWED TO GO TO THE BATHROOM WITHOUT SOMEONE SUPERVISING YOU, AND THAT PERSON WILL ONLY GO WITH YOU IF THEY MUST GO THEMSELVES! AND DON'T THINK IT'S UNFAIR, BECAUSE WHEN I WAS A CHILD, MY MOTHER MADE ME HOLD IT IN AND WOULD NOT STOP TO LET US GO TO THE BATHROOM UNLESS SHE OR MY FATHER HAD TO!"

Jack thought: Was everyone in that generation crazy?

"And on a happier note," said Uncle Peter, calming down, "it is time to get ready to go to the magic show."

Jack was truly disappointed. He was hoping that his punishment would be that he had to stay home.

* * * *

Uncle Peter parked his van at the parking lot of the carnival after looking for a spot for ten minutes. Jack was horribly carsick from all the circling. Then everyone went out of the van and walked to the entrance of the carnival.

"It's two-twenty, and we have ten minutes before the show

starts. Let's go to the stage and see if my brother is there," Peter said.

They walked through the carnival to the stage, and they looked in every seat to find Peter's brother. Finally they found him in the front row, where he had saved a block of seats.

"The show is about to start," said Lenny. "Sit down, everyone."

So they sat down and waited for the show to begin. Finally a woman got on the stage. "Good day," she said. "On behalf of the city of Thorntown, I'd like to welcome you to the fifty-second annual Thorntown Days Festival!"

Everyone applauded.

"I hope everyone is enjoying the third day of the festival, but for now, please welcome Mr. W, our magician!"

Chapter 30

"Good afternoon, everyone," said a man in a black suit and tie. "I am Mr. W., master of magic and illusion."

"He is the best magician in this area," said Lenny softly.

"Everyone has the power to do magic. And sometimes you do not need any equipment at all but knowledge. For example, I am going to pull my finger off right now in three ways."

"The first finger to be pulled off is the thumb. I am going to put my thumb in the middle of my other hand and pull it off. One, two, three," he said, and he pulled his thumb off.

"Now I will pull off the next two fingers, starting with my pointer finger. One, two, three," he said and pulled off his pointer finger. Then he pulled off his middle finger.

"Those are just simple tricks you can learn at any joke shop. Anyone can be a magician. And magic tricks often have secrets that have two classic origins: they can involve science or hidden knowledge, or they can be made by misdirecting the audience's attention. If you do not know the secret, you will not figure out the trick. You will think it is simply magic.

"To start off, we will have a misdirection trick. Now, I could misdirect you by screaming, "LOOK BEHIND YOU!" If I did that, I would be a bad magician. I do not need that. For this trick, I need a deck of cards, and here it is. It is a normal deck of cards. But I have the ability to name any card and then be able to, on my first try, take it out of the deck. Let's see if it works now. I promise that I will take out of this deck a three of diamonds."

He shuffled the deck.

"Now I will see if I can find it." He looked in the deck and said, "I have found it." Then he took the deck out of his hands and all of the cards fell to the stage except one card, which was the three of diamonds.

Everyone applauded. Jack put his hands over his ears since it was too loud for him. To him, applauding was like someone saying to the crowd, "FIRE!" and the crowd starting to shoot their guns. And he hated shows of any kind, particularly magic, since he had a hard enough time figuring out how ordinary reality worked—magic and things that didn't make sense to ordinary people were ten times as confusing and stressful to Jack.

"Now, that trick involved misdirection. This next trick involves science. You see, science involves chemicals, and those chemicals can do things that seem magical. For example, we all know that vinegar and baking soda react and release a gas that makes the mixture seem to rise to the top of the container, which is the secret of model volcano eruptions. But suppose I didn't tell you that? Not telling the whole truth is another way of making a trick seem like magic.

"For this trick, I am going to try to make solid out of liquid. Here is a small plastic cup. I will pour my magic formula in this cup and wait to see what will happen. In the meantime we will do another science trick. One thing that occurs in the lives of some parents is that some children go through a phase where they love to get wet. Therefore, for this trick, we would like to have a child volunteer come up if they wish to get wet. Raise your hand and I'll call on you."

A boy in the middle row was picked and walked up the stairs to the stage.

"Now, what's your..."

Everyone gasped suddenly. The cup that had that liquid poured in suddenly had foam pouring out of it.

"I see what you are looking at. The trick worked! We have turned normal water into solid foam," Mr. W. said, and to prove it he took a knife to show that the foam was solid.

"But back to you. What is your name?" asked Mr. W.

"Thomas," said the boy.

"Well, Thomas, let me show you something. Here are four buckets. Two are filled with water and two are empty. To show you that there is indeed water in the buckets, I will take the two buckets filled with water and pour them into the empty buckets," said Mr. W.

He took the two buckets and poured water into the empty buckets.

"Now I will take this bucket of water and pour it on you," he said. He took the bucket and put it upside down on top of Thomas. But no drops of water came out. Everyone clapped.

"Hey, what's going on?" Mr. W. said. "I'll try again." Then he took the other bucket and put it upside down on top of himself. Water instantly poured on him.

"All right, I'll try again," said Mr. W. Then he poured more water from one bucket to another bucket and put it upside down on top of Thomas. No water came out.

Everyone clapped again.

"All right, I'll try again. And if nothing comes out, I'll give you one dollar," said Mr. W.

Then he poured more water from one bucket to another and put the bucket upside down over Thomas. Water instantly poured on him.

"Let's hear it for Thomas, who did a wonderful job participating." Everyone clapped and cheered.

"For my next trick, I am going to bake apple pie. Because I am a magician, I use invisible ingredients. I am going to use this Pyrex glass pan because Pyrex is known for its ability to withstand high temperatures. But I must warn you that Pyrex might shatter or explode if it is put under the broiler in an oven, or if liquid is added to it when it is hot."

Mr. W. held up the Pyrex pan for the audience to see. "You can see for yourselves that the pan is empty. I am going to get the stove now," he said, and he left the stage and returned with a stove on wheels and plugged it in an outlet on the stage.

"Now I will start the oven," said the magician, "by turning on the knob that starts preheating the oven The knob labeled PREHEAT will do the trick." He turned the knob until the electronic screen on the stove read PREHEATING OVEN TO 350 DEGREES, and put the empty pan into the oven. Then he walked back to his table full of stuff. He picked up a black blanket and a bouquet of red flowers. He put the black blanket over the bouquet, then opened it, and the flowers had changed from red to yellow. After that, he put the blanket over the yellow flowers and they changed to blue.

Everyone cheered.

He took the blue flowers and put them back on the table and picked up a paper bag and a cereal box. He put the cereal box in the paper bag and then crumbled up the paper bag as if nothing was in it, and everyone cheered.

"Now," said the magician, "one thing that I carry around, like everyone else, is spare money. But because I'm a magician, I carry money for other reasons. Magic reasons. You see, some people want to take my money, and so I have to be prepared to regenerate that money. Look at this wallet," he said as he picked it up, "that I am holding. It has one dollar bill in it. But this wallet has the power to recreate money. Therefore, if someone stole it, I would be able to recreate it."

He walked around the stage, and the money suddenly caught fire and was burning up. Everyone laughed.

"What's going on?" asked the magician. "Oh, look, my money is on fire! I'm glad it didn't burn a hole in my pocket. I guess I will have to put it out."

So he put the dollar back inside the wallet and removed it. When he did, it was back to normal as if it had not been burned. Everyone cheered.

"Now, for my next trick…"

DING! A bell rang.

"That means the pie is done. Now we will see if my invisible ingredients have made a pie," said the magician.

The stove opened and he pulled out a pan full of apple pie, which shocked Jack and everyone in his family.

"I will serve the pie to anyone who wants to eat some at the end of the show. In order to be safe, I am turning off the PREHEAT knob on the stove.

"For my next trick, I am going to show you something. It is a coloring book. But this coloring book is an empty book." He flipped the pages to show that it was empty. "This coloring book can read minds. If everyone visualizes a picture, any picture, in their heads, this coloring book can take those pictures and print them onto the pages. On the count of three, all of your visualized pictures will be inside the coloring book," said the magician.

Jack was terrified. He had horrible trouble visualizing pictures, as he thought in words. And he was afraid that the magician would yell at him if he didn't visualize a picture, since his picture would show words on the coloring book page. So he tried, but then the magician called out, "THREE!"

Jack was not finished, so he hoped that the coloring book did not have enough time to pick up the words that he visualized.

"Now it is time to see the pictures you thought of," said Mr. W. He flipped the pages and there were pictures of animals, plants, towns, and homes. Jack was relieved that his picture of words was not in the coloring book.

"These are black-and-white pictures," said Mr. W. "But since this is a magic coloring book, what if we color them? Since you were able to visualize pictures, you should be able to visualize colors. At the count of three, visualize colors for the book."

This also caused Jack problems. When he visualized red, he visualized the word **RED** instead of the color itself. He hoped that the coloring book would not fill one of the pictures with the word **RED** instead of the color red. Finally the magician said "THREE" and it was time to see if the coloring book did put words in one picture because of Jack's thoughts.

Jack, however, did not need to be terrified. When the magician flipped the pages of the coloring book now, it was full of color pictures without the word **RED** anywhere.

Everyone cheered.

"Now I'd like to do a trick that is similar to getting your ears pierced. Who in the audience has their ears pierced?"

A number of girls and boys raised their hands.

"Except this is a trick about piercing balloons. All right, I know what you're wondering. Balloons? Wouldn't a balloon pop when it was pierced? Not always. That is because I use special balloons that do not pop. Here it is. And here is a needle," said the magician as he showed the white balloon and needles, "that I will pierce the balloon with."

The magician took the balloon and put one needle in it. The balloon did not pop. He put a second needle in another spot on the balloon and once again, it did not pop. He put a third, fourth, fifth, sixth, seventh, eighth, and ninth needle in the balloon and it still did not pop. But Jack knew that it could still pop. He was holding his ears so that if it popped, he would be prepared for the loud sound. The magician put a tenth needle in the balloon and it still did not pop. He said, "We have now put ten needles in this balloon, and we are lucky that it has not popped yet. But I am determined to put more needles in it." When the eleventh needle touched the surface of the balloon, it popped.

Jack held his arms tightly around his head. Everyone cheered. To Jack, it sounded like a dull roar.

"Now, for my next trick we are going to need a volunteer, so anyone who wants to come up, please raise your hand," said Mr. W. People raised their hands and Mr. W. picked someone.

Jack thought it would be just anyone, but he was wrong. Mr. W picked his cousin Erin. Jack felt no jealousy even though a normal child would, and he was thankful that Erin was picked. He had no desire to go up there.

"Now," said the magician, "what is your name?"

"My name is Erin," said Cousin Erin with a big smile for him and then the audience, as if she were auditioning for a play.

"Now, before we start this trick," said Mr. W, "I am going to give you a lesson about other cultures. In Asia, people practice different religions. One of those religions is called Buddhism. Buddhism is a religion that preaches tolerance of all religions, as well as not harming or killing any other living creatures, as that upsets the balance of nature. Buddhists are well known for practicing meditation. Meditation is a state of calmness where one forgets their troubles and sits silently for long periods of time. Sometimes during this calmness, Buddhists have ritual chants. The leader of some services is called the Dalai Lama. Today I am going to let Erin experience Buddhist meditation. But in order for her to be a true Buddhist, she must dress like one. Therefore, Erin, I would like you to put on this meditation robe."

The magician continued talking as Erin put on the robe.

"Now Erin will wait here as I build a platform for her to meditate on," said Mr. W. The magician took two chairs, and put a black board on top of the chairs. Then he said, "Now, Erin, it is time for you to sit cross-legged on this board."

Erin smiled, batted her eyelashes at the audience, then got up in the robe and sat cross-legged on the board. Then the magician moved the robe so that it covered the entire board.

"Now, you are to sit completely still with your eyes closed in meditation," said Mr. W. "And do not get off the platform until I say you can."

Erin batted her eyelashes one more time, then closed her eyes and was still. Then Aunt Eva called out, "Great job, sweetie! You're my angel!"

Mr. W. said to Aunt Eva, "Ma'am, I would like to ask you to be silent. Meditation only works in silence. You may talk after the trick is done."

Aunt Eva looked flustered. She wasn't used to being lectured.

Mr. W. walked around the platform, and the magic began. Mr. W. removed one chair that supported the platform. After that, Mr. W. removed the other chair that supported the platform. Jack was shocked. Now Erin was not only meditating, but she was being levitated. Then another surprise came. Mr. W. removed the platform that Erin was sitting on, yet she did not fall down. This shocked everyone. But the magician was not done with the trick.

He took a hula hoop and put it around Erin five times to show that she was indeed levitated. The trick, however, had to come to an end. The magician put the platform back under Erin, then put the two chairs back in place and said, "Your meditation is over. Please step off the platform."

Erin opened her eyes, got off, took off the robe, curtseyed, then returned to her seat. Everyone was cheering.

"What's going on? What happened?" asked Erin.

"The magician levitated you," said Aunt Eva. "How did you feel?"

"All I felt was sitting on a platform," said Erin.

"The magician took the platform away. How could you have been on one?" asked Aunt Eva.

"I was," said Erin.

"You couldn't have been. The entire audience saw it being

taken away," said Aunt Eva.

"Of course I was," said Erin.

"DON'T CONTRADICT ME!" roared Aunt Eva. "YOU WERE IN THE AIR WITHOUT ANY SUPPORTS!"

"Please stop yelling at her," said Uncle Peter. "There obviously is an explanation to the magic trick. Erin, what your mother is trying to tell you is not that you are wrong, but not to tell anyone what you felt, since it may give the trick away."

"That's right, Erin. We'll talk about it after the show," said Aunt Eva.

Erin sat down, furious. Once again, her mother had spoiled her great moment.

"Now, for my next trick, I am going to need a boy volunteer. Please raise your hands again."

This time almost every boy in the audience raised his hand. Everyone except Jack.

Jack had his arms wound tightly around his head. But in the sea of raised hands, especially since all his cousins had raised their hands and were waving them, somehow the magician misinterpreted Jack's nonverbal message. Somehow the magician thought that Jack's upraised arms meant he wanted to be picked.

"How about the boy in the front row wearing the red shirt?" the magician called out, pointing at Jack.

Everyone looked to see who the lucky boy was. Everyone except Jack, who had his eyes closed in terror.

"Come on," Bobby whispered. "You're the only boy in the front wearing a red shirt! He means you!"

"Jack, go up! You've been chosen!" said Aunt Eva.

Jack unwrapped his arms and realized that the entire audience was waiting for him to stand up. It didn't occur to him to disobey, since to Jack, helping a magician was just as horrible and just as compulsory as tying his shoes in school.

Jack stood up and took slow, small steps up to the stage. Every step made him a little more fearful. His heart pounding, he walked to the magician.

"Now," said the magician, "What is your name?"

Chapter 31

Jack was shaking in his shoes, not knowing whether he could utter even a sound.

"J-j-j-j-j-j," he said as he continued stuttering in terror.

"Yes, what is it?" asked the magician.

"J-j-j-Jack," said Jack in extreme fright.

"Could you say that again? I couldn't hear you."

"J-j-j-j—"

The magician quickly realized that he had made a bad choice, so he announced pleasantly, "I think this young man would rather not be up here. Why don't you all give him a big hand for trying as he goes back to his seat."

The magician patted Jack lightly on the back. It was one of the first kind things anybody had done for him that day.

But when Jack went back to his seat, almost no one clapped. A few hands made a little noise. His two aunts were furious.

"Jack, you've embarrassed us in front of all these people," said Aunt Mary.

"Let's get out of here," Uncle Peter said.

"But we want to see the end," Bobby protested.

"Yeah, that's why we came!" said Brittany.

"You can blame Jack for spoiling your time," said Uncle Peter.

Then he motioned for everyone to get up and leave. Jack's cousins all gave him looks of anger and fury as they left. Jack couldn't understand *why* they had to leave, since the magician had already picked someone else, and walking away seemed a whole lot more inappropriate than staying to watch the end.

He was confused, too, about Uncle Peter. One minute he seemed nice, then the next minute he was just as bad as the rest of the adults.

"I'm hungry," Erin said as they walked away from the magician's show area.

"Okay, kids, we'll buy something to eat," said Uncle Peter.

So Aunt Mary, Aunt Eva, Uncle Peter, Jack, and his cousins all walked to a ticket booth, got tickets, and ordered hamburgers, hot dogs, French fries, and a salad at a food booth.

"The nearest tables are this way," said Uncle Peter.

They walked to a table, put their food down, and sat down.

"I'm not hungry," Brittany whined. "Can't we go on a ride first?"

"Yeah," said Bobby. "Can't we go on at least one ride?"

"Who wants to go on a ride?" asked Uncle Peter.

Everyone except Jack raised their hand. You can imagine how Jack felt about machines that twirled him and turned him and rocked him back and forth. He couldn't even stand riding in the backseat of a car, so a Ferris wheel was like a medieval instrument of torture.

"Okay, Jack, since once more you're the *only* one who doesn't want to do something, *you* sit here and guard the food. And don't eat any," said Aunt Mary.

"O-o-kay," said Jack, who was still too terrified even to think about food."

"Actually, Mary, Brittany, Bobby, and Erin, you go find a ride. Jack and Peter and I are going to have a talk," said Aunt Eva.

The others walked to the carnival.

"Jack, I'm sure you understand what you did was wrong," said Uncle Peter.

"What did I do wrong?" asked Jack.

"You disobeyed the magician! He asked you to give your name and you wouldn't!"

"I was scared," said Jack.

"Scared or not, that does not excuse you to misbehave. We came to see this magician for fun! Why aren't you having fun like we are? Don't you understand the sacrifice we had to make to take you here?"

"If it is such a sacrifice, why did you do it?" said Jack. "I'd be happier if you didn't."

"Because it is my duty. Getting married to your aunt means I am legally related to you and so I must sacrifice time for you.

Why can't you enjoy things like your cousins? It's as if you don't belong in this family," said Uncle Peter.

"What else did I do wrong?" asked Jack.

"You behaved horribly in front of the entire audience. That magician should not have taken your side! You were lucky he did, since not many people would," said Aunt Eva.

"Aren't we all scared of something in life?" asked Jack.

"Yes, but we must overcome that. Otherwise you'll never be able to get a job," said Aunt Eva.

"Life requires getting a job, but life does not require helping magicians," said Jack.

"HOW DARE YOU TELL ME WHAT LIFE IS ABOUT?" roared Aunt Eva. "I'VE BEEN HERE LONGER AND THEREFORE I KNOW! YOU'RE ONLY A CHILD!"

"Well, this is enough," said Uncle Peter. "Let's go find the others. I'm hungry. Jack, stay here and guard the food."

Jack blinked. Here was yet another example of inconsistency. Peter was mean and rotten one minute, then kind and reasonable the next. Maybe he just hadn't been a member of Jack's family long enough. Within a year he might be as consistently mean and rotten as everybody else.

Jack was so exhausted that he put his head down to rest. The next thing he remembered was a hand on his shoulder roughly shaking him awake.

"What did you do, Jack?" Aunt Mary screamed. Behind her Erin was glaring at him, but there was something besides anger in that glare. Jack had trouble reading faces, especially when he was tired, but he thought he saw something else—was it guilt or excitement—in his cousin's expression?

"I didn't do anything," he said, for the hundredth time.

"Well, look, you idiot," said Erin, and Jack looked.

The hamburgers, hot dogs, French fries, and salad were all eaten Only crumbs and empty plates remained..

"Peter!" said Aunt Eva. "Why did you leave him alone?"

"Who?" asked Uncle Peter.

"Who indeed?" Aunt Mary chimed in.

Then once more, every eye turned on Jack.

Chapter 32

"Why are you like this?" asked Uncle Peter. "I mean, I have known you for only four days, and yet you have caused more trouble and embarrassment than any child I have ever met. Do you hunger for attention? Is that why you ate all the food—as a metaphor? Is it a thrill to you to risk punishment for misbehavior?"

A *thrill?* thought Jack, sorry he had ever even considered that this man could be nice.

This was going too far. It was not a thrill to be punished. It must be a thrill to them, however, to abuse power and falsely accuse the innocent.

"I'm sure there is enough food for you to eat. Why would you eat other people's food? You're not impoverished and destitute. You don't come from a rich family, but at least you come from a family that successfully supports itself," said Uncle Peter.

"Everyone, because of Jack, is going to have to starve until they get home" said Aunt Mary.

"Thanks a lot," said his cousins sarcastically.

"I didn't…"

"WHAT LIES! OF COURSE YOU ATE THE FOOD! THE FOOD HAS BEEN EATEN AND YOU WERE THE ONLY PERSON HERE."

Jack had a sudden thought: If constantly claiming to be innocent didn't work, maybe he should simply start pleading guilty to everything.

"All right," he said. "I did eat the food. I waited until all of you were out of sight, then I took each and every hamburger, hot dog, drink, and piece of lettuce, and stuffed them in my mouth, and I made sure that not a single crumb or drop of ketchup remained on my hand or got on my shirt, since you are always yelling at me for being a slob, and then I ran and washed my hands anyway, since they are now, as you can see, perfectly clean—"

"You don't have to make a speech," Aunt Eva said, "but he's
right about something. Jack can't eat anything without making an
utter mess, and his hands and clothes are completely clean." She
turned quickly. "Erin, let me see your hands."

"Why?" Erin said, surprised.

"What were you doing for so long when you said you had to
go to the bathroom?"

"What are you saying?" Erin cried. "Are you accusing me?"
"I was in the bathroom. See?" She held out her hands.

Everyone looked closely, even Jack. The hands looked freshly
cleaned, though, he thought, maybe she ate all the food, *then* went
and washed her hands to destroy the evidence.

"Very well, Erin," said Aunt Eva. "I'm sorry I accused you.
You're my perfect, beautiful daughter, and Jack had no business
to accuse you."

"But I didn't—" Then he remembered his new plan. "You're
right. I shouldn't have accused you, my sweet and innocent
cousin. Name the punishment."

"Well, let's see," said Aunt Mary. "I think you should be
required to socialize again for the next two days. That's a fitting
punishment because it teaches you something. And I must say, I
think our punishments are working. You have made great
progress, I feel, from what you have just said."

"Thank you, Aunt Mary," said Jack, his suspicions confirmed.
To please them, he would *have* to lie and betray himself.

If that's what it meant to be normal, he understood why crazy
people often chose to live in lunatic asylums. At least there, they
were protected from the insanity of the real world.

One day later

It was now 10:30. For the past thirty minutes, Jack, in
Bobby's room, had been doing command after command for
Cousin Erin in Tuesday's socializing. It wasn't even stuff that was
needed. First she asked him to take off her coat, though she only
had put it on one minute before. Then she asked him to open her
suitcase and find her teddy bear, which he had already found

thirty minutes ago in her suitcase. (Erin put it back in to frustrate him.) She also asked him to do other things repeatedly to tease him, such as put hair bows back in that he already had taken out.

"Haven't you ever had to do this yourself?" asked Jack.

"No, I haven't. My father always did it for me," said Erin.

"Then after my parents divorced, my mother started doing the things you're doing."

Jack knew he was getting nowhere, so he decided to shut up. "What do you want me to do now?" asked Jack.

"I want you to go into my suitcase and find my red dress," said Cousin Erin.

So Jack went into her suitcase and found a red dress.

"I'm sorry, but that is not the red dress I was talking about," said Erin.

"What dress do you want? This is the only red dress in that suitcase," said Jack angrily.

"Look harder and you'll find another dress. Put that one back," said Erin.

Jack put it back and looked in her suitcase and found another red dress. "Here's your red dress, Erin," said Jack.

"Now, Jack," said Erin, "please look away while I take off my red shorts and pink shirt. And give me my red dress."

Jack gave her the dress and looked away. Erin took off her clothes and folded them. Jack knew, however, that if he did not turn around when she was done, she would get angry. So Jack turned around hoping she was ready for another order.

When he did, he gasped. Erin was completely naked.

"Aaaaahhhh!" gasped Jack. He looked away.

"Jack, why did you look at me? Didn't I tell you to turn away?" asked Erin.

"I thought you were done," said Jack.

"I wasn't. I will tell you when I'm done," said Erin.

So when Erin said he could look, he did, only to be bombarded with another command: "Now please take these clothes back to the suitcase."

He did. Then Erin said, "Are you hungry? I would like for us to get some snacks in the kitchen."

"Fine, Erin. At least, I can get out of this room."

"Follow me to the kitchen, Jack," said Erin.

They both walked to the kitchen. Aunt Mary was there.

"We're hungry, so can we get some snacks?" asked Erin.

"All right," said Aunt Mary.

Jack and Erin sat down at the table. He noticed that the digital message on the stove read "PREHEATING BROILER TO 500 DEGREES."

He looked right next to the stove. A huge glass baking dish was sitting there full of something. Obviously that dish was going into the stove.

"What is the glass dish made of?" Jack asked.

"Pyrex," his aunt said.

The glass pot was made out of Pyrex? The magician said that Pyrex might shatter or explode if it is put under the broiler in a stove. It could set the house on fire.

No one would want to have the house on fire, or have something blow up in the stove. And there was Aunt Mary, making tea in the microwave, unaware of the danger. But this unforeseen plague was coming. Soon, Jack and his family could be dead meat. He had to save them.

"Aunt Mary!" called Jack.

"What?" said Aunt Mary.

"If you put that glass pot in the stove, it will blow up," said Jack.

"What will blow up?" asked Aunt Mary. "Nothing is going to blow up. You're crazy!"

"The pan is going to blow up, Aunt Mary," said Jack.

"How can you say that? Do you have any evidence that it will blow up?" asked Aunt Mary.

"Yes. That pot is made out of Pyrex. The magician said yesterday that Pyrex shatters if it is put under the broiler in a stove. And that stove is preheating the broiler before the pot goes in," said Jack.

Aunt Mary shook her head and walked out of the kitchen. Cousin Erin got some snacks for both of them.

"Why did you try to scare me and my aunt about the Pyrex?

Don't you know how that made her feel?" asked Erin.

"It's true. But Aunt Mary won't believe me," said Jack.

"How can you know? You're just a child. Do you have any proof?"

"The magician said—"

"You're crazy. I'm getting out of here for a while."

Jack stayed there, terrified. No one was listening to him, even though their lives were in jeopardy. If the pot blew up in their stove, the explosion could start a fire that would potentially burn the house down. Why couldn't they understand? This was a matter of life and death.

Aunt Mary returned, saw that the broiler had reached 500 degrees, and put the pot in the oven. Jack was afraid to move, expecting the explosion like an angry, fire-breathing dragon.

Where was Erin? Jack thought. As he walked out of the kitchen, he heard people talking in Brittany's room. Obviously someone was in there, so Erin could be there. He had to find out what was going on.

The moment Jack tried to open the door, however, Aunt Mary walked into the hallway.

"Jack, what are you doing there?" asked Aunt Mary.

"Erin and I are playing a game where I am waiting for her to knock on the door and address me as a fake person," lied Jack.

"Well, at least you two are playing," said Aunt Mary.

"By the way, Aunt Mary, enjoy your last moments of life," said Jack. "When you put that glass pot in the broiler, it is going to blow up and potentially burn the house down."

"Jack, why are you so obsessed with the glass pot all of a sudden? It's not going to burn down the house! If you bring up the pot again, I'm going to tell your mother," said Aunt Mary.

She left and Jack attempted to open the door again. It was locked, so he put his ear against the door and listened.

"We have to do it now," said Brittany. "We have to tell him."

Him? Jack thought. *What was going on?*

Chapter 33

Brittany opened the door to her room.

"Listen," said Jack. "I don't know what game you're playing, but something strange is going on. Why is no one believing me about the pan that will blow up in the oven? Everyone, including you, heard what the magician said yesterday."

"Before we explain anything," said Brittany, "we would like to know why you're trying to scare us about the Pyrex pot."

"Explain? What's there to explain?" asked Jack.

"All right, all right, I'll tell him," said Bobby. "But we'll have to close the door. If mother finds out, then we're in trouble."

Bobby closed the door and then said, "Jack, I am so sorry for what has happened."

"Sorry?" asked Jack.

"I'm sorry for what's happened. For years I have felt sorry for you. But my parents won't let me show my sympathy to you," said Bobby.

"And when I attempted to play with you," Bobby added, "my parents banned us from interaction. You know the story.

"So this time, right after you came, I decided that I wanted to teach our parents a lesson. I figured if I started misbehaving, eventually I would get caught, and my parents would realize that I was no different from you. Then maybe they would be nicer to you, and we could all play together by choice, not by force."

"What?" asked Jack. "What are you talking about?"

"I'm sorry, Jack," said Bobby, "but no matter how obvious our pranks were, my parents always blamed you."

He continued, "I also wanted to get our parents' attention. I wanted them to realize that we are misunderstood children with feelings even if we came last. But I knew that I could not do it alone. I needed help.

"So I tried to get Brittany and Erin to help me," said Bobby. "I knew that if the girls knew that it was to help you, they would not try to help. So I told them it was to get our parents' attention.

We planned six things to do that were bad, and we would watch how our parents reacted. First I would do something bad, then we would take turns. After all six things took place, if they hadn't caught one of us, we would reveal ourselves one by one, and confess the truth.

"The second day of our visit we went to the zoo. It was my turn to do something, so I turned off the lights in the reptile house. My class had a field trip there, and I happened to see the circuit breaker box. When I saw that my parents accused you about the event, I felt sad because my initial attempt had failed."

"Then it was my turn," said Erin. "I ripped up the phone book in the hotel room. The adults blamed you again."

"Although it was kind of fun," Brittany giggled, "to see someone else being blamed for a change."

"Shut up," said Bobby.

"Sorry, Jack," Brittany said.

Bobby continued. "It's just that I could see over and over that my parents are capable of blaming kids for everything, with no evidence at all. It makes me realize that they are wrong when they accuse and punish us."

"Why didn't you tell me?" asked Jack. "Does this mean that you three were responsible for everything else?"

"Yes, Jack, we were," said Bobby. "I will not deny it. When I saw that the first two attempts failed, I tried to get the girls to stop, but I failed. So I decided to just keep to the original plan. I took the wedding ring and hid it in my drawer, where you found it. I felt so sorry for you."

"But if you felt sorry for me, why is everyone so mean to me?" asked Jack.

"You may never have realized this, but all of us are scared of getting punished," said Bobby.

"The night before the wedding I faced a moral dilemma. My deepest desire was to teach my parents a lesson, but it seemed as if the more I tried, the more I got you in trouble. So how could I try to teach my parents a lesson and also continue to have loyalty to you? I didn't have to bother. The girls continued with the plan. They said it was part of their secret sisterhood or something."

"You wouldn't understand, Bobby. You're a boy," said Erin.

"During the wedding," Bobby continued, "I saw you make mistakes and I felt so sad. You see, what I couldn't understand was why they didn't choose me to be the ring bearer. After all, I was available and would have been a better choice, since I am one year younger than you. And besides, the other nephews Peter had were perfectly desirable. But I was silent, since the wedding, which actually was a very funny occasion because the computer was involved, was going on."

"When you were in the receiving line," Brittany said, "I got an idea. I would cut a piece out of the wedding cake."

Erin continued, "When the receiving line was still going on, Brittany took her red knife that was in her pocket all along and cut a slice of the wedding cake, and then hid it quickly so no one would know. She figured that no one would blame you since you're allergic to cake. Then she purposely left her red knife there so you would have to be declared innocent."

"But it still didn't work. When I saw that you were yet again blamed for something you couldn't have done, I was shocked," said Brittany. "After all, there was no real reason at that time to blame you. There was evidence that you were innocent, in the form of my red knife, but this incident showed how mind-blind my parents truly are."

"But why didn't you tell me before?" asked Jack. "Throughout this visit, I have seen small pieces of evidence showing that you, Bobby, and Erin were possible suspects."

"It's amazing that only you were able to notice all the evidence," said Bobby.

"Tell us what you saw," said Erin. "We want to know if at least someone noticed our clues."

Jack was afraid to say anything. What if this was another trap?

"Continue, Jack," said Bobby. "No one is going to hurt you."

So Jack told them all about his suspicions, about the evidence he had uncovered piece by piece and had kept to himself.

"But now you must tell me the rest," he said.

Bobby continued: "After the wedding, I felt defeated and helpless. We had tried four times to teach our parents a lesson and every time we tried, not only did we fail to teach our parents a lesson, but I got you in trouble even more. So I realized our plan was going nowhere and officially gave up.

"But Erin and Brittany did not. At Uncle Peter's house, Peter asked us to go to the bathroom and Brittany went in and stuffed the toilet with toilet paper. This set the stage for the toilet to overflow. When you were blamed yet again, I felt so sorry. But not only did I feel sorry, but we also were angry. We HAD to teach our parents a lesson. And I wanted to now—to teach my parents a lesson about you.

"Erin felt the same frustration that I did. She had to find a way to get our point across about our parents. She realized the magic show was not a time to do anything, but when you fell asleep while you were told to guard the food at the end of the magic show, she realized that this was her golden opportunity. She threw away the food when she was supposed to go to the bathroom. But then when we saw you getting blamed again, we realized that since we are children, we would never win. The meeting that you walked into right now was a meeting of surrender," said Bobby.

"But if you did this to help me, why have you been so mean to me? Why didn't you tell me before?" asked Jack.

"We wanted to find the right moment to tell you," said Bobby. "When my parents go into one of their rages, they attack everyone, and we didn't want that. We wanted to tell them when they were calm. Unfortunately, we never found an appropriate time. And we also have been driven by fear. You may be terrified of seeing my parents, but you only see them one month per year, and I have to live with them. If we do not support our parents, we risk being punished ourselves. We did not want that. Our parents are the kind of people that are willing to fight until you give up. They will not surrender. And also, there is no privacy in this house. Everything seems to be connected to everything else, so no matter what we do, my parents always find out. If we told you the truth, my parents would find out."

"But then how have you been able to come together and talk about this plan? Wouldn't your parents have found out by now?"

asked Jack.

"We met in the middle of the night," said Bobby, "when my mother and father are asleep. We would meet inside a closet. But still, we were terrified every minute of being caught."

"Now I feel sorry for you," said Jack. "I get to spend a lot of time by myself because of my autism."

"But you now know what's going on. We were also meeting here because we were talking about telling our parents about this. And we are planning to tell them tonight," said Bobby.

"Tell whose parents?" asked a voice outside the room.

Then Jack's heart began to pound as Aunt Mary walked into the room and saw Jack with his cousins.

"Good!" said Bobby. "Now we can tell her! This is our chance!"

Chapter 34

"Why is everyone all gathered here?" asked Aunt Mary, who entered the door.

"We were playing together," said Brittany.

"Bobby, you know that you are not allowed to play with Jack."

"Uh, Mother, there's something we need to tell you," said Brittany.

"Well . . ."

"Speak up. I'm not going to put my life on hold waiting for a child."

"Go on, Brittany," said Erin. "Tell her. Tell her the truth. Tell her everything."

"It's about Jack," said Brittany.

"He's innocent," Bobby finished for her.

"Innocent? How?" asked Aunt Mary.

"Well, you probably know that Jack has been misbehaving quite a lot more than usual," said Brittany. "Well, that's because some of those things you have blamed him of doing he didn't do. I know who is really guilty."

"Really? Who?" asked Aunt Mary.

"Me," said Brittany.

"And me," said Bobby.

"And me, too," said Erin.

"I shut off the power," said Bobby.

"And I tore up the phone book," said Erin.

"I stole the ring," said Bobby.

"I cut the cake," said Brittany, "and I stuffed up the toilet."

"And at the carnival, I ate the food," said Erin.

Jack looked at Aunt Mary. She was completely shocked.

"Well, I am astounded and ashamed of the three of you!" she said. "You have performed acts that are inexcusable! All of you will be punished severely. But it is not like you to misbehave. Why did you do it?" asked Aunt Mary.

"Don't you get it?" asked Brittany. "Don't you know why we did it? Haven't you figured it out and learned your lesson?"

"I have no lesson to learn. I am an adult, and it is my job to teach, not to learn,"

"Is it also the adult's job to be stupid?" said Brittany. "We're your children, not your—what did Uncle Frank call us?—your lab rats!"

"We're angry about the way you treat Jack," said Bobby.

"Jack?" Aunt Mary laughed. "How can you possibly defend Jack?"

"Because we are no different from Jack. He's our flesh and blood. And we're no better off than he is. We all come last," said Bobby.

He continued, "Hasn't your brother Frank taught you anything? Or has the failure of your own life angered you so much that you tune out other people? Frank has more sense than you. People, even children, should be respected and admired. And although adults have power, the power you are wielding is not power. You are guilty of power abuse..."

"POWER ABUSE? YOUR STANDING UP TO *ME* IS POWER ABUSE!" roared Aunt Mary.

"No, it is not," said Cousin Brittany. "The more you fight, the less you'll get in the long term. Human history shows this. The nicer you are to people, the more power you'll get in the end. When you win the support of people, you'll get power over them. We only wanted to teach you a lesson in compassion. We wanted to teach you to look at evidence and logically find the real culprit rather than assuming it's Jack's fault just because he's autistic."

"Brittany," said Aunt Mary, "I will not take it anymore. *That's one.*"

"I will not stop until I am heard!" said Brittany.

"Brittany, *that's two.*"

"I will not stop either!" said Erin.

"Brittany *and* Erin, *that's three.* Now your punishment will be—"

Suddenly a sharp smell filled Jack's nose, and he could not stand it. It was the smell of smoke. He held his breath so he would not have to smell it.

"Jack, why are you holding your breath?" asked Aunt Mary.

"There's... smoke... in... here," said Jack slowly so he would have to breathe as little as possible. "I can't stand the smell."

"There's no smoke. You're just lying the way you lied about the Pyrex," said Aunt Mary.

Then suddenly the unthinkable happened. There was a loud BANG, and the unmistakable sound of an explosion and glass shattering took place. Jack fell to the floor, crying.

"What happened?" asked Bobby.

A shrill beeping noise filled the room, and Jack screamed.

"The smoke detector!" said Aunt Mary. "It's gone off!"

"What's happening?" asked Brittany.

"You stay here. I'll go check!" said Aunt Mary. But before she left the room . . .

"FIRE!" roared Jack's father running into the hallway. "THERE'S A FIRE IN THE KITCHEN! EVERYONE GET OUT OF THE HOUSE!"

Chapter 35

"Get out of the house!" Aunt Mary screamed. "I'll go see what happened!"

Everyone except Jack ran out of the room. He wanted to see for himself whether the Pyrex had indeed blown up. As he was running down the hall toward the kitchen, he heard a loud scream.

"AAAAAAAAAAAAAAAAAHHHHHHHHHHHHHHHH!"

It was Aunt Mary. Jack ran faster. He absolutely had to see for himself.

He burst into the kitchen and saw that the oven door was open. Giant flames were shooting out of it. Aunt Mary was on the floor, moaning. Her clothes were on fire!

"Why didn't you leave the house like I told you to do?" she shrieked when she saw Jack, and she coughed after speaking.

He realized, though, that if he did save himself, no one could help her. Even though she was his mean and rotten aunt, he could not see her die if he was able to do something about it. That was what separated him from his aunts and uncles. He may have hated them, but he never wanted any of them dead. His aunts and uncles, however, frequently talked about certain people they would be happy about when they died. He ran to the sink to pour a glass of water. But that wouldn't help. He needed a lot more water. He needed a hose.

There was a hose hooked up just outside the side door. But what should he do? Aunt Mary told him he must NEVER turn on the hose—no exceptions! She was already furious at him. Dare he disobey her at a time like this? What should he do? He was so confused. He always tried to follow any rule he could comprehend, but—

Her life was in danger! Jack could not bear to see her burn to death, no matter what the rule was. He would have to disobey her and risk punishment. He had survived her punishments before. Quickly, he ran out the door, turned on the hose, and pulled it back into the kitchen. Twisting it to full stream, he doused Aunt Mary from head to toe. She screamed in fury.

He didn't care whether he would get in trouble or how Aunt Mary felt. This was a matter of life and death. When she was thoroughly soaked, he knew that he had to turn off the stove. But how? Then he remembered from the magic show. The magician had told them about Pyrex, and also showed them how he had used a knob labeled PREHEAT to turn the stove off and on. Luckily, this stove looked like the same kind of stove used at the magic show, so he found the knob and turned the stove off. After that he doused the stove with water. And he doused himself as a precaution.

Then he did something else he was absolutely forbidden to do. He called 911.

After he gave the address, he hung up the phone and went to his aunt. She was now unconscious. Taking several deep breaths, he grabbed her by the elbows and somehow pulled her out of the door and onto the ground of the side yard. He had to get her out now or else the side door exit would become blocked. In the distance, he heard the sirens wailing. He covered his ears.

Everyone suddenly came running into the side yard. Jack was now outside right next to Mary.

"Mary, are you all right?" Jack's mother cried.

Aunt Mary couldn't answer just yet.

"The whole house may burn down," Bobby said, trying to hide his natural boyish excitement.

"But my *things* are in there!" wailed Erin. "I want my suitcase!"

"I'm sorry, but we're not going to let you go back in to rescue your suitcase," said Jack's mother.

Erin began to cry. "You don't understand! T-those are the things that I have had for y-years!" she sobbed. "I need them!"

Although autistic people are often accused of being mind-blind and lacking common sense, Jack for once understood his cousin.

"Erin needs her things the way she needs her heart," he said. "People need a heart to live, and so Erin needs those things.

Besides, I need my suitcase."

"I'm sorry," said Jack's mother. "You can try to comfort your cousin, but she still is not going to get her way. And Jack, there is no way we will go inside a burning house to get your suitcase."

"But I have to have *my* suitcase," said Jack, since he had had that suitcase for six years and wasn't willing to let it burn to death.

Erin ran to the back door to get back inside, since the side door was blocked.

"Erin, no!" Jack's mother yelled.

"Susan! Marvin! Mary! Are you all right?"

Suddenly Uncle Hayes and Uncle Frank came running into the side yard.

"What's going on? The fire department called us at work to let us know about the 911 call." asked Uncle Hayes.

"What happened?" said Uncle Frank.

"Something blew up inside the stove," said Jack's mother.

"Why would something blow up inside the stove?" said Uncle Hayes. "Is everyone safe?" He looked around at all the people. "Where is Erin? And where is Jack?"

"Oh my God, they went back in!" Jack's mother screamed. "They wanted to get their suitcases."

"We're going in," Hayes cried.

But then Erin stumbled into the side yard with Jack from the back door, carrying her suitcase. Her clothes were on fire, and she was screaming.

Jack ran out and grabbed the hose again. Pressing the release quickly, he doused his cousin thoroughly, though he was careful not to get her suitcase wet. Panting, she stared at him, for once unable to think of anything nasty to say.

Just then Aunt Mary seemed to wake up. She looked around and started screaming. "JACK, PUT DOWN THAT HOSE! DIDN'T I TELL YOU—"

"Jack just saved your daughter's life," Frank interrupted.

"WHAT?" echoed Mary, Uncle Hayes, and Jack's parents.

"The firemen are here!" Bobby cried.

Jack looked at the driveway and saw a fire truck. Five firemen ran out from the truck in their fireproof suits.

"The fire started in the kitchen," said Hayes, taking charge. "Something blew up in the stove."

"Don't worry, sir," said one fireman. "We'll take care of it."

"Now, I want all of you to sit down at the fence," said another fireman. "That is far enough away so that you will not get hurt while we put the fire out."

Working as a team, the other firemen rushed into the house.

After what seemed like hours, the firemen finally put out the fire. They left the kitchen and walked through the entire house to see whether there was any fire left in the building.

One of the firemen came out to talk to the family.

"How much damage was done?" asked Uncle Hayes.

"Well, you should be thankful your house is still standing," said the other fireman. "Fires often burn the entire house down. To tell you the truth, the kitchen is completely destroyed. The walls and floor are all burnt to a crisp, and everything was damaged. You'll have to redecorate, I'm afraid. Be grateful no one was hurt. From what I hear, the quick actions of this brave young man saved two lives."

Jack didn't know what to do. For the first time in his life, someone was actually proud of him. And what was even more confusing, he felt proud . . . of himself. It was a feeling so new and strange, that he didn't quite know how to process it. He felt close to tears.

"Well, our work is done here," said the other fireman. "And remember, everyone, if there is a fire in your house or you think there is one, you can always count on the fire department to come and help you. Good luck."

They took the fire hose back into their truck, left the house, and drove away.

"Well, we can all relax now," said Uncle Hayes. "The fire has been put out."

"Wait a minute," said Uncle Frank. "We can't relax. Jack just saved Mary's life, and Erin's life too. And maybe your house as well. It was he who called 911, wasn't it, Jack?"

Jack looked down, but he nodded. He was afraid someone

was going to punish him for using the telephone without permission.

"You owe him your life, Mary. You have to thank him."

Mary looked flustered. She also was feeling new things.

"I don't know what to say," she replied.

"Jack, you have to think of the thing Aunt Mary must do in order to repay you. *What is the deepest wish in your heart?*"

Chapter 36

"Go on," said Uncle Frank. "It is your turn to shine."

Jack thought hard, and then he thought of something. All morning he had tried to help prevent the fire but no one listened to him. Throughout the entire visit, whenever he tried to tell the truth, no one listened. The reason why no one understood him was not because they *couldn't* understand him, but because everyone refused to listen to him.

He now knew what he had to wish for.

"I understand that you are my aunt, Mary, and that you legally are bound to have authority over me. Therefore, I am only asking for a small task, one that can be performed by all of you," said Jack. "One that can be performed right here without anyone moving an inch. I am going to tell you something, and my cousins will too, and the only thing I ask you to do is to listen to us. The reason why you do not understand us is because you refuse to listen. And I hope in the future, you will remember to listen to everyone, even children."

"I refuse to be lectured by a child," said Aunt Mary.

"You are going to listen to him," said Uncle Frank. "And if you don't, I am going to treat you the way you treat your children."

"All right, then," said Aunt Mary.

"My three cousins committed six crimes during this visit, and I have been innocent all along," said Jack. "But the reason why they performed the acts was to teach you a lesson. They wanted to show you that I was not the only one who potentially could misbehave in this family. They could too. They also wanted to see how you would react, and they found out that even with no evidence whatsoever, you instantly assumed that I was the person at fault—even though if you looked at the context, you would have realized that during the time the situation happened, I was not present. They also wanted to get attention. They wanted to tell you that they had feelings and a mind of their own just like you, and you were not accepting that because of your belief that children are inferior. Before punishing them, think of what you've done. All they wanted was what I wanted you to do—listen. And they wanted you to regain common sense. For it seems that you had trained yourself to associate me with troublemaking and everything that happened became my fault even if it was not."

"What am I supposed to do about it?" asked Aunt Mary. "What I have done is in the past."

"Are you crazy?" said Uncle Frank. "There is a lot you can do. You can apologize to Jack for starters."

"I can't do that."

"You must. It is the right thing to do, and I'm sure you want to do the right thing for your child to see," said Uncle Frank.

"If I apologize, my kids will never respect me as an authority figure."

"On the contrary. It will make them respect you a great deal more."

"All right, if I have to. But I must remind you that this is highly unorthodox," said Aunt Mary.

Uncle Frank laughed.

"Jack, I apologize for what I have done to you. And I will try to listen to you under the condition that you listen to me," said Aunt Mary. "But since you saved not only my life but Erin's life, I owe you a second wish. Name it."

"I have something I would like to ask you to do for my second wish," said Jack. "I would like to be able to play with Bobby again."

"Well, I—" Aunt Mary began.

Then her husband Hayes cut in. "My boy, your wish is granted. I rescind my order. I'm proud of you, putting the safety of women and children ahead of your own. You'd make a fine soldier after all."

Chapter 37

Twelve days later

October 28, 2001, was a sad day for most of the Thatchers.

Two days earlier, Great-Aunt Edna had passed away after saying her last words: *Remember who you truly are.* And now they were in the car going to the graveyard for the burial, after they had attended the funeral at the First Methodist Church of Cyclone. They were driving down State Road 38 to Graveyard Street, which would take them to the cemetery.

Jack, however, was not sad. Things became a lot better for him since the fire. The fire destroyed the kitchen and parts of the living and dining room, and some of the insulation inside the walls had to be replaced. That was basically it.

Everybody congratulated him for saving Aunt Mary's and Erin's life, and they started to listen to him and to his three cousins. Jack was able to play with Bobby again, and they played with each other every day. Today Jack was allowed to wear his comfortable clothes under his dress clothes. No one was able to tell, and he wasn't in pain. It was amazing how nice adults could become once they learned to be flexible toward children.

The funeral procession pulled into the cemetery driveway.

Uncle Hayes, Aunt Mary, Uncle Peter, Aunt Eva, Uncle Frank, and Jack's parents all got out. Then Jack and his cousins got out of the cars and van.

"Okay, everyone, follow me," said Uncle Hayes.

Jack looked around him and saw tombstones everywhere. Realizing this would take his mind away from the funeral, he started reading aloud from the tombstones in the cemetery:

HU A	W FE
HARM H. MARTENS	GERTJE N. MARTENS
BORN 11-12-1833	BORN 06-07-1836
DIED 12-04-1905	DIED 03-12-1915

```
              O   O
          IN GOD WE SLEEP

HU   A                      W FE
ANTHONY BOSCO              MARIA S. BOSCO
BORN 10-19-1866            BORN 04-02-1868
DIED 3-19-1952             DIED 09-01-1959

   AUGHTER                    O
ELIZABETH B. BARBONE       JOSEPH I. BOSCO
BORN 02-22-1897            BORN 12-25-1889
DIED 11-05-1989            DIED 11-06-1971
```

"What's going on?" asked Uncle Hayes. "Who's talking?"

"Jack is," said Uncle Frank. "And I think he's trying to tell us something."

"JA-ACK!" roared Uncle Hayes. "WHY ARE YOU—"

"Stop yelling at him!" said Uncle Frank. "Remember, you have to listen to him."

"All right, fine. Jack, why were you talking?" asked Uncle Hayes.

"I was j-just reading tombstones," said Jack.

"Why are you reading tombstones?" asked Uncle Hayes.

Now it was Jack's turn to tell the truth. Uncle Frank was backing him up.

"I was just interested in the tombstones," said Jack. "I do not think there's anything wrong with that."

"Now Jack—"

"He did not do anything but talk to himself, Hayes," said Frank. "He is still going to attend this funeral just like us. One of the other rules that an authority figure must remember is to only enforce rules that are essential. Reading the tombstones is not going to stop him from attending this funeral, which he knows very well he must do."

"I can't believe it!" said Uncle Hayes. "My brother has become just like Jack!"

"Besides," said Uncle Frank, "why don't we ask Jack whether he wants to attend the funeral?"

"I do," said Jack. "I cannot say no to attending this funeral, for if I do, I will be asking for too much, and I will be guilty of power abuse."

"You are right, Jack. Let's go to the funeral."

Then Hayes went to be with the others.

"I'm glad you stood up for yourself," said Uncle Frank. "But I'm also glad that you are willing to exert limits on yourself. My siblings do not seem to know how to do that."

They walked to a row of chairs in the cemetery that was shaded by a tent. Up ahead was the steel coffin that lay above the hole that was dug for the burial.

Then a man walked up to the front of the chairs and began to officiate the funeral.

At the end of the funeral, the coffin was lowered into the ground, and Jack decided to read more tombstones on his way back to the car. He was curious about the people who were buried here. Despite their mere appearance on a marker, they all had lived lives, though now they were dead. That is why people have cemeteries: to remember those who are dead, to preserve their memory, and to make sure that when a person dies, they will not be gone completely. One of the saddest things about a cemetery is the vast difference in lives. One person may have lived to be 95, but the person next to him was 23. There are also tombstones with just one date on them. Those were babies who died when they were born. It shows you how fragile life really is.

The tombstones he read were:

```
ALBERT JEFFERSON
BORN AUGUST 12 1880
DIED FEBRUARY 26 1973
```

```
MARY ADAMS JONES
BORN APRIL 10 1864
DIED MARCH 27 1897
FOREVER AN ANGEL
```

GEORGE G. LOEW 1828 – 1910	SARAH HIS WIFE 1842 – 1929

CHARLES McCAY WILLIAMS, II
BORN JUNE 25 1853
DIED AUGUST 10 1854

BELOVED SON AND BROTHER

FORT O

HU A JESSE FORTSON 1783 – 1827	W FE MARY W. FORTSON 1783 – 1827
O THOMAS FORTSON 1815 – 1885	**AUGHTER** MARTHA F. BREWER 1801 – 1884

"Why is Jack talking again?" asked Uncle Hayes.

"Hayes, I thought you agreed we could let him read the tombstones. He's only saying them to himself," said Uncle Frank. "And besides, he *did* attend the funeral."

"It is impolite to speak during a funeral procession!" said Uncle Hayes, but he realized that arguing was futile. "You'll make him think he has the right to boss us around! You're turning him into an adult!"

"On the contrary, I am not," said Uncle Frank. "Jack knows very well that he's only a child and that you have authority over him and know better than him. He knows very well that he must check his power. After all, if he did not, then he'd be guilty of the same crime he accuses you of. If he felt like he had total authority, he would have refused to attend this funeral. But his willingness to attend reveals that he knows not to abuse power."

They all went back to the cars and drove away. Forty minutes later, they were back home. Jack was so happy he had been able to read the tombstones. Ever since that fire, he had been treated much better. Frank was right. Sometimes it takes a life-threatening emergency to change a person's destiny.

Epilogue

Two days later

It was now October 30th, and it was also the day that Jack would leave and return to his own home. In ten minutes, he would be leaving, but for now he was sitting with Bobby and talking about how fun it was that they could play together again.

"It's been three years, cousin," said Bobby. "But finally we are together again. Thank you for choosing this as your wish."

"It's a pleasure," said Jack.

"You know, I'm glad my mother didn't believe you about the Pyrex blowing up," said Bobby. "After all, if it weren't for the fire, we wouldn't be playing here."

"I know this may seem weird to you," said Jack, "but I believe that there is a force that humans cannot perceive that connects their actions together. Whenever a person does something, he invisibly starts a cycle of events which results in a larger action. For example, when your mother didn't believe me, she had no idea that there would be a fire, that I would save her life, and she would be forced to listen. Because she did not listen, she started a cycle of events which made her do something she did not want to do, but, when forced to do it, made me and you happy."

"I do thank you, however, for using your wish to help us as well as yourself. The average person, when asked something like that, would wish for material objects, such as roller blades, or Nintendo games," said Bobby.

"Even though our lives have changed, there is still a problem throughout the entire world. Since children are not represented in any law-making body, no one can understand their feelings. But even so, most houses are run as a democracy, not as an oligarchy or dictatorship," said Jack.

"And I also want to tell you one more time," said Bobby. "Congratulations today on winning our Scrabble game. That is the first time I have been beaten in Scrabble for a long time."

Jack's parents walked in.

"It's time to put on your shoes and get in the car. We're all packed and ready to go," said Jack's mother. "Bobby, you can come out if you wish to say good-bye."

"Well, I guess it is now time," said Bobby.

Jack put on his shoes and walked outside to see that the car was packed and they were almost ready to go. Jack's parents were outside, waiting at the car.

"Jack, stay here near the car. We still have to say good-bye," said Jack's father.

Then Uncle Hayes, Aunt Mary, Cousin Bobby, and Cousin Brittany all came out of the front door. Erin had left 10 days ago on October 20.

"Before we say good-bye, I would like to take the time to take a picture of everybody," said Jack's father. "So we can remember this occasion. So I would like Bobby, Brittany, Jack, Hayes, Mary, and Susan to please go to this tree and stand."

Jack obediently went to the tree with everyone else, even though he could not stand flashbulbs. For the first time since he could remember, a tree was not being used by his aunt or uncle as a place of punishment.

When everybody was standing together, Jack's father said. "Are you ready? One…two…three."

The flashbulb went off, but Jack closed his eyes to protect himself just before it flashed.

"Thanks, everyone. There will come a day when the only way we can remember this event is with the picture I just took. Now Jack, say good-bye."

Jack then went to Uncle Hayes and hugged him.

"Good-bye, Jack," said Uncle Hayes. "Thank you for saving your Aunt Mary's life."

Jack then went to Aunt Mary and hugged her.

"Good-bye, Jack," said Aunt Mary. "Thank you for saving my life and…and…for teaching me an important lesson. I'll never forget it. I promise."

Jack then went to Cousin Bobby and hugged him.

"Good-bye, Jack," said Cousin Bobby. "I will definitely miss you. And I hope that my parents will let me play with you at next year's gathering."

Jack then went to Cousin Brittany and hugged her.

"Good-bye, Jack," said Cousin Brittany. "Thank you for helping me and Erin and Bobby get some attention."

Then Jack went to an empty place in the yard and waited until everyone else was finished saying good-bye. When that was over, he went into the back seat of his car and waited for his parents to finish packing the trunk.

Two minutes later, Jack's father got in the car. When Jack's father started the car and drove it out of the driveway, everyone was waving at them.

Five minutes later, they were on the open road.

"I'm so proud of you," said Jack's mother from the front passenger seat. "You learned so many lessons this month!"

"What?" asked Jack.

"You learned to stand up for yourself, for one. And you saved two lives," said Jack's mother.

"And two suitcases," Jack reminded her.

And I guess he actually *did* learn some lessons.

As Jack sat silently in the car, slowly getting closer to home, he knew that the happiness he felt now would not last. After all, he was going to have to go back to school. At least not being at school was one benefit that came with being at Uncle Hayes and Aunt Mary's house.

Although Jack knew he was going to have to return to his miserable, misunderstood life, he also knew this experience had changed him. For a brief period in his life he had not been the underdog. This was a period where he had performed a heroic act, broken rules, risked severe punishments, and had come out victorious.

So what had he learned in his heart? I don't think he really knew. Perhaps he did not need to know. All he needed to know was that even though he had been hurt by so many people in his life, this visit was the time and place designated by God where he would be able to shine.

As the Bible says, *For everything there is a season, and a time for every matter under heaven,* and this was the time and place for Jack's recognition.